Arianne Richmonde's full-length novels in the Pearl Series, *Shades of Pearl*, *Shadows of Pearl*, *Shimmers of Pearl*, *Pearl* and *Belle Pearl* follow the tumultuous and heart-rending love story between Pearl Robinson and Alexandre Chevalier. All five books are bestsellers in erotic romance. The first three books are also available in an e-box set as *The Pearl Trilogy*.

What people are saying about the Pearl Series:

"There is one regret I have about reading this series—that I waited so long to read it."
—*New York Times bestselling author Nelle L'Amour*

"Just when I didn't think there would ever been room in my life for anyone but Christian Grey, along came Alexandre Chevalier! Christian who?"
—Cindy at *The Book Enthusiast*

"The best erotic romance series I have read to date."
—*Megan Cain Loera*

"If you like 50 shades of Grey and the Bared to You series, you are ABSOLUTELY going to LOVE The Pearl Series."
—*Books, Babes and Cheap Cabernet*

"CALL THE FIRE BRIGADE my house is burning down from Alexandre's sexpertise!!"
—*Island Lovelies Book Club*

"This is a MUST READ!!!!"
—*Sugar and Spice Book Reviews*

"The twists and turns left me in pieces. Other times, it was so sweet or incredibly sexy that I didn't think I'd be able to get enough. I found it very hard to put it down and loved every second of it. A definite page-turner."
—*The Book Blog*

"We LOVED the journey these books took us on. The storyline is great and the sex scenes do NOT disappoint. Ms. Richmonde also gives us lush scenery and exotic locales, and there are a LOT of plot twists. Trust us, you will NOT anticipate the twists and turns of this story."
—*The Book Bellas*

"Some of the HOTTEST sex/love scenes I've read. I could really feel the attraction and desire that Pearl and Alexandre had for each other. Their chemistry was amazing and their need for each other leapt off the pages. Arianne Richmonde did a wonderful job, not with just the story and characters but also with her skillfully crafted descriptive writing. The whole series has simply captivated me."
—*Swept Away By Romance*

"Don't miss out on this amazingly hot and smoldering read…you will love it!"
—*Two Crazy Girls With A Passion For Books*

"I LOVE LOVE LOVE Alexandre!"
—*The Literary Nook*

"A heart wrenching love story you won't forget."
—*E McDonough*

"What an amazing series this is. It will knock your socks off. Getting to know Pearl and Alexandre is definitely a must. Arianne Richmonde is a very talented story teller."
—*Mary Elizabeth's Crazy Book Obsession*

"I was hooked from the very first page. I had many mouth hanging on the floor moments because I was just so surprised as to what I was reading. I swear you won't see it coming."
—Debra at *The Book Enthusiast*

"I love how this author writes; she made me believe I was watching the whole thing like a film in my head. I would highly recommend this to all who love a great love story with sex, that would be most of us then, 5/5 Stars."
—*Confessions of a Bookaholic*

"A FREAKING awesome story filled with so much drama…oh, how I loved the drama. It was a big page turner for me and when things got crazy oh how I got sucked in!"
—*Momma's Books Blog*

"I am a fan of the 50 Shades of Grey series and the Bared to You series. As I liked both this one was a surprise and I loved it. I thought this was better than both of them put together. I found a new author who can't write fast enough."
—*Reviewer*

"The twists and turns that happen are amazing—stuff you just don't see coming."
—*WhoAreYouCallinABookWhore*

"Before I knew it, I was completely entrenched in this story. The descriptions. The emotions. I loved these characters. I hated these characters. I loved these characters again. I didn't know who to trust and who was lying. Between the mystery, the lies, and the hot sex… my head was literally spinning and going to explode."

—*Love N. Books*

"If you haven't read this series yet, put it on your Must Read list!! I look forward to more from Arianne Richmonde!!"

—*Sassy and Sultry Books*

"I loved the older woman/younger man dynamic of this series. The love scenes are passionate and raw. A complete love story from beginning to sweet end and I enjoyed every single word…"

—*Martini Times*

"I couldn't turn the pages fast enough. This book was HOT and sexy. Ms. Richmonde gave the reader a little of everything."

—*Wine Relaxation And My Kindle*

"Alexandre is one of my original Book Boyfriends right up there with Fifty."

—*Mommy's A Book Whore*

"Awesome; full of heart, tears and much laughter. It flows together and feels so real and true I forgot I was actually reading a story. I love these characters. If you want to read something great, get these books."

—*Dawn M. Earley*

Shades of Pearl

by

Arianne Richmonde

About the Author

Arianne Richmonde is an American writer and artist who was raised in both the US and Europe. She lives in France with her husband and coterie of animals.

As well as ***The Pearl Series*** she has written an erotic short story, *Glass*. She is currently working on her next novel, a suspense story.

The Pearl series:

The Pearl Trilogy bundle (the first three books in one e-box set)

Shades of Pearl
Shadows of Pearl
Shimmers of Pearl
Pearl
Belle Pearl

To be advised of upcoming releases, sign up:
ariannerichmonde.com/email-signup

For more information on the author visit her website:
www.ariannerichmonde.com

Acknowledgements

To every one of my amazing readers who demanded more of Pearl and Alexandre. Thanks for all your love and feedback. ***The Pearl Series*** would not have been possible without you. Thank you to all the bloggers and readers who recommended my books to their friends and followers. Your tireless support and enthusiasm have me in awe. Thank you so much.

1

Park Avenue is broken into a patchwork of glimmering colors, the streets a slick, shining wet as rain makes mirrors of the red and green of the traffic lights. I am mesmerized by the windscreen wipers of the taxi cab washing away the deluge of a sudden summer downpour that has taken the city by surprise.

I love New York City in the summer rain, a relief from the muggy air. But today it threatens to make me late for my appointment. I always aim to arrive early because, by nature I'm disorganized, so I need time on my side. I ask the driver if he can go any faster, if he can pull a miraculous short-cut out of the bag, but no, he and I are both aware that that's impossible. The traffic is lugging, straining; all we can do is be patient, all I can do is calm myself, take a breath and remember that work is not the be-all and end-all of my existence. So what if I'm late? Does it really matter in the big scheme of things, in the giant picture of life?

Life – that's something to mull over. I wish work wasn't so important to me, but I cling on to it like a piece of driftwood in a stormy ocean. Work is all I seem to have right now. I've just turned forty, I'm divorced, single - I live alone and don't have a child. Work is my lifeboat.

I sit back into the scuffed seat of the cab and look through the notes on my iPad.

The conference will be packed, my boss has assured me. Replete with an international crowd from all corners of the globe. It's the biggest I.T convention of the year and I know I won't fit in. Nerdsville here I come. I know very little about this world, and the only reason I have been summoned to go is to see if I can connect with two of the people who will be speaking today. They are a brother and sister from France who have made a small fortune, seemingly overnight, not unlike Facebook computer programmer and Internet entrepreneur, Mark Zuckerberg. This duo is young, too. She's the business and he's the brains, apparently. They started a social network company, HookedUp, a sort of Twitter cum social dating interaction which, although not so popular in France, went pandemic here in the U.S. Everyone has joined, even married couples, even me - which is really saying something as dating is a game I play badly; I've had no luck and I've all but given up.

My company, Haslit Films, wants to do a documentary about this pair of siblings. Not so easy. They are very private and rarely do interviews. They don't go to openings or parties. They don't do Red Carpet. There was a big piece about them in the New York Times, but other than that they are a bit of a mystery. He, Alexandre Chevalier, is twenty-four and she, Sophie Dumas, is ten years older, his half sister from a previous marriage. They share the same father. This much I know. But I can find only one photo of him on the internet and he's wearing a hoodie, his face practically masked - he looks like a typical college student. His sister stands beside him, her hair in a neat chignon – looking formidable, poised. HookedUp is going from strength to strength. Rumor has it they are looking to sell or go public but nobody can be sure. All this, I need to find out.

I stare out the cab window and sigh with relief as the traffic speeds up. I think about all the millions out there trying to find a mate, trying to get 'hooked up' - and smile to myself. When was the last time? Two years ago? It was a rebound disaster waiting to happen, or rather, I was the rebound waiting…hoping to find love again. I hadn't expected my divorce to knock me sideways the way it did. I didn't even love him anymore. It was mutual. There was nobody else involved, we just drifted apart. We had gotten to the point where we couldn't even watch each other eat. Yet when those papers came through, the ink hardly dry, I cried myself to sleep for weeks. If Saul and I had had a child, at least that would have given me some sort of purpose, a perspective - but there I was, a two-time miscarriage vessel, empty, null and void - my sell-by date looming.

It's funny how others see you, though. So many of my friends were envious of my life. They still are. 'So glamorous,' they purr. 'So free'. No homework to deal with, no snotty nose to wipe, no husband's dirty socks to pick off the floor. Instead, a fabulous, well paid job with a fabulous, successful film company making top-notch documentaries, meeting fascinating people…and yet. Yet what? What excuse did I have, *do* I have to feel unfulfilled?

Perhaps everyone feels this way, no matter what cards they hold. Always looking for something richer - something or someone more satisfying to fill an empty hole. Turning forty didn't scare me until after it happened. 'But you look amazing,' said friends after I'd blown out forty candles on my birthday cake. The 'but' spoke volumes. Tick-tock. Tick-tock.

That last date I went on, just after my divorce - what a fiasco. I thought it might give me confidence – make me feel stronger but I found myself tumbling into bed with a man I hardly knew, after he'd taken me out to an oh-so-expensive dinner. I think he felt I was dessert, and I can only blame myself as I offered myself up as such, accepting a 'night cap' at his apartment. Just thinking about it now makes my mouth pucker, as if I had a lemon in my mouth. Bad sex. Grappling, groping, sweaty hands on my breasts, the poking and panting. Ugh, just the thought of it. He sent me flowers the next day, saying what a wonderful evening he'd had. He was so keen. So well-meaning. So clueless.

Not that I'm any expert. No. Sex has rarely been good for me. My ex-husband was very attractive but his idea of foreplay was rubbing my groin as if I were a horse needing a good rub-down. Rhythmic efficiency.

It seems that men have read about the clitoris (the Big C), the nerve-rich locus of women's sexual pleasure, and think it's a target to be zoomed in on *immediately*. All those women's magazines don't help, either, that go on endlessly about multiple orgasms - something that has eluded me like a fugitive on the run…forever out of my range. Perhaps it's all a conspiracy and the big M O, or rather, Multiple 007 doesn't actually exist…just a fantasy that we all believe in.

It reminds me of my old Al-Anon meetings – a place for family members of alcoholics to find solace and talk to one another. That was before my eldest brother died, when my family was struggling to understand his alcoholism - his personal demons which were ripping us apart. I was searching for help, for answers. The meetings, for some odd reason, were ninety-eight percent women. Once we'd all gained each other's trust, we started to explore other problems and to really open up with one another - problems not related to our families, but our own deep secrets, which turned out to be collective insecurities. Sex came up. Of course, doesn't it always? We had all sworn honesty, not to judge each other, not to share our experiences with anyone outside the room. It turned out that many of the women there - in fact, *most* of the women there - had unsatisfactory sex lives, if any at all. Several bowed their heads in shame when they admitted they'd never reached orgasm through penetrative sex. Others, that they couldn't bear to have their clitoris touched (manhandled), or they felt too self-conscious to have their partner go down on them. We all laughed about *that* scene in *When Harry Met Sally*. So true. Women faking orgasms so they can get to sleep, take the kids to school, or just get it over and done with. But you still soldier on, still hoping for that magical person who can wave a wand and make it all happen - hoping that same person will be your soul mate, or at least, that you'll have a good deal in common. *Or* that your present partner, or husband, will wake up one day and find you gloriously sexy, and that his top priority in the world is to give you carnal pleasure and become a veritable god in bed.

As for me? Right now my confidence is wobbling and wavering with desperate insecurity like a child learning to ride a bicycle way too big for her. Sex, or any kind of a relationship, is the last thing I feel equipped to navigate my way around. On paper, I look good. Had a great education, a degree from Brown in

Comparative Literature. I worked my way up from research and I am now a producer with Haslit Films, a job I love. I own my own apartment, a one bedroom co-op on the Upper East Side. I travel to a different place in the U.S every year for a ten day vacation, usually in September when the crowds have died down. My life is wonderful.

But I'm single.

And, just to add salt to the wound, I haven't reached that exclusive O during sex with a partner of any kind, for nearly eighteen years.

The conference center is all a-buzz. There are placards filled with names and seminars. *Deep Dive: Best Practices for Wireless and Mobile Management, Operations and Security.*

Selecting the Right Platform Solution.

Cloud-based Convergence of Desktop, Communications & Social Apps: Microsoft Office 365 vs. Google Gmail/Docs.

Social Media as the Top Malware Delivery Vehicle - How to Protect Your Network.

I scan the list to find out what I am looking for, but cannot see the French sibling duo anywhere. I make my way to the ladies' room and check myself in the mirror. I see a blonde woman staring back at me with her flecked blue-gray eyes, wearing a tight gray pencil skirt and fitted white T-shirt, her bra making her breasts seem larger than they are in reality. Cheating. That's what we females do whenever we can. The woman is familiar yet, every time I see her, it shocks me that she is *me*, a person who only yesterday was climbing trees and asking her mother for more ice-cream. It sounds like a cliché, but where did all that time go? Who is this woman looking back at me? This seemingly self-assured lady with marshmallow insides who hides her insecurity with designer clothes and a bright smile – who is she? I open my old, oversized, leather bag and take out some high, nude platform pumps, slip off my sneakers and put on the shoes, one foot at a time, leaning against the wall to balance myself, swapping comfort for extra height. My five foot seven frame is now several inches taller.

I wish I had a sweater now; the air conditioning is up high, my hair is soaked from the rain – no wonder we get summer colds in New York City. I inspect my face in the mirror and wish I could magic away these crow's feet that have nestled themselves so comfortably on my face. I put on another layer of mascara which brightens me and makes me feel younger. I never wear foundation; the beauty of getting older is the absence of pimples. Reading novels on my co-op's shared roof terrace has given me a golden, sun-kissed glow – no need for blusher at this time of year. I dab on a touch of pinky-red lip gloss, let down my damp, wavy blond hair from its pony tail, and consider myself ready to enter the world of I.T.

I move back to the lobby and stand in line, waiting to collect my name tag. "Ms. Pearl Robinson," I say to the man behind the desk.

He hands me my badge and I pin it on my T-shirt. I read a banner which says: 'THE #1 meeting place for the global business technology community,' and for some odd reason, I feel nervous.

I clear my throat. "Um, excuse me but I've never been to one of these business technology conferences. I'm trying to find one of the speakers today. Two of the speakers, actually."

"Yes, ma'am, how can I help?"

"Can you direct me to Alexandre Chevalier and Sophie Dumas?" I'm aware of my voice. I feel ridiculous trying to make the Alexandre come out with a French accent. My French is limited, to say the least. Restaurant French. Directions French. It occurs to me that if I take the Alexandre and the Dumas and put them together I have Alexandre Dumas, the French author who wrote the swash-buckling adventure, *The Three Musketeers.* But this Alexandre is a recently graduated college kid - a geek who wears a hoodie and probably keeps pet rats in his bedroom.

"One moment," the man replies, "let me see...the HookedUp guys? I believe that-"

All I can hear is a booming voice behind me, chatting excitedly. "Everybody was talking about Data Center last year. This year, did you notice that hardly a word was spoken? Did you not notice that? I mean, dude, the buzz instead is about software-defined networks, decoupling the network control plane from the data plane and using the OpenFlow protocol to give servers, which inherit network control, access to devices such as switches and routers."

I turn around and glare at the bearded guy behind me speaking double-dutch. Then I say to the man at the desk, "I'm sorry, I couldn't hear you, what were you saying?"

"That the seminar is over ma'am. The HookedUp guys? It finished, like, twenty minutes ago."

"But my schedule said 11am."

"It was brought forward by an hour. You should have been informed if you'd booked ahead."

Booked ahead? What is this, Broadway? "Are they speaking again? At a different time?" I ask, knowing I've blown my chance of ever seeing this elusive duo.

"No, ma'am. That's it. It was quite a coup getting them here. The audience was the biggest we've ever had. Sorry you missed out."

"Me too," I mutter.

I think how disappointed my boss will be whose idea it was to do this documentary. I feel so unprofessional. I should have double-checked the hour. The duo wouldn't submit themselves to an interview just, 'Come and see us speak at the InterWorld show on the 12th – we'll talk then.' I secretly wonder if I subconsciously willed this to happen - messing it all up. Surely my own project can now take preference? I've been hatching and researching an idea for a year now, a venture that really interests me, something that deserves worldwide attention. *The Aftermath of World Aid* is its working title. What happens to the billions of dollars that never reach the victims after a natural disaster? Everyone digging into their pockets to unwittingly fund corrupt governments - siphoned-off aid – money in the wrong hands. It's a political hotbed. Nobody wants to tread on toes.

My other ambition is to run a special on arms dealing. People talk about world peace but how will that ever happen as long as dealing in arms is legal? As long as its trade is used as world currency by governments? If the profit were taken out of war, if war was no longer business, surely then wars would end? At least, on such a terrifying scale.

My reverie is broken as I hear my cell phone vibrate in my bag. I fumble about for it, my hand wading through my sneakers, hairbrush, iPad and a thousand other things which make my handbag feel like a training tool for women's welterweight boxing.

I look at my cell, holding it out at arm's length. Another annoying thing about getting older - my eyesight is not what it was - yet it's not bad enough (yet) for me to have to wear glasses. Uh oh - my boss calling via Skype. Her picture comes up on my iPhone screen, her smooth caramel-colored face poised with questions, her large hazel-brown eyes expectant.

"Hi Natalie," I say with a hint of a sigh that I can't manage to keep to myself.

"So it's been cancelled," she says in more of a statement than a question.

As usual she's one step ahead of me.

"No, not cancelled, it was moved forward. I've just missed them."

"Darn."

"I'm so sorry, Natalie. It's all my fault, I should have checked. Look, I'll track them down somehow. I'll get onto it. I promise."

"You know what? Forget the whole idea. These guys are obviously not up for it. They're too hard to get hold of. We don't have time to be messing about with subjects that are not interested in collaborating with us."

"Really? You mean that?" I ask, relieved.

"Really. Get your butt back into gear on one of your other topics, we'll figure out something else."

My lips curve into a subtle smirk. I'm thinking about the tsunamis....Japan, Sumatra, Thailand. The earthquake in Haiti. Maybe she'll green-light my *Aftermath of World Aid* project after all.

"Okay, I'm going to grab a coffee and we can talk," I suggest.

"I have a few ideas in the making."

"Oh yeah, I know you do," she replies, laughing. "But, honey, I'm out the door now. I need to pack and I have a ton of stuff to take care of first. And just to be clear, please don't disturb me while I'm in Kauai, I really need this break."

"Okay, I promise."

"You'll be okay for two weeks without me to guide your skinny ass?" Natalie is being ironic – she knows I can hold my own at work. *I hope.*

"Not so skinny," I joke. "Have a ball, Natalie."

Natalie was single until I introduced her to my father – but that's another story. She has two teenage daughters and, luckily, her sister is coming to stay to look after them while Natalie takes a deserved break in Hawaii. By the time she returns, I'll have a nice package to offer – I'll work hard on my presentation and come up with a choice of projects.

I head across the road for a coffee.

It's both a comforting and disconcerting fact that there's a franchise coffee shop on practically every corner of NYC. You don't have to go far to feed your addiction. I shuffle through the door, now back in my sneakers – New York City sidewalks do not favor high heels for any period of time. You can tell how long someone has been living in New York by their footwear. Comfort first. Heels are for visitors. Or women from New Jersey.

I stand in line and ponder over the rich choice I am presented with. A wave of guilt washes over me as I mentally tot up the money I've spent on superfluous coffee breaks over the years – money needed by charities, for water wells somewhere, for a child's education. Stop! Life isn't fair. Yum, *Mocha Cookie Delight…coffee blended with mocha sauce, vanilla syrup, chocolaty chips, milk and ice.* Or a *Vanilla Cappuccino - coffee flavored with vanilla and blended with milk and ice – and fewer calories.*

A man's voice interrupts my chocolaty train of thought.

"So how did you enjoy the conference?" His accent is foreign, his voice deep and melodic.

I look up, feeling now dwarfed in my flat sneakers, petite against his tall, solid frame. The first thing I notice, at eye level, is the definition of his pec muscles underneath his sun-faded, pale blue T-shirt. He's tanned; I see he has a name tag just like mine from the InterWorld conference, which reads: ***Alexandre Chevalier.*** My gaze rises higher and I observe a pair of penetrating peridot-green eyes rimmed with dark lashes, friendly yet intense, looking down at me. His hair is dark, his face unmistakably European - yes, dare I say it, he even looks French, the profile of his nose strong, the jaw defined. He's so handsome I feel a frisson shoot up my spine. He's smiling at me. My stomach flips. I'm speechless with surprise.

"Your name tag," he clarifies. "Were you at that conference around the corner?"

"Yes, I was." I can't say any more. I feel like a teenager. My mind is doing acrobatics, trying to figure out why his presence makes no sense at all. This man must have borrowed the tag of the real Alexandre Chevalier. Why?

He's at the front of the line, now, talking in French to another woman. She looks familiar. I feel an inexplicable pang of jealousy. Absurd! I don't even know him. *Get a grip!* But then realize–

"I'll pay for whatever this lady's having too," he tells the woman serving behind the counter, and he pulls out a wad of notes. I notice a stash of hundred dollar bills which he is trying to surreptitiously stuff back into his jeans' pocket, without drawing attention to himself.

He turns back to me and looks at my name tag. "For Pearl," he adds, rolling his tongue around the R of Pearl.

My name suddenly sounds beautiful, not like a pseudonym a hooker might use, which is what I was relentlessly teased for in high school.

"Pearl," he says again. "What a beautiful name. I've never heard that before. As a name, I mean."

"Well, my parents were kind of hippies. Thanks for the compliment, though. I'll have a….a…um, I'll have a *vanilla cappuccino,* please. You really don't have to do that - buy me my drink, I mean."

I fumble about in my 'handbag' - although it seems more like an *overnight* bag - and try to locate my wallet. I'm not used to strangers buying me drinks. My fingers can't seem to find my wallet, anyway. I often fantasize about inventing an inside handbag light that switches on automatically whenever you open it – I'd make millions – they'd be sold at supermarket checkouts nationwide. My bag is pitch dark inside, I can see nothing.

"And what's your name?" I ask, still not believing that this man before me is Alexandre Chevalier, the twenty-four year-old nerd in the hoodie, as he appeared in the online photo. This Alexandre is sophisticated – looks way older than that. Even though he's just in T-shirt and jeans, he's stylish. Very Alpha Male - yet oozing *je ne sais quoi.* I could describe him as 'beautiful' but he is so much more than that. There is an aura surrounding him of power and sexuality yet blended with an unassuming sort of friendliness as if his good looks are accidental somehow.

He laughs. His teeth flash white and are almost, but not quite

- perfect. An almost perfect, ever so slightly, crooked smile - disconcertingly sexy. "Very funny," he replies tapping his long fingers on his ***Alexandre Chevalier*** name tag. "Oh, this is my sister, Sophie."

The Sophie sounds like Soffy. His accent is disarming me. I think of those classic, 1960's French films - Alain Delon movies - yes, he does have that air about him - a young Alain Delon - mixed with the raw, untamed sex-appeal of Jean Paul Belmondo in his prime – What was that film? Ah yes, *À Bout de Souffle* - *Breathless* was its translation. That's how I feel now…

Breathless.

Sophie locks her eyes with mine and smiles at me. She's smartly dressed, elegant. We move forward to shake hands. My fingers brush across Alexandre's T-shirt for a second and I feel the hardness of his stomach. I catch my breath. I want to blurt out about our company, Haslit Films, who I am, why I have a name tag for that conference, but I find myself behaving like a character from a TV sitcom - Rachel from *Friends*, or Lucy from *I Love Lucy* - compelled to tell fibs, invent some cover-up. I feel as if my hand has been caught in the cookie jar, and then wonder at my own absurdity. *What cookie jar?* I haven't done anything wrong! I can feel my face flush hot and know that if I were the type of person to blush red - these two strangers would be able to detect the embarrassment glowing in my cheeks.

"What a coincidence," I say, tossing a coin in my head about whether to explain everything.

"Really why?" Sophie asks.

But I go all *Rachel* again and find nonsense spurting from my lips.

"Well, just that you were at the conference and so was I."

I suddenly think that if I tell them about my film company and why I was at InterWorld, they'll think I've been stalking them. Trailing behind them, pursuing them into the coffee shop like some low-grade paparazzi reporter for a cheap newspaper. The fact that Alexandre Chevalier is no longer a rat-loving geek locked in a dark room programming codes, unnerves me. He looks like a movie star. He's as rich as one - maybe more so. For some reason I can't come clean.

They are chatting away in French to each other. Good, eyes are off me. *Damn, why did I take off my heels?* I feel so insignificant - so low down. My jittery hand gropes about in my monster bag again, and my fingers feel the sharp points of my shoes. The fingers wander about some more. Ah, the wallet, *phew*, I can feel it. But my heart jumps a beat when, for all my fumbling, I can't locate the keys to my apartment! *Why is this man making me so nervous?*

The alarm on my face must be obvious, as he asks, "Is everything alright?"

"Well, for just a second, I thought I'd lost the keys to my apartment. Ha ha. I mean, that second is still ticking," I tell him, my voice rising higher. "The keys don't seem to be there."

"One iced vanilla cappuccino, one iced coffee and one black shaken iced tea," the server announces.

Before I've even lifted my eyes from my bag, Sophie has grabbed her drink-to-go, and says, "Nice to meet you, Pearl. Maybe see you around sometime." And she adds in French to her brother, "*À plus*," and she's off, out the door and onto the street.

"I had got the drinks to go but do you want to sit down?" he asks. "Have a better look for your house keys? A man's life is so much simpler – we carry everything in our pockets."

We find a couple of free armchairs and sit down. His cell phone buzzes. I slip on my high pumps, just for good measure - no pun intended.

He smiles at me. "Excuse me, do you mind? I need to get this call."

So polite. I don't even know him and he's already bought me a drink and asking me if I mind him taking a call. He looks embarrassed as he speaks in hushed tones into the phone.

"What's it like? Is it worth that inflated price?" he murmurs.

I'm looking through my bag, but curious about his conversation, so keep an ear inquisitively cocked – if I were a dog, my ear would be raised. Ah, here they are, those elusive apartment keys, always giving my heart a run for its money. I swear - that pumping, lost-my-keys-lost-my-phone-lost-my-wallet adrenaline is going to give me a literal heart attack one day.

"Okay," I hear Alexandre say, "I'll buy it. Yes, even at that price - it's a one-off - I might not get this chance again. Yes, wire the money. Okay, bye Jim. Thanks."

I want to ask him what he was talking about, but don't dare to be so snooping.

The look on my face, however, must give away my curiosity, as he reveals to me, "A vice of mine. My sister's sure to disapprove."

"Oh? Why?" I ask innocently.

"She thinks cars are for getting from A to B, and one's enough."

"Buying another car, huh? How many do you already have?"

He looks almost ashamed. "More than I need."

"A collection?"

"You could say that. But they are all works of art in their own right."

"So what's the latest?" I ask, feeling envious. I don't own a car. Wish I did but I live in New York City, for goodness sake. The garage alone in my neighborhood would cost practically the same as rent. And if you park it on the street you have to remember to move it all the time for the street cleaners, so it won't get towed away. Fines. An expensive hassle. Of course, Alexandre Chevalier wouldn't have that problem.

"It's an Austin Healy. I have a weakness for British classics."

I know how expensive that must be, but I play dumb. "Do you have an *American* car?"

"Of course. When in Rome. I drive a Corvette." *That rolled* R *again…uum…Cooorr – vette.*

"You *live* here? I thought you might be just visiting?"

"Yes, I live on Fifth on the Upper East Side, overlooking Central Park. I'm very fortunate," he adds.

I look down and then up at him through my lashes. I haven't flirted like this for years. "I live on the Upper East Side, *too*! Seventy-ninth and Third. Lucky you, overlooking Central Park. That's anybody's dream."

"Not my sister's. She prefers to live in Paris. She hates New York."

I blink at him. "Well. Paris. Yes, well, I guess *Paris* must be the most beautiful city in the world."

He's biting his lower lip with his gaze set on my face, and it's sending a jolt of electricity through my body. "You've never been?"

"No, I'm ashamed to say, I haven't," I reply. "But I intend to."

"Don't be ashamed. You're lucky you have something wonderful to look forward to. Like, if there's a great book you haven't read - a classic. It's a happy thought to know something wonderful is in store for you. Waiting with open arms to welcome you."

I smile. "That's a refreshing way of looking at it. Funny you should like classics. Me, too. I love Russian novels and I adore old movies and re-runs of 50's and 60's TV sitcom shows like, *I Love Lucy, Bewitched* and *I Dream of Jeannie.*" I realize how dumb that sounds. "Silly really. I love old songs too, especially from the 70's. And you're a lover of classic cars?"

"They've been tried and tested. Loved too. You know what you're getting. You're sure to be rewarded with quality." His green eyes now look flecked with tiger-gold. *Is he flirting with me?* My stomach is fluttering again - when he said those words, 'tried and tested' it churned. *Does he think older women are 'tried and tested' too?*

"Fifth Avenue and?" I ask, immediately realizing I sound like a stalker.

"Fifth and Sixty Second. I wanted to have a green view. A view to Central Park - and more importantly - a good place for my dog."

"You have a dog?"

"Rex. But he's still in Paris. He's at my parents' house for the moment until I bring him here. My whole life," he says with a smile, "is designed around Rex. I made sure the apartment here had a spacious roof-terrace, too. It even has trees and a patch of lawn up there. Ready for a life of comfort. Me? I'd be happy with a dark little cave somewhere, but only the best for Monsieur Rex."

I laugh. "What kind of dog is he?"

"A black Labrador. All black, except he wears a smart white

cravat on his chest. One of the advantages of France is that you can take your dog anywhere. To restaurants, even. Especially, black Labs. President Mitterrand had a black Labrador and ever since then, they've been very respected creatures in my country."

My eyes widen. "Seriously? You can even go to smart restaurants with your dog?"

"I usually call ahead to be polite. I book the table and then add, 'Oh yes, just one thing, do you mind if I bring my dog along, you know, he's just a typical *Black Labrador.*' They always say yes. But I'll tell you a secret-"

He leans forward and, oh so slightly, rests his hand on my knee. It starts to quiver, goose bumps shimmer along my thighs, my arms.

"What's the secret?" I ask, my voice sounding like a small child's.

"He's not pure Labrador. I think he's got a little Pit-Bull in him. He has a wide face and compact thigh muscles that feel as if they're made of rock. He's the sweetest dog that ever lived. The sweetest, the gentlest. You know Pit-Bulls were originally bred to be nannies? To be guardians to babies and young children – to watch over them?"

"No, really? You're kidding me."

"I'm serious. A whole lot of vintage photographs have been discovered from the Victorian age. American Pit-Bull Terriers were used as baby-sitters. Unfair they've been given a bad rap and their loving natures abused. In France, they were forced to be sterilized some years back, but my Rex has some Pit-Bull genes in his blood, I'm sure. They were never considered dangerous in the olden days."

Don Gaire Oose....dangerous...his accent is so alluring. "That's fascinating," I say. "I never knew that. I'm crazy about dogs. I had one as a little girl. She was a Husky."

"Huskies are beautiful."

"Mine - she was called Zelda, she had one blue eye and one golden eye. She was a real stunner. But she'd run off whenever she could. They're real escape artists, Huskies. She was okay for the first year, but as soon as she turned thirteen months she started doing her own thing, escaping, getting into mischief. She killed chickens, unfortunately. One day she ran off and didn't come back. We never knew what happened. It broke my heart. Since then I haven't had the courage to get another dog."

Alexandre brings his palms up to his face and covers his mouth with genuine empathy. "That's a very sad story. I'm so sorry. You'll have to meet Rex. I'm organizing his move – should be in the next couple of months."

An invitation? Is this for real? "I'd adore to meet Rex – he sounds lovely. So why did you choose to live in New York?" I ask, not wanting this conversation to finish. Ever.

"France is one of the most beautiful countries in the world. Fine wine, great cuisine, incredible landscape - we have a rich culture. But when it comes to opportunity, especially for small businesses, it's not so easy there."

Small businesses? His company is worth millions! No - billions, even.

My sitcom alter-ego is rearing her naughty, lying head again. "You own a small company? What do you do?"

He narrows his penetrating eyes. Every time he does that, it sends shivers coursing through my body. "That's why I was at that conference," he explains. "I was answering a few questions, giving people some tips, you know, advice from my own personal experience. It's done nicely my company."

Nicely? So modest.

"What were *you* doing at the conference?" he asks me. "Sorry, that's very prying." He looks down and takes a gulp of his iced-coffee. I observe the cupid bow of his top lip pressing on the cup. Then he takes out an ice cube and starts sucking on it. I catch a glimpse of his pink tongue licking his lips. Butterflies circle my insides again. *Control yourself, Pearl, he's sixteen years younger than you!*

"Your English is so good," I marvel, steering him away from me and my story. I don't want to tell him why I was at the conference. "Your vocabulary, words like *prying*. Where did you learn your English?"

"I lived in London for a few years. But I started speaking it when I was young - self-taught from video games, mostly. All the best games were in English. There was nothing in French when I was a little boy. All the technical vocabulary for the Internet was also English. I was forced to learn if I wanted to have fun. Not to mention song lyrics. I learned a lot that way, too. My favorite bands were all American or British."

"You must enjoy your work, then?"

"I don't really consider it work. I'd be doing it anyway, even if I wasn't getting paid for it."

"Is that what you do, then? Internet and computer stuff?"

"Yeah, I started a company with my sister. She was single at the time, you know, no boyfriend, and an obsessive Twitter user. It was she who came up with the idea. A Twittery way to get a date. Get 'hooked up' as the Americans say. It started from there. I'm a programmer. Amongst other things."

"HookedUp. Is that *your* company?" *I should be given an Oscar for best performance. Or slapped in jail for most wicked liar of the year.*

"Yes, that's me," he says simply.

"Wow, doing okay, I guess."

"Yeah, we've been lucky. And I love what I do which is the most important aspect."

"So what are your hobbies? When you're not doing technical stuff?"

"Oh, I'm a sucker for anything technical even when I'm not working. Cars, electric guitars. I love gadgets. You probably think me pretty foolish - a typical guy."

"Boys toys," I laugh. "Men usually like gadgets. Do you fly a plane?"

"No. I have my cars. I like feeling the ground beneath the wheels." He looks at me intensely.

Ground beneath the wheels – why does that sound so evocative?

"So you don't fly about in a private jet or helicopter?" *Where did that ridiculous question come from? - I'm beginning to sound like a chat show host.*

"I think my carbon footprint is bad enough as it is – no, I rarely travel by private jet or helicopter. Although, now you mention it - not a bad idea for Rex," he says, deadpan. "It would be way more comfortable for him to travel that way. What about you?" he asks. "Private jet?"

"Not unless you count the water-jet thing on my toothbrush private."

His defined lips curve into a subtle smile. "You haven't told me much about yourself, Pearl."

Oh no. What do I say? Luckily, he's European. I've noticed they rarely ask you directly what you do for a living; they consider it bad manners.

"Well," I begin, "I like writing. One day, I hope to pen a

screenplay."

"Really? I love theatre. I don't know much about screenplays or movies, but I adore going to the theatre. Actually, I prefer a good play to a novel. Molière, Voltaire, Jean-Paul Sartre, Camus. We have pretty bad translations of Shakespeare into French – they just don't do him justice – another incentive to perfect my English. I've seen some great plays in Paris and London. My sister used to be an actress. She got me into plays. Theatre is her passion."

"It sounds as if you two are really close," I remark, amazed at how sophisticated he is, and how well read. He seems so much older than his years.

"I guess we are."

"So when you're not going to the theatre, or working, or zipping about in your beautiful classic cars, what do you do to relax?"

"Let's see. I love rock-climbing."

"Not so relaxing, though."

"Not physically, but for your mental state of mind, it's great. You have to concentrate so hard on what you're doing - it cleanses the mind from all the clutter. A bit like meditation. Not that I meditate, but you know, I can imagine. It's not a team sport, it's boring for any spectator – it's about personal satisfaction, personal goals."

"You sound as if you're very accomplished at it."

"I've climbed a bit. Rock climbing involves strength, control and finesse. Using the muscles in your arms and legs to pull yourself up a sheer rock-face takes strength and control. Using your brain to place your hands and feet so that your muscles can do their job - that's finesse."

I study the *finesse* of his chest, his lithe, tanned arms, and see where he gets his worked-out physique from. But he's not overly muscley, not exaggerated. There's no bull-neck there, no bulging, bulky biceps. He's long and lean but not too slim, either - he has definite substance.

"I tried rock-climbing once," I tell him. "I was terrified but I could see the attraction to the sport. It was fun, I'd love to try it again someday." I'm aware that I'm fishing and he takes the bait.

"Really? Would you like to come with me? My sister hates it. I can never get anyone to go with me."

"Your girlfriend doesn't like rock-climbing?" I hear myself spurt out and wish I had a mouth-plug.

"My girlfriend?"

Oh no, he does have a girlfriend, after all.

"I'm unattached," he lets me know.

I sigh with relief and hope he hasn't heard my body heave gratitude. I sip a long, long mouthful of cappuccino through my straw. "I'd just *love* to come rock-climbing with you."

I notice he's watching my mouth clamped around the straw, and I feel self-conscious. I wipe my mouth – fearful that I have foam on my upper lip and it looks like a moustache.

"Great," he says, not taking his eyes off me. "How about the weekend?"

"You mean this weekend, or next?"

"That's right, today's Friday. It's all a bit last minute and I have something on tonight so it might—"

"What?" I ask, panicked he'll change his mind.

"It's too hot to climb midday in summer, so I usually set out very early. I mean, I often spend the night there – makes it easier. But it's already Friday so—"

I am waiting; my breath uneven. The cappuccino is gurgling, swilling in my stomach. *Please don't let me be sick. Please don't let me throw up with anticipatory nerves.*

"I mean," he continues, "if it doesn't seem too forward to ask you for the weekend–"

"Not at all!" I exclaim way too keenly, too desperately, a desperate non-housewife, with a sudden longing of nothing else but to rip off this young man's clothes…but then panic sets in again. *Who am I kidding?* No way could I sleep with his man! I'm, what, sixteen years older than he is. I wouldn't have the confidence. My body isn't like it was when I was twenty-two…I wouldn't even want him to see me in a *bikini*, let alone…

He must be reading the alarm on my face. "Don't worry, Pearl. We'd have separate bedrooms, of course."

"Yes, of course. Separate bedrooms," I repeat pathetically, relieved, but wishing I had more gumption, more confidence to jump his bones. Be more like Madonna or Demi Moore.

"Actually," he breaks in. "I know another place we can go climbing that's closer to the City. It's only ninety miles Upstate – we can drive there very early and come back late, all in one day. Is this all too last minute?"

"No, it's fine," I say, now disappointed. I've blown it. I've sabotaged my one chance to spend the night with him.

"Great, I'll retrieve you at….what about seven o' clock tomorrow morning? Is that too early?"

Retrieve, how quaint. His accent is killing me. "No, seven's perfect."

I give him my address, my phone number and when I stand up in my high pumps my legs are as wobbly as Jell-O. *Forty years old? Really? I could have sworn I'd had my sixteenth birthday party just last week.*

2

All night I was tossing and turning, going over our conversation in my mind. I wish I'd pressed 'record' on my iPhone app so I could now play back what he and I said to each other in the coffee shop. I realize my fleeting fantasies of Alexandre finding me attractive are just that - fantasies. He needs someone to hang out with. He said it himself in so many words…his sister hates rock climbing. He needs a sister figure, he feels at home with older women. He just wants me to go along for the ride. Hang out. Nothing more. *Get a grip woman, this man is too young for you. Or rather, you are too old for him.*

But just to be on the safe side, I went to get a pedicure yesterday. The least I can do is have pretty feet. I also made a dash to my hairdresser. Roots - the bane of my life. My first gray hairs came early; I was only twenty-nine. Thanks, family genes. I read about those Thirteen Day Bergdorf Blondes who have their blonde heads re-touched every thirteen days, so they look like cool, natural, ice-princesses. I, too, have to keep an eye on the thirteen day thing, but for a different reason - those white 'evil-step-mother' hairs pop through in all the obvious places – around the temples on the parting line. I go for my natural color, dark honey-blonde. And if I keep a sharp eye on this impending granny situation, not letting thirteen days pass, I manage to fool everybody. People usually take me for thirty-something. That's why, if I were to become famous overnight (don't we all have those fancy flights of the imagination?) I would never do one of those reality TV shows when they're trapped on a desert island or in the jungle. I need my hairdresser. And in emergency situations (if she's not available) - my Honey Blonde 8.3.

The phone rings and my heart starts pounding. It's 7am sharp. It's the doorman calling to say my visitor has arrived and he's waiting downstairs in the lobby.

I never pegged myself for a car fanatic but when Alexandre opens the door for me and I slide into the passenger seat, my skin tingles with anticipation. I sink into the bucket of the seat – vintage cars smell so good - and stretch out my legs, raise my arms into the air - it's a convertible - and I glow with girlish glee. The sky is clear after yesterday's rain and it looks as if we are in for a day of sunshine.

Alexandre is grinning as we move off, the engine humming loud beneath the great long hood of this glorious sports car. He drives one-handed with his left elbow jutting over the sill. "She's a 1968 Chevrolet Corvette C3. What a roadster! She packs four hundred and thirty-five horses under the hood. The '68 was the first year of the third generation of Corvettes—" he stops himself mid-flow. "Sorry, I'm sounding like a real car nerd."

"Yes you are," I reply, and then laugh. "She's beautiful, though. I love the color."

"LeMans Blue, the original color. That's what made me fall in love with her. Same color as your eyes, almost." He looks over at me and winks.

My eyes? It's his eyes that have me so weak. I can't believe he just said that to me. *I get it - this must just be what Frenchmen do. Disarm women with heady compliments, even if they aren't true.*

"This model," he goes on, "is underestimated. I've driven her all over America and she's never let me down once."

"You said you had a collection. What other cars do you have?" The wind is blowing my hair and I do up another button of my jacket.

"Really? You're interested?" he asks with a look of surprise.

"I'm no expert, believe me, but everyone loves a pretty car, don't they?" Knowing he likes British classics I throw out the first name that comes into my head. "E-Type Jaguars are impressive."

"Ha! You've got excellent taste, Ms. Robinson. You know something? When the E-Type first came out Enzo Ferrari, himself, called it the most beautiful car ever made."

"A Ferrari – now that's a fancy car. Do you have one?"

"No. I'm a Lamborghini man. There are too many posers cruising about the Côte d'Azur with Ferraris that they can hardly drive. An exquisite car, that can't be denied, but too much of a cliché for my own personal taste."

"So you don't use cars as babe magnets?" I joke.

"Actually, it's usually men who are attracted to my collection. I'm a man-trap, unfortunately."

"What's your Lamborghini like?" I ask, clueless.

"It's the *Murciélago.*"

"That means bat in Spanish."

"Exactly. It looks like Batman's car. It's outrageous. It's a stunning design. But it was actually named after a brave bull called Murciélago which fought with such spirit that the *matador* chose to spare its life, a virtually unheard of honor."

I grimace. "I hate bull-fighting."

"Me too. There are two things I can't understand in this world – cruelty to animals and cruelty to children. Oh, and women too – I don't understand how anybody could physically hurt a woman."

"Even if the woman agrees?"

Alexandre furrows his brow and stares at me hard for a second. "Why would any woman agree to being hurt by somebody?"

Uh, oh, where's my mouth plug? I find myself stuttering and wish I hadn't said that but then I dig myself in deeper and blurt out, "Whips and handcuffs are all the rage right now – rope is flying off the shelves at the hardware stores."

He narrows his eyes at me but I blabber on, "Well….a friend of mine……there are a bunch of books….so many erotic romances these days with a BDSM and bondage theme to them – they've gotten everyone curious…I mean women seem to be intrigued by the whole thing." *Shut up, Pearl, what made you come out with all that?*

"France has a tradition of literary erotic writing," Alexandre tells me. "The Marquis de Sade, Anaïs Nin, Pauline Réage - you know, the one who wrote *The Story of O*? But any sort of sexual slavery is a real turn-off for me."

"But what if it's consensual? You know, the dominant role-play with the submissive female – if it's an agreement between both parties?"

"It depends how young the girl is. Any woman under twenty-five is underage for that sort of role-play, in my opinion."

"But *you're* under twenty-five!" I exclaim, alarmed, and immediately wish I hadn't come out with that. *My God! He considers himself underage.*

"How d'you know how old I am?" he asks, and I can feel my face go hot.

"Just a guess," I lie. *Please don't ask me how old I am.*

"Almost right. I had my twenty-fifth birthday several months ago, actually. But I'm old for my age. I'm different, Pearl, I grew up way before my time – I was wise in all manner of things before the age of fourteen. Also, I'm a man. Young women are still vulnerable, still discovering the world and in my opinion it's not right for a girl to get involved with that sort of kinky stuff. It could be damaging psychologically as well as physically."

"Wow, you have very old-fashioned morals," I remark, surprised at his conservatism.

"Each to their own, but for me that sort of practice is so *not* erotic."

"What if it's the other way round? With some–" I am about to say, 'some Mrs. Robinson type,' but stop myself. *I* am Mrs. Robinson in many people's eyes…. being forty, hanging out with a younger guy – having designs on him sexually. Pearl Robinson - Robinson is the *last name* I need right now. My lips curl up at my silly pun.

"Well, being male that's hard for me to imagine because as a teenager, I happened to love more mature women and always had older girlfriends but I suppose a boy, in certain instances, could also be vulnerable."

"Well, millions of people might disagree with your attitude. Most people believe anyone is a fully-fledged adult at eighteen."

"You see?" he exclaims. "That's what's so strange about this country. You can whip and tie a girl up at that age with her consent but not offer her a glass of wine, or you'd be breaking the law."

"You're right, I hadn't thought of that. Most states you have to be twenty-one to drink."

"Anyway, wielding a whip is not my cup of tea, I can assure you, Pearl. Even if it is consensual. I can't imagine wanting to hurt a woman. Females are the gentler sex and should be treated with respect. Wanting to tie up a person and spank or whip her is something I could never do. I can't imagine how anyone could seriously get off on that."

I catch a glimpse of Alexandre's face and he looks angry as if I've touched a nerve. *Mama Mia, what made me steer the conversation in that direction? He must think I'm a pervert! Now I've really blown my chances.*

But then he adds with a wry smile, "A little harmless dress-up, maybe. A little food-play, but nothing that could *hurt* any-one."

Food play? Dress-up? My only contribution to dress-up was when I put on some heels and asked my ex-husband to do it to me with my shoes on. He didn't get it at all, told me to take them straight off. Seriously, is this what turns Alexandre on? Dress-up? Food? What kind of food? Mick Jagger and his legendary Mars Bar, shoved up you-know-where, type of food? (My brother told me that – is it true, I wonder)?

"Speaking of food, Pearl, you must be starving, I bet you didn't have time for any breakfast. I picked up some fruit and croissants and a couple of bottles of freshly squeezed orange juice." He leans behind him and produces a bag of goodies. "We can stop off for a coffee if you like or just wait until we get there."

"I can wait."

"Really? *Can* you?" The way he looks at me when he says it makes me wonder if there's a *double-entendre* somewhere. His eyes seem to be undressing me and he runs his tongue along his bottom lip ever so slightly. Perhaps the *double-entendre* is my imagination, and maybe he's just innocently licking his lips. Whatever, I'm feeling the heat between us.

Then he says, "As well as literature there are lots of erotic French films, too. Here, I'll play you the soundtrack to this famous one from the 70's – *Emmanuelle* – maybe you know it."

He puts on the music and I do recognize it – beautiful and very sensual. There's something about a man singing in French which is a real turn-on. Alexandre hums along to the tune and winks at me again. I sense a tingling in my groin which takes me by surprise. Our conversation about sex, the erotic music, the deep vibration of the Corvette's heavy engine makes me throb with desire. I wriggle in my seat just looking at him - his defined arm muscles flexed at the steering wheel, and he looking so handsome, driving this sexy femme-fatale of a car with such control - all this is excitingly new to me, truly unexpected.

I feel a pulse between my legs.

It's amazing how just ninety miles away from New York City you feel as if you're on a different planet. When we arrive at Shawangunk Mountains - pronounced Shon-gum and known simply as 'The Gunks' - Alexandre informs me that this is one of the best places for rock-climbing in North America and has a steady stream of eclectic visitors from all over the world. It is also home to several conservation groups. The scenery is breathtaking. Lush green stretches as far as the eyes can see, topped by imposing white and gray quartz cliff-bands, several miles wide, shooting up from the earth like proud monuments.

Alexandre has thought of and organized everything – packed water bottles, sunscreen, bug-repellent, even a spare camera in case I forgot mine (which I had) and, of course, his own gear. The guide will bring mine. I see Alexandre is a man quietly in control of situations – organized, methodical, leaving nothing to chance. He behaves way older than his years and has a cool sophistication about him, too. No wonder he's been so successful at such a young age.

"That's where we're going to climb along the Shawangunk Ridge. Up there where you see that tower?" he says, pointing. "That's Sky Top."

There's a stone tower perched on top of a mountain with a craggy rock-face below of pale golden stripes, creating from afar a series of patterns like old men's distorted faces etched into the rock formations. It looks terrifyingly vertical. Each horizontal stripe adding age to this natural masterpiece of nature. It's awesome in the real sense of the word.

"Sky Top is home to about three hundred rock climbs like Strawberry Yoghurt, Petie's Spare Rib and Jekyll and Hyde. Don't you just love the wacky names? It's private property and has been off-limits to climbers for more than ten years but we'll be having lunch at Mohonk Mountain Lodge so we're all set up. You look nervous, Pearl. Don't be, our guide knows these climbs like the back of his hand so you'll feel quite safe. I've been here several times - I know them too."

Our guide, Chris, is young and enthusiastic and looks like a surfer. He has a hard tan and deep crow's feet around his sun-weathered eyes. He claps his arms around Alexandre and says, "Hey, man, you made it. My favorite frog in the world."

"Very funny. This is my friend, Pearl. What have you got planned for us today, Chris? As I told you on the phone, Pearl's just a beginner, so we don't want to scare her with any overhangs - go easy on her today."

"Frog?" I ask.

"Don't mind me, just teasing," Chris cackles.

"As you probably know, we French get called Frogs by half the world – can't think why. Don't worry, when you come for dinner I won't serve you frogs or snails."

"You cook?" I ask Alexandre.

"A little."

Chris squints at the mountains before us. "I thought Pearl could start with Finger Licking Good this morning and see how we go."

We make our way along the trail until we come to a clearing beneath a massive rock-face. Chris goes through endless instructions, teaches me knots, commands, names of bits of equipment and safety checks. There is so much to learn and I kick myself. *Why did I agree to this?* The truth is, I lied to Alexandre. I have never been rock-climbing. Well, I once went with a group of friends in Idyllwild, California, so technically I did *go*. I even put on the gear but the rock-face was so daunting, I was too chicken to go through with it. I am a novice and I'm too ashamed to tell him. I've never, ever climbed more than several flights of stairs. It's too late now to come clean without humiliating myself further.

Alexandre helps me step into the leg loops of my harness and tightens the straps around me, hitching me up so it's snug against my pelvis and hips. When he touches me I sense my heart race. The shoes feel as if they are four sizes too small but they both assure me they are the perfect fit for good grip. I'm also given a helmet – uh, oh, not such a sexy look, but at this point, peering up at the rocky wall in front of me, I need all the help I can just to stay alive.

"You said this was for beginners," I grumble.

Alexandre looks amused. "It is."

"But I can't climb that!"

"Yes you can. Rock climbing is about faith, Pearl. Faith in yourself. Believe that you can overcome anything and you will. Trust me."

"I'll try," I say, not completely convinced.

"Good girl," he says tapping me on my behind. "Now climb up that rock-face and remember, don't look down any further than your feet. Keep going higher and higher. Take your time, don't rush, don't panic. Just believe in yourself. Now, I'll go up first, I'll be leading. There will be this rope connecting us. If you fall I'll have you – the rope will catch you, hooked into pre-placed bolts in the rock, so don't worry. Chris is down here with you. He'll be coaching you all the way. Trust him. He's been doing this for years, he's a pro."

I watch Alexandre as he climbs without hesitation up the sheer rock-face, clipping the rope into nooks and crannies. Easy for some. Meanwhile, Chris is explaining more technical stuff to me, how the ropes work, the carabiners.

He explains, "Now, whenever possible, Pearl, you should try to do most of the work of climbing using your *legs*. In the ideal case, climbers try to keep their centers of gravity over their feet and then push upwards with their legs. Only use your arms and hands just for balance and positioning."

"But where do I put my feet?" I squeal, looking up at what seems to be an almost smooth surface.

"You'll feel your way as you go and I'll guide you. Little itty-bitty notches and indentations – that's what you need to feel for with your hands which will, in turn, guide your feet into the right positions. Those shoes you're wearing have a lot of grip. Imagine you're climbing a ladder, it's that simple. But keep your weight down on your toes, not your heels."

"I *wish* it was that simple." My palms are sweating with trepidation.

"Here, dip your hands in this," Chris says, and I put the tips of my fingers into a little bag he offers me, filled with what seems like white chalk.

Alexandre is way up high, lodged on a small ledge, waiting for me. "Ready?" he shouts down.

I nod and take a sip of water to ease my nerves. Trembling, and I haven't even started.

"How much experience do you need to have to lead a

climb?" I ask Chris, double-checking Alexandre's prowess – *can I trust him?*

"There's no set answer to that. Leading is an art form, make no mistake, and it requires an incredible amount of climbing experience - stress management, decision making, route finding, rope management, gear placement, anchor systems, climbing technique and God knows what else, to be brought together all at once. You need to have a good head on your shoulders, and it helps to be mechanically inclined. I wouldn't let Alexandre do this if I didn't trust him implicitly. This is an easy climb but he's led some pretty tough ones. Don't worry, you're in good hands."

I know what Alexandre was talking about – Concentration with a capital C. I have never been so focused. They say the rope will catch my fall but I can't trust the equipment, I need to do this on my own, rely on myself. I gingerly put my foot on a hold and try to push my way higher. I manage and feel elated.

"See that little orange-colored knobby bit just up at the level of your thigh?" calls Chris. "Raise your left foot up there and push up through your toes."

"No way! Are you crazy?" I yell. "That's miles away! I can't lift my leg up that high and keep balance."

"Yes, you can," shouts down Alexandre. "Climb like a cat — quiet, deliberate, and precise. Picture the move, and then execute it. Use your feet as you would your hands. Pick out the place for your hands first – plan your move. Take your time, this isn't a race."

I raise up my left leg. Yoga has nothing on this.

"Now balance yourself," Chris calls up, "with your right hand. Lift your arm higher. Try to climb in an X shape with your hips being the middle of the X. Hang with your arm straight.

Your skeleton can take much more of a load than your muscles can."

Skeleton. Cat….which?

"Up you come, up you come," Alexandre coaxes.

After what seems like decades, I finally pluck up the courage to raise myself up. I feel myself falling, my insides churn and drop to my groin, but miraculously I manage to balance myself with my right hand in time. I'm spread-eagled against the rock-face. My elbows and knees are already scuffed and scratched.

"Bravo!" cries Alexandre.

"And now what?" I scream into the rock, my mouth kissing the stone. The sun is getting warmer now. I'm pressed like a starfish, immovable, terrified. All this to try and impress Alexandre but I must look like a total fool. My right foot starts to shake uncontrollably.

"Okay, I can see you've got sewing-machine leg," Chris bellows. "That's because the heel of your foot is hanging too far down and your leg is starting to shake like a sewing machine. This is very normal for a beginner. Don't worry, just apply more weight to your toes so your calf muscle spasm can stop."

I do as I'm told and he's right, my leg stops shaking. Almost. I push up again and am amazed at myself. The impossible is melting away. I feel free, invincible. I hook my fingers onto a tiny crevice, and what is a small opening feels like a crater to my sensitive hand. Everything is magnified by a thousand. Every indentation. Every chirp of a bird, every whistle of breeze, every miniscule scar on the rock-face, which I use as my life-line to cling onto. I can smell the rock. It is alive with molecules. And right now it's my best friend in the world. We are as one, the rock and I. I am a daughter of nature. I can think of nothing else except my hands and feet, the rock and my next move. Like a cat I push up once more. I'm not even listening to their instructions any longer; I'm trusting my own instinct, following my intuition. I'm higher now. I can no longer even hear what Chris is saying, he's so far below. I look up and see Alexandre smiling at me but I don't smile back. I'm too inside my own intense moment.

"You're nearly here. You're doing great," he cheers on. "Grab that bit that's jutting out to your right, above your head."

"I can't, it's too high."

"Yes you can. Just do it."

I reach up but feel myself slipping. Oh no! Mother of Mercy, what's happening? I can feel my body lose balance, I'm going to fall, I'm going to kill myself. I yelp. I slip. But at the last second my right foot finds a hold and I'm re-balanced, hugging the rock-face once more.

"That's a tricky bastard that tiny crack, isn't it?"

"I almost fell," I pant.

"But you didn't. I knew you'd find that hold – you were positioned right," he says. "Well done, chérie, well done."

I'm in reach of him now. Just one more push and I'm there on the ledge with him. Did he just call me chérie? Or was I imagining it? I make one final heave, my leg quivering with exhaustion and I'm there, hurling myself onto him.

He catches me and hugs me tight in his arms. "I'm so proud of you, you did great. Good girl." His skin smells of sun and open air, and something else wonderful – a happy memory I can't quite place. He takes my hand and kisses it with a flourish, then raises my other and kisses it too, but more slowly this time, his lips soft against my fingers. I can feel the breath of his nostrils, gentle like an imperceptibly warm breeze, and I go limp in his strong arms, my legs buckling under me with fatigue.

We're in Alexandre's beautiful LeMans Blue Corvette heading back to New York City. I'm stretched out in the front seat going over all the sweet details of the day in my mind. It was arduous but probably one of the most satisfying days of my life. While I was getting my breath back after the first climb, mentally gearing-up for another assault on my limbs, I watched Alexandre and Chris scale a rock-face with overhangs, called *Sound and Fury*. Alexandre maneuvered his body with grace and precision – I was in awe, especially knowing how hard it is to cling on almost vertically, let alone upside down horizontally! They discussed it afterwards, describing their 'free-swinging ape-man moves' and it was true, they looked like agile monkeys – it was nail-bitingly tense to watch. Then I did another climb after lunch, harder than the first, and felt as if I'd conquered the world. It was exhilarating. We took lunch at the luxury resort hotel, The Mohonk Mountain House, situated right on Mohonk Lake. It looked like a Victorian castle, with balconies and tall windows and replete with period decor. I guess this must have been where we would have stayed had my face not registered such alarm yesterday. Shame.

I am wary of my desire to please this man. I have never felt this way before. At least, not since my early years when I wanted to please my father while learning to ride a bicycle. The determination to get it right and earn approval from Alexandre is shocking.

I'm mulling all this over, enjoying the car ride, when he turns his head and says with a little smile:

"You've passed the second test."

"Second? What was the first?" I ask bemused.

"You can't guess?"

"No."

"You have no idea?"

"No, not a clue."

He smiles, says nothing, and I'm racking my brains wondering what the first test was.

"Give me a hint," I plead.

"You'll find out, soon enough."

I picture myself wearing the helmet today, my ungainly positions, my elbows and knees scratched all over, and wonder if he's teasing me. The music is loud - a soulful, dusky voice surrounds us, singing about giving over your heart. I feel vulnerable and know that if I did give Alexandre my heart he could break it.

I ask him, "What's this great song? I don't think I've heard it before."

"By an artist called Rumer. Doesn't she have a lovely voice? The song's called *Come to Me High.*"

The lyrics speak my mind. I *am* on a high. A high from the feeling of staring death in the eye. Of course it wasn't really that way, the ropes could have caught my fall, and did at one point on the second climb – but still, every nerve in my body has been awakened by the thrill of today. The buzz of fear, the fear of failure, and the thrill of the way Alexandre makes me feel inside.

"You should feel proud of yourself, Ms. Robinson." *That R again. That sexy accent.* "You've really piqued my interest," he purrs in a soft voice.

He puts his hand on my bare thigh and I feel a shiver run up my spine. I'm wearing a thin cotton skirt which he pushes a couple of inches higher up my leg. His fingers linger on my flesh and I'm too stunned to stir. He starts to move them softly, one hand edging towards my crotch, but oh so subtly – so much so I wonder if I'm imagining it. His other hand is on the wheel. I can feel that pulse deep in my groin again. I look at him. So gorgeous! His chest muscles are ripped from today's action. I saw him change out of his T-shirt and put on a linen shirt before lunch, and I nearly passed out. His skin was smooth, tanned and flawless with just a small amount of body hair in between his pecs. Just thinking about his body now makes me throb with desire - his elegant fingers imperceptibly still resting on my upper thigh – I feel as if my heart-beat is between my legs. But then, he takes his hand away, back to the steering wheel. I let out a sigh of frustration. He's tormenting me with this tease.

"Tell me about yourself, Pearl. You're a mystery to me. I know you're brave and up for a challenge. I know you like dogs, and I can sense you're smart. What else?"

I feel as if he's asking, what else do you have to offer me? I can't seem to answer him. I rack my brains for something clever to tell him about myself, something impressive. I'm still wondering what the first test I've passed is. Rock-climbing being the second – but the first? "I don't know what to say, really," I begin. "My life is pretty hum-drum compared to yours."

"I doubt that very much. Tell me about your family."

"Well, my mom died three years ago. Of cancer."

"I'm so sorry."

"Yeah, it changed my life, we were very close. I'm only just getting over it. I mean, you can *never* really get over it but I'm finally accepting what happened. My dad lives in Hawaii and owns a surf shop."

"Another passion of mine. So you surf, then?"

"No. No, not at all. I've never even tried. He left us when I was six years old to go 'find' himself. He did. He found himself. Found himself a new wife, too. I guess I always associated surfing with abandonment. I went to see him last year – see if I could lay a few ghosts to rest. I wanted to tell him what I thought of him, unleash all my anger."

"And?"

"And….well, it didn't work out that way. The second I laid eyes on him I burst into tears and all I could think about were all those wasted years between us. We hugged like two long-lost bears. He had such a kind face. I fell in love with his little-boy-lost look, just the way my mom had done all those years ago, and I couldn't help but forgive him. He was lonely - his second wife had died several years previously. All my anger melted away. We talked every night watching the moonlit waves, drinking cocktails under the stars. Then he came to Manhattan to visit me. We keep in touch by e-mail - Skype every week. You know, I'm so glad to have him in my life, even after all the heartache he caused."

"And what about brothers and sisters, you have them, too?"

"I have a brother who lives in San Francisco. Anthony. We see each other once in a while." I want to tell him about my late brother, John, who died of an overdose ten years ago but I can't seem to bring myself to mention his name.

"Does Anthony have children, a wife?"

"No, he's gay. He lives with his boyfriend, Bruce. What about your parents?" I ask.

"Well, I had a similar upbringing to you. My mother was a single parent. It was just the three of us. 'The Three Musketeers,' she called us. All for one, and one for all. We were very close. Still are."

"Oh, I thought when you said that your dog, Rex, lived with your parents, your dad was–"

"My step-father. She re-married when I was sixteen."

"Ah. Is he nice?"

"He helped me and my sister set up our business. He's a good man. And most importantly, he's a great husband to my mother."

"What about your dad?"

"I don't talk about him. Ever."

"Oh, I'm sorry."

I want to ask him why. But I can see his eyes alight with fury, his mouth shut tight as if a floodgate has just been opened and streams of polluted water are flowing uncontrollably and it needs to be locked shut again. His look scares me. The charming Frenchman has turned. His face is dark with resentment. Is it resentment? Or am I reading him wrong? Perhaps he misses his father. I wonder if he is still alive and what the story is, but I'm too nervous to ask. I quickly change the subject.

"So, tell me about—" we both burst out simultaneously, our voices in unison. We laugh.

"You first," I say.

"No, you. What were you going to ask me?"

"Just about your work."

"Me, too," he says laughing. "I was going to ask you about what *you* do." *Phew, his furious scowl has dissipated.*

"I was just going to ask you about the way your company is linked to charities," I venture.

He narrows his eyes. "How do you know that?"

"I read a piece in *The New York Times*. How all the advertising for HookedUp automatically gives a percentage to charity."

"That's right. People like giving to charity but they *don't* like giving to charity, if you see what I mean. People want to, and often do, but when they have their hard-earned pay check in front of them, bills take priority, especially in these tough times, and charities lose out. This way, they don't even have to think about it. It's done for them."

"You mean the advertisers pay?"

"Exactly. But they have such a massive audience that it's worth their while. Everybody wins."

"So how does it work?"

"It's really simple. Three percent of all advertising revenue goes straight to a multitude of different charities hand-picked by me and my sister. It sounds like nothing but you'd be amazed how much it adds up."

"So what are your charities?"

"So many. All varied. Children in need. Water wells. The blind, deaf, and mute. Setting up schools in remote areas all over the world. There's one called The Smile Train that fixes hare lips, cleft palates and deformities, and there's another charity, I forget its name now, that helps with cataracts. Such simple operations that can transform a life. Then there are our personal favorites - women's shelters to safeguard them from domestic violence, and animal protection associations. We even have a donkey sanctuary on our list."

That's the second time he's mention domestic violence, I notice.

"A lot of people object to that," he continues. "They think humans should always come before animals. But you know what? They can fuck right off. Until we all learn to treat creatures with respect, there isn't much hope for the human race."

Passion is dancing in his eyes again and he stares hard at me without smiling, maybe testing me for my reaction.

"You're preaching to the converted," I let him know. "I agree, animals are God's creatures, too."

I relax back into my seat and wonder more about who this man really is. He has me fascinated. So young to have such feisty, strong opinions, yet he seems way, way older than his years. His mother raised him and his sister, alone. Tough. I think of my own mother and the agony of her death, the cancer eating away at her insides when she was too young to leave this earth. "What about cancer research?" I ask, thinking of her. "Do you support those charities, too?"

"You see, I know this is a sensitive subject for you, Pearl - losing your mother to that awful disease - but that's a tricky one for me. All our charities are vetted to make sure they're not linked with any upsetting practices. As long as any particular cancer research center is not using animals to test on, that's great. There's stem-cell research now, there's no excuse for anybody to be testing on animals."

"You're getting into deep water, there," I say, tears welling in my eyes. I quickly look down so he doesn't notice.

"Sink or swim."

"What do you mean by that?"

"In this life, you have to make choices. You have to take sides. I have to make tough decisions in my line of work every day of the week. I can't say yes to everybody. Plus, I have to make a stand. Nobody is being forced to use HookedUp. The list of charities is right there for anyone to investigate. If they don't like the way we do things, fine, they can drink their tea elsewhere."

I burst out laughing. He loves expressions that have to do with tea. Living all those years in England, perhaps. My laugh is nervy. I wanted to be angry with him but I find myself beguiled by his strength, by his overconfidence, his pride. And his quirky sense of humor.

"Do I amuse you, Pearl Robinson?"

"*Drink their tea elsewhere* – I love that. Especially the way you say it."

"Are you making fun of my accent, Ms. Robinson?" Alexandre's half-cocked smile lets me know he's enjoying being teased. "My turn," he continues, more seriously now. "I was about to ask you about *your* work. You said you write. Tell me more."

"Actually, I make films. Documentaries."

There, I said it. He'll probably realize now, why I was at the conference.

"An activist, then."

Good, he's not put two and two together.

"I have my ideas. And yes, often they are quite controversial. Topics for discussion and thought."

"Like what, for instance?" he asks.

"We did something on pharmaceutical companies. The hold they have over the world. The exorbitant sums of money they earn, often at the expense of poor nations."

"So you like to kick up a storm?"

"I like to reveal the truth."

I say this but it has struck me that there are all sorts of truths I am masking from him. Not to mention my age. Thank God he hasn't asked me that. Yet.

"You have your own company?" he wants to know.

"No, I work for someone. Her name's Natalie. She's actually

visiting my father in Hawaii. She left today on vacation. Ironic, that - that my boss should hook up with my dad. Didn't see that coming when I introduced them." The hook-up word, again. Clever name for a social media site.

"Keep it in the family. What's she like, your boss?"

"Smart. Beautiful. Opinionated. Tough to please." Sounds like I'm describing Alexandre himself.

"From New York?"

"Yes. From Queens. But she lives in Manhattan now."

"French origin?"

"No, why do you ask that?"

"Because Natalie is a really common name in France."

"I don't think she has French roots – she's African-American."

"Seems like your dad lucked out. She sounds interesting."

"She is. It complicates things a little having two such close people to me, together in a relationship but I'm getting used to it now."

We've been talking so much I hardly realize that we've already arrived outside my building. It's now dark. Alexandre parks the car by the curb next to my apartment block.

"Well, here we are. Thank you, Pearl for a wonderful day." *Wonder Fool.*

"Thank *you.* You've awakened my senses."

"Oh, that's just the beginning, believe me," he says enigmatically.

I catch my breath and feel my mouth part. *The beginning? Please say he's not just kidding.* I'm hoping he's going to kiss me. But abruptly, he gets out of his side, walks around and opens the car door for me. I scramble out of this low Corvette, trying to look composed, but my legs are momentarily splayed apart, showing off a flash of my white panties.

He undresses me for a second, his eyes in a half-closed bedroom, *come hither-and-fuck-me* look, noticing the color of underwear I have on - I'm sure of it. He bites his lower lip and I feel those butterflies again.

"Would you like to come in? Have a bite to eat, a glass of wine?" I offer.

"No, Pearl. Thank you, but I have an early meeting tomorrow."

"But tomorrow's Sunday," I protest, having somehow whipped up a dinner à deux for tonight, a romantic interlude and at least a long kiss between us.

But it's clear to me now that our 'date' has ended. He's been toying with me. Amused to see me all flustered, turned-on and worked up. He's a professional charmer. Of course he doesn't want any romance with me. *He's twenty-five years old!* He's probably going off to dinner somewhere else, *with* someone else, and then on to a trendy club to dance the night away with her - some nubile sex-pot, before fucking her senseless and then taking her out to a fabulous Sunday brunch somewhere tomorrow. *Stop!* I say to myself. *Enough! He's taken you rock-climbing - you've had a great time. Leave it at that.*

"I had a fabulous day," I say.

"Me too."

"Really?" I ask with an unwanted tinge of disbelief in my voice.

"Really. It's been fun. Night-night. You'll be tired and will sleep like a baby. Get some rest, your body needs it."

If only, I mull, he knew what my body *really* needed. It has been awoken, and now awake, it is *pining* for attention.

He walks me up to my door and then presses a light kiss on my lips. No tongue, no exploration, just a gentle, soft kiss. "Night Pearl, take care."

"Night," I murmur, my voice small.

I turn to go inside and the doorman lets me into the lobby. "Good evening Mrs. Robinson, did you have a good day?"

"Marvelous thanks, Dervis."

"Oh, Mrs. Robinson. One thing - I'll be on vacation this week. There'll be the new boy here taking my place. Luke."

"The skinny one with dark hair?"

"Yes. That's right."

"Okay, thanks."

I turn my head and look through the glass of the wrought-iron door to see Alexandre's expression but he's already revving up his car and driving off. He didn't even say he'd call. Who knows? I guess I'll never see him again.

3

The following day is slow torment. All yesterday's fun is being marred by my own insecurity and post-mortem blues. I almost wish I hadn't met him, my senses being stirred, like hearing a beautiful piece of music for the first time. Or a poem. And then having it snatched away from you forever. *How can this whippersnapper of a man have this effect on me?* I think of my last name, Robinson, and feel a wave of clichéd embarrassment surge through my veins. *The Graduate* - Mrs. Robinson. How apt. Except I am *Ms.* Robinson now. At least *Mrs.* Robinson got to see it through. At least *she* had guts. There I was, last night, like some simpering fool as I said goodbye. I should have taken the reins. Pounced on him. Okay, it would have only been one night probably, but one night of bliss, surely? Now I have nothing.

No, that's not true, he's done me a favor – he's made me realize that there *are* fish in the sea. There is life after divorce. And I can, literally, climb a mountain.

As if reading my thoughts telepathically, my brother calls. His usual Sunday call. Comforting.

"Hi Anthony."

"So where are you having brunch today?" he asks.

"I don't know," I answer despondently.

"Hey girl, you sound happy. What's up?"

"No, I am happy. Really. Just—"

"What?"

"Just a guy."

"Hallelujah! I never thought the day would come. Tell me more, girlfriend."

"Stop that 'hey girlfriend' talk, Anthony."

"Seriously. Who is he?"

"A young guy."

"How young?"

"Twenty-five."

He hoots with laughter. "Cradle-snatcher."

"Shut up."

"So, how was it?"

"That's just the problem. It wasn't. Nothing happened."

"Oh, I see. So you're just *friends*?"

"Maybe not even that."

I tell him about our day, all the details about Alexandre, rehash our conversations. Anthony is silent for a beat. He is never silent.

"Speak. Say something," I plead.

"Just forget him. I don't want to see you get hurt."

"You mean, I'm past my sell-by date and this man is way too young and gorgeous for me?"

"I didn't say that."

"You didn't have to. I can hear it in your voice. Even in your silence."

"Look, Pearly. He's uber-rich, he's young, he's sexy. He must have pretty girls throwing themselves at him. Especially, with his French accent and his drop-dead-delicious body. Girlies wet their panties for that stuff. He's probably your typical Latin Lover kind of guy who has a woman in every port."

"You're right. But why can't I be one of those women in one of the ports? The Port of New York."

"Go out there, and now that this youngster has whetted your appetite – or should I say 'wetted' your appetite – start dating guys *your own age* and get laid by one of them."

"But I haven't found anyone else attractive. For…for… *forever*. That's the problem!"

"Well, if you're happy to dry up like some old prune, be my guest. I'm just trying to offer some brotherly advice. Look, I've got to go - we're running late. I'll call you next week, okay? By that time you'll be over him. At least he didn't get into your panties *and then* not call, or you'd *really* be obsessing. I know how women are. They want forbidden fruit."

I frown. "So you're already assuming he won't call? Thanks for the vote of confidence. And why should he be so forbidden?"

"Hello? Pearl! He's almost half your age."

"But what about Madonna? Her boyfriend–"

Anthony cuts short my sentence with an exasperated sigh followed by a palpable silence. It cuts like a knife. Madonna, his heroine. Madonna, the Holy Grail.

"I know, I know, I can't compare myself to Madonna."

"No, you can't. Bye sweet pea. Take care. And don't do anything rash. Love you."

He hangs up and I'm left feeling bereft and tiny. He's right. I've got to be realistic – I must forget Alexandre.

I start doing my usual Sunday morning tidy-up. I go down to the basement and do laundry, do some dusting, put away clothes and generally sort out my apartment and the tangible things in my life.

I love my apartment. It's my little haven. Full of my favorite books (self-help, classics like Graham Greene and sad Russian novels by Tolstoy and Dostoyevsky - just to remind me how heavy life is – and children's books like the Beatrix Potter series, The Wind in the Willows, and books about dogs). Interesting taste. Varied, to say the least.

I have a mixture of modern and figurative paintings on my walls. Originals, no prints. I love to support new, young painters and always keep an eye out for up and coming artists. Some of the works have appreciated in value but I don't care about that. I only buy something if it speaks to me, if it tells me a story. I have a dark wooden, four-poster, antique bed from France draped with off-white linen, and an art-deco table with four chairs for the times I have my girlfriends over. No men, apart from my father, my brother and the pizza delivery guy have set eyes on my apartment. I'm a loner. This place is like a sanctuary. It's private. It's me in a nutshell, and I find it hard to let anyone crack it open.

My phone is ringing again. Anthony to apologize for being such a negative schmuck? No, it's Daisy calling, my British friend who's been living in New York forever. I pick up.

"Hi Daisy."

"Hi sweet cakes. Brunch?"

"A hundred percent yes. I'm starving. And feeling unattractive. Maybe you can bolster me up."

She chortles with laughter. "*You*? Unattractive? You make me sick. Wish I had your beautiful blonde hair, your perfect body."

"I'm old."

"Oh pl—*ease*."

"I feel old."

"You *so* don't look your age. You could pass for thirty."

"Still too old."

"Too old for what?"

"I'll tell you at brunch."

We are downtown in The Village on the outside terrace of the restaurant where we've chosen to eat, blessed with another sunny day. The young and beautiful are wandering by in polka-dot dresses and designer shades, some with designer dogs. I'm people-watching and glugging down a Bloody Mary with extra horse-radish sauce, for kick and punch. I've wolfed down my Eggs Benedict and I'm ready for my third drink. This is unusual for me – I don't usually have more than a glass or two of wine.

I can hear my words slurring, morose pessimism thick in my voice. "Why do you think I haven't dated all this time? It's too raw, too painful, that's why."

Daisy is married with a child. She has forgotten what it's like *out there*. She's looking fresh-faced and jolly; her husband has taken her daughter, Amy, to the park for the day and Daisy has a few hours free. Her dimpled cheeks and curly red hair make her look like a grown-up *Annie*.

"Bollocks!" she exclaims. "You've been locked away at work and have not even given dating a chance. Anyway, it sounds like this Alexandre guy is into you."

"That wasn't my brother's opinion."

"Yeah, well, this happens every week. After you've spoken to Anthony you always seem to want to slit your wrists."

I say sarcastically, "I haven't noticed that."

"Families – often they do more harm than good. Take what he says with a pinch of salt. Look, Alexandre fondled your thigh, kissed your hand like some romantic, courtly knight from the Medieval Age. Come to think of it, isn't that his last name? Knight?"

"Alexandre Chevalier."

"Exactly. Chevalier means knight in French."

"That's right, I'd completely forgotten that. My French is pretty poor. I can speak some Spanish, though."

"Listen, he took you away for the whole day, treated you to everything, including a beautiful lunch at that fancy resort."

"But that doesn't mean he finds me sexy."

"If you looked like the back end of a bus, believe me, Pearl, he wouldn't have bothered. He must be interested to have invested a whole day with you. Men are basic. They don't do favors, they do what they *feel* like doing."

"I'll tell you something interezz - ting," I slur, the Bloody Marys making me bold. "When he had his hand on my thigh, I thought I saw a big rock in his jeans. I assumed it must be his wallet but later, when I looked again, after he'd taken his hand away, it had gone down. Could be my imagination—"

"You see? He had—" - she lowers her voice and looks about to check nobody is listening - "-a *hard-on* when he touched you."

"So then, why didn't he ask to stay over? Or at least come in for a night cap? Or rather a 'knight cap,' " I joke, tweaking my fingers in quotation marks.

"I don't know. Odd behavior for a man in his twenties. But, apart from that, it does sound as if he really fancies you."

4

Nearly a week has gone by. No news from Alexandre. Such a bullshitter, giving me hints about inviting me over for a meal, going climbing again, et cetera.

I have thrown myself into work, re-editing some old projects I had put aside and doing massive amounts of research on all manner of controversial topics. I'm grateful that Natalie is away so I don't have to fend off questions and nosey wonderings about why I am so quiet this week.

When I get home from work, Dervis the doorman is back from his vacation, his large Hungarian frame looking a few pounds heavier.

"You look relaxed, Dervis," I tell him as he opens the door for me. "Did you have fun?"

"Yes, thank you, Mrs. Robinson. I just stayed at home but it was very pleasant. Very pleasant indeed." I notice a sheepish look on his face. "I'm so sorry, Mrs. Robinson. There's a package for you. The new boy put it in the store room and I've just discovered it."

"When did it arrive?"

"It had Mrs. Meyer's dry-cleaning with it which was delivered last Tuesday so it looks as if it has been there for a few days. It came by hand delivery."

"But it's Friday today."

"I apologize. Luke has made several other mistakes and has already been dismissed. He won't be working with us anymore." Dervis goes to retrieve a large, gray box wrapped in a white, velvet ribbon, and hands it to me.

"Thank you, Dervis. Oh, and by the way it's Ms. - not Mrs."

"Pardon?"

Poor Dervis can't get his head around feminist American culture.

"I'm not married anymore, Dervis," I explain. "Mzz is better for me than Mrs." I smile at him sweetly.

I ride up in the elevator and race to my front door, but typically, I can't find my keys. In a panic, I empty the entire contents of my handbag on the floor. I discover them. They were hiding themselves, lodged in my address book. Why I still have an address book when all my numbers are in my iPhone, I do not know, perhaps the weight of paper reassures me. Or the infallibility. I fumble with my keys and unlock the door. This package is making me nervous.

I walk into my messy bedroom, place the box on the bed and stare at it. It is not my birthday. My heart is racing. *Is it possible that….?* No, surely not.

I open the box. Inside is another one, also donning a ribbon, the box much smaller. I lift off its lid and again, another box, oblong in shape. Also, tied with a ribbon, but one made of silk.

My hands are trembling. Another box now – in pale blue leather edged in gold, but it isn't new. It is slightly tattered. I open it. It's velvet-lined and has the name of a Parisian jeweler of *La Place Vendôme* inside - the most expensive jewelry quarter in Paris. The box is antique. I can't believe what I'm seeing. *Did the young doorman make a mistake? Surely this must belong to Mrs. Meyer on the eleventh floor?* I check the name on the first box again, **Ms. Pearl Robinson**, written in large, black letters. No mistake.

I gaze at the stunning piece of jewelry nestled in the leather box: an exquisite double strand of pearls with a diamond and platinum, Art Deco clasp. This definitely looks vintage – they don't make designs like this anymore. There is no way this is a copy. And the worn blue box – unquestionably antique.

I lift the necklace out of the box, delicately. It's a choker; the pearls perfectly round, graduating very subtly in size - fine lustrous pearls with overtones of cream, rose and hints of pale honey and bronzy gold. I hold them up to the light – the myriad colors shimmer with unfathomable depth. I cannot count the different shades; if I were an artist and had to paint them I'd need to mix at least forty hues of subtle colors to do them justice. I think of their origin, each pearl starting its life off as a grain of sand locked in an oyster shell – how each one turns into a perfect, complete jewel. Naturally iridescent, polished by nature, not man.

I unhook the intricate clasp of the necklace and walk to the large mirror in my bathroom, terrified my fingers will fumble – *please don't let me drop this work of art on the floor!* I lay the choker around my neck, the clasp at the front so I can see what I'm doing. A perfect fit. Its beauty is breathtaking. I gasp. My namesake - Pearl. My nose starts to prickle as tears well in my eyes, now glistening like pools of water – like the pearls. I stare into the mirror in disbelief. Nobody has ever given me a gift this special. *But no note? Nothing?* I go back and search amongst the boxes on my bed and inside one of them I find a small envelope. I open it. A handwritten card reads:

Pearl,

These Pearls belonged to a unique Parisian lady called Delphine Aimée. This necklace was a wedding present from her husband, designed especially for her. She was a happy woman, a shining star ...one of the greats. This choker will bring you good luck. There are precisely 88 pearls. Eight is a lucky number.
Eighty-eight is an untouchable number. It is the symbol of infinity – the double directions of the infinity of the universe. It is the period of revolution, in number of days, of the planet Mercury around the sun. It is the number of constellations in the sky. It is the number of keys on a piano.
It is your number, Pearl.

Alexandre.

I am suddenly aware of how embarrassing this situation is. Days have passed since the gift was delivered. Not knowing, I haven't called to say, thank you. He must think me the rudest, most ungrateful woman that exists. I can't believe he hasn't called me to check I'd received the package. Surely he must be worried.

How valuable is this piece of exquisite jewelry? It doesn't bear thinking about. Where, now, did I leave his business card?

I find it in the kitchen and call. No answer. His voice-mail picks up. I leave a message, my speech garbled, my apologies profuse with jumbled explanations as to why I haven't called.

I go into the bathroom, quivering from the surprise and excitement of the last fifteen minutes. I need to relax. Friday evening is my weekly personal hygiene, me-time. I check my roots. They're fine. My pedicure still looks perfect but I need to do my legs and double-check my underarms. I strip off my work clothes, brush my teeth until they squeak, and run the bath. I need a good long soak to ease away the stress of the week and the tension of worrying if Alexandre will return my call. Perhaps he has given up on me by now, wishing he'd never given me such an extravagant gift. Maybe he'll even demand the pearls back. Punishment for being so ill-mannered. Can I accept such an expensive gift? Perhaps he got them in a foolish moment, a hasty decision which he now regrets. I must be prepared for that, prepared to let them go.

My beauty regime begins. I take out the cold wax strips – I can't be bothered with salons, it takes too long, so I always do this myself in the privacy of my own home. It's quick, painless, like ripping off a Band-Aid – I've been doing this since I was fifteen and proud that I've never let a razor near my skin. This way, the hair grows back sparse and soft, not stubbly as it does with shaving. I had my bikini line dealt with years ago – electrolysis did the trick, but I regularly give my pubic hair a neat, close trim with a round-ended pair of small scissors. No gray down there, thank goodness. When that day comes it'll be a full Brazilian, all the way.

I look at myself in the long mirror – I'm naked, except for the pearl choker; I look like a vintage hand-tinted photograph of a 1920's glamour girl, my make-up still on but my body nude. I clip my hair up and try to take off the necklace. It won't come off. I don't want to force it, God forbid something should happen. Can you wear pearls in hot water? Suddenly, I fear they could melt. *No, that's absurd, of course they wouldn't.* I climb into my nice, warm, bubble bath, laced with aromatherapy oils, lie back and pick up the book I've been reading but haven't been able to concentrate on. As usual, I start thinking about Alexandre Chevalier but now my reflections are tempered with sweet hope. He bought me a gift! And not just a box of chocolates (which in itself would have been enough of a thrill) - but an out-of-this-world, one of a kind necklace.

Unique. Precious. Personal. With a beautiful message -the number eighty-eight with all those meanings.

How *Romantic.*

I let my hands explore my body, massaging the oily water around my knees, my elbows. I take care of my skin in this way - it keeps me soft. I rub the heels of my feet and in between my toes and soon my fingers wander northwards. I have Alexandre's buffed-up torso in my mind's eye, the sexy glint in his expression, his prowess as he climbed that rock, the texture of his messy dark hair, the smell of his skin and the huge, hard bulge I could see in his pants when he touched my thigh. I sense a throbbing tingle in my groin and slip my middle finger inside myself and rub the sweet-smelling water around me, gently on my clitoris and up around my mound of Venus. I think about my anatomy and suddenly coin a new V word inspired by the number eight: the number of infinity, and eighty-eight, double infinity. V for vagina.

V for Vajayjay. And now V for V - Eight.

Or just plain "V," vagina sounds so clinical.

And what about V for Venus? That's a good one - so much prettier than just plain vagina.

I can hear the house phone ring but I ignore it, I'm not getting out of this heavenly bath. But then my cell starts buzzing. I reach for it on the edge of the tub.

"Hello?"

"I'm downstairs," a familiar voice says.

My heart misses a beat. It's Alexandre. It must have been Dervis calling on the land line to let me know I have a visitor. Alexandre is here in the building!

"I'm in the bathtub," I say.

"Good," Alexandre replies, "I'll join you."

"Pass me onto Dervis," I say.

I can hear Dervis's breathing on Alexandre's cell. "Dervis, you can let him come up," I tell him.

"Okay Mrs. Robinson."

I scramble out of the tub and quickly dry myself. The pearl necklace is glistening, even more now, with drops of oily water. I wrap a huge white towel about me and glance into the mirror which is all steamed-up. I wipe a corner away and see my mascara is smudged, my eye-make-up dark, like coal. I swab a little away with a Q tip and let my hair down. My doorbell is buzzing. I feel my heart thud and I go to answer it.

I open the door. He's more striking than I remembered. He looks disheveled, his dark hair unkempt, his shirt half unbuttoned. He's wearing flip-flops and his feet are elegant and clean. He has a huge bunch of the palest pink roses in his grip, and a bottle of chilled champagne.

"I've missed you Pearl," he says, taking a step towards me.

I feel myself go weak.

"You're wearing the necklace," he observes, running his fingers on the nape of my neck. I tingle all over.

"It's the most stunning thing I've ever seen. I can't thank you enough."

"It's normal," he replies, which I think translated directly from the French means, 'you're welcome'.

No, it's not normal! I want to shout out. But I say, "Are you sure? I mean, I shouldn't accept such a generous gift."

"You *have* accepted this gift, Pearl. You're wearing it and it couldn't suit you more. So stop protesting and come closer." He puts the flowers and champagne on the hall table and takes me in his arms, pulling me tight to him. "You look beautiful," he whispers, staring into my eyes. "How perfect those pearls look on you."

He pushes me against the wall and plants a gentle kiss on my mouth. I gasp. Then his tongue opens my lips apart and he begins to explore slowly around my mouth, licking me softly. My jaw is slack, my breath fast, hungry to be as close to him as possible, greedy for more. The points of our tongues touch and I feel a spasm of desire shoot through my body. Then our mouths are full of each other, tongues probing, locking together.

He pulls off my towel, stands back from me as if to take in the image. "Beautiful," he says with approval. His mouth traces itself around my throat and shoulders - then my nipples which his tongue licks deftly, flicking around each areola until both are erect. He simultaneously strokes the small of my back and buttocks with the tips of his fingers, running them lightly along the crack of my butt. I moan with pleasure. I feel how moist I am between my legs, my V-8 swelling hot. I lower my eyes and notice the huge bulge in his jeans and I gasp in anticipation.

He sucks one nipple and then takes it gently in his teeth but without hurting me. "I'm going to have to do things to you, Pearl. I want you so much. But you know that, already, don't you?"

"I wasn't sure," I say in a thin voice.

I reach for his crotch but he stops me. "Not yet - ladies first," and then he moves his tongue around my breasts again. "I love your tits, they're perfect - your skin's so soft."

His hands are now firmly around my waist. He licks one nipple and lets his fingers walk down one of my thighs. His large hand cups my mound of Venus and I feel one finger slip inside me.

"So, so wet," he murmurs, biting his lower lip. "You're making me rock-hard, chérie. I'm going to have to do something about that. You're really asking for it, aren't you, Pearl? So soon? And I haven't even started yet."

He adjusts his position so he is standing behind me, my back pressed up against his torso – I can feel his hard-on. His thumb is inside me now, his palm cupping the entirety of my vulva. He's holding me as if I were a six-pack! It feels incredible.

"So juicy," he breathes, grabbing the champagne and flowers in the other hand and pulling me close behind him, thumb still inside me, his palm pressing hard against my clitoris. "Come on, let's have a drink – you'll need to put these flowers in water."

I'm on tiptoes tottering in front of him, his hand maneuvering me, thumb still inside, slowly circling as if he is steering me. I feel him with every step I take - gently pushed ahead by him, his palm pressing my sweet spot. I lean back for a second and press my back against his torso. I feel his erection through his pants up against me - his hand still controlling me as if I were a glove puppet. So dominating! But it feels really erotic. Then he softly lets me go. I'm nude, panting, wet as an oil slick, not understanding what has just happened. I turn round to face him - he's smiling, amused.

"Let's have some champagne," he suggests.

"Let me put something on," I reply, confused.

He runs his finger up my spine and feels the choker around my neck, fondling the pearls with the tips of his fingers. "You've already got something on."

"Some clothes," I whimper. I feel vulnerable, exposed. It's as if he has control over me. No man has ever seen me this way. Nude with a choker of Art Deco pearls around my neck like an exotic dog collar. Yes, as if I were some expensive dog on a leash to be pulled and led this way and that! To be *manhandled*. I'm in my own apartment yet, for some reason, I feel helpless.

He holds me by the wrist and pulls me closer. "No clothes. Why would you want to put on clothes? You're so sexy as you are. So beautiful."

"I feel—"

"I forbid it."

He's French. Maybe the translation has come out wrong. The word 'forbid' sounds ridiculous. Like a command. So young, but evidently domineering. But then I see a humorous smirk on his face and I realize he's teasing me.

But before I can protest, he's on his knees, running his tongue around my navel and down towards my wet opening. His head is underneath me now and his five o'clock shadow is brushing against my thighs and along my cleft. He starts licking me slowly, softly, as if I were an ice-cream on a sweltering day, under, over, around, up inside, running the tip of his tongue around to catch the melting bits. I'm groaning now, the pleasure is indescribable.

"So sweet," he murmurs. "You taste delicious. So, so ready for me. You have no idea how much I want to be inside you."

And then he stops.

"Come on," he takes my hand. "I think you need a glass of champagne."

I'm a wreck. I stand there, stupefied. Naked. Hot with longing. Desperate for him to lead me to the bed and fuck me. *What's he playing at?* I want him inside me. Right *now*. But he's talking about having a glass of champagne and putting the roses in water! Still holding my hand, he leads me to the kitchen. As if it's his own apartment, he starts opening cupboards and looking for a vase.

"Up there on the left, second cabinet," I say with disbelief - my groin on fire.

I watch him fill up the tall, glass vase with water and arrange the glorious bouquet of pink roses; pale, pale pink, like some of the highlights and shades of the pearls. Before he starts rummaging about for glasses, I climb onto a chair to locate my special, crystal, champagne glasses that I was given by my mother for a wedding present. Never used. How ironic, they, like the choker are also original Art Deco. They're shallow *coupe* glasses like saucers – the sort in 1930s Hollywood movies, when champagne flowed in fountains and *femme-fatales* smoked with silver cigarette holders.

Just as I've reached up for them, as I'm still standing on the chair, I feel Alexandre's hand slip up between my thighs again.

This yes-no tease is driving me to distraction. I nearly drop the glasses. I look down and see his head planted between my thighs, forcing them apart. I splay my legs a little. His soft hair is tickling me, brushing against my clit like silk. I close my eyes in bliss. He spins me around, his strong hands clamped on my hips. I can't move, I'm being manhandled again. He has my backside now in his face. I can't see him but I can feel him gently parting my buttocks with his fingers. His tongue starts licking between my crack. Up and down. Wow this feels incredible. *Thank God I had a bath and I smell of sweet oils,* I think to myself, as I whimper with pleasure. My hands cannot touch him, I'm still holding the champagne glasses and I don't want to drop them. He pushes my back down a touch so I am now leaning slightly forward, bending over, still standing above him on the chair.

"Relax, chérie," he cajoles, and I am too turned on to disobey.

His palm is cupping me, my clitoris throb-tingling as he slips his thumb inside and circles it, touching on my inner front walls. The base of his palm putting pressure against my clit – I'm flexing my hips back and forth. I'm really wet. This feels so….*oh my God*! His tongue is licking me up and down along the crack of my buttocks once more. Licking, flicking, darting, probing. He's still palming my clit. I think I'm going to come. That would be a first. All my sensations are deep and hot inside - my brain is like a marshmallow…

My mind is going into a tunnel of black and then flashing pink and red and …*oh wow,* his thumb is pressing and circling rhythmically in a place at the front of my walls, in a place, oh….ah…, ah, *ah.* I feel every nerve inside me as I implode with pleasure in this deep, undiscovered zone, deep inside me. I cry out – this is the most intense, throbbing orgasm of my life.

He holds his grip firm as I writhe with ecstasy, letting the orgasm spasms of my pulsing, tingling nerves climax in waves, until slowly, very slowly it calms.

He takes his thumb and hand away and licks my juices from his fingers. "Hmm, tasty," he grins, looking up at me. He lifts me down from the chair and sets me on the floor, gently. He grabs the champagne bottle, takes the glasses from me and places them on the kitchen counter. He pops open the champagne and pours, as if what he has done is the most normal occurrence in the world.

I'm a quivering wreck.

"You like that, then?" he asks with a crooked smile.

My jaw hangs open. "That's never happened to me before. That was new. Where you had your thumb has opened up a completely new….a new–"

"I must have hit your G-spot."

I have read about this famous G-spot but was beginning to believe it was a myth. "It felt….how can I describe it? It felt *deep*. So intense."

He smiles knowingly and narrows his eyes as if to say 'that's just the beginning.' *Does this man realize what he has just done?* Oh yes, I think he does. He has a confident air about him as if he does this every day of the week.

"Well, I got to do a little exploration of your body so I had an idea," he says humbly.

I'm still in a state of wonder. Shivering with amazement. He seems to know my body better than I do and we hardly know each other.

"Are you cold, baby?" He looks concerned. A gentleman and

a rogue rolled into one. I'm not cold, just shaking with post-orgasm ecstasy. He takes off his loose linen shirt and puts it around my shoulders. I drink in his torso. I close my eyes for a second and, like flash photography, or when you've been staring at something bright, the image makes an imprint on my brain. His stomach muscles ripple into segmented compartments – not a six-pack, no, that's far too crass a word to describe what I see. Nor the statue of David, whose penis is a sad let down and makes his body look like an excuse – no, I know what's beneath Alexandre's pants and I have a feeling it's beyond substantial. His body is superb; a work of art.

He catches me ogling at him and smiles, oh so subtly. He knows the effect he is having on me. Oh yes, he knows all right.

He leads me to my living room and places me on the chaise longue as if I'm his patient recovering from an operation. That's how I feel. Shaky, trembling with wonder at the skill of my doctor who has just discovered something about me, that I didn't even know myself.

I sip my champagne; we're christening my crystal glasses. A real celebration, I think. *That elusive G-spot was targeted!* The champagne is delicious - no wonder - it's Dom Pérignon - Marilyn Monroe's favorite. Music is playing softly on Alexandre's iPhone – I recognize it – Bach's *Air*…so beautiful and soothing. He is sitting beside me, wearing only his jeans. I notice his lovely feet bare – elegant, each toe pleasing to the eye. He's unbelievably handsome and I try not to stare too hard. I can't decide if he looks like a pirate or a gentleman – a mixture of both, I think. Like a pirate, he took me by surprise.

He has me transfixed, bewitched. I scrutinize his even features, his strong, straight nose, his defined jaw, his full mouth, and I wonder what it is that makes a person attractive. It isn't just the looks - no, it's a glint in the eye, the way a person laughs. Alexandre laughs a lot, his conversation interspersed with chuckles, which makes him seem carefree, light. But I saw that dark side last weekend, the flash of fury when he mentioned his father. And nobody as wealthy as Alexandre can be that sweet. He must have a ruthless edge when it comes to business, or some kind of killer instinct.

The Dom Pérignon has made me tipsy, not drunk, but gloriously relaxed. Alexandre is stroking my body, running his long fingers along its entirety, caressing me with a feather touch. Every once in a while he kisses me, soft kisses on the lips, before he lets his tongue dance with mine in a hungry embrace. I'm feeling needy; a longing is pulsing through my veins. How can that be? I have just been satiated. My legs keep opening wide with a will of their own. I want him to make love to me. For some reason, I want more. I feel less self-conscious now, half nude with nothing on but his shirt and the pearl choker, and he, still in his faded Levis, with a look of quiet contentment on his face.

It is dusk outside; the sky is turning orange and throwing a golden glow through the west-facing windows of my living room. I can feel the warmth on my face and an immeasurable sense of relaxation courses through my body as if I were a rag doll. He could do anything with me now. I am his.

He takes a swig of champagne and kneels at the far end of the chaise longue and pushes my legs akimbo. He blows softly between them and darts his tongue out touching my clitoris with the tip of his tongue, almost imperceptibly. I groan and wriggle on my back.

"You're so sensitive, aren't you Pearl? You like it soft, don't you?"

"Yes," I whisper.

"How do you like to come, chérie?"

But I already have come, I think. Doesn't he realize what a big deal for me that already is?

"Hum?" he asks.

I'm silent. What can I say? I can't tell him the truth. I can't tell him that I'm basically unable to orgasm with penetrative and oral sex.

"Tell me about your first time," he urges. "Not the first time you had sex but the first time your little pearlette exploded."

My pearlette. How dainty. What a beautiful way to describe it. Only a Frenchman could come up with that.

I don't have to think hard. I remember as clearly as if it happened yesterday.

"There was the very first time in the bathtub with the shower-head," I admit, almost shamefully. "The pressure of the water got me excited and I had a spontaneous orgasm. It was a huge surprise. I was ten when it happened. And then, soon after that when I was crossing my legs really tightly. I was taking an exam and the pressure, the fear and the panic gave me an orgasm – I didn't even touch myself."

He is still caressing me. I touch his arms and stroke the hair on his head. He's running his tongue along my thigh now and his pinkie finger is tapping my clitoris so gently like the delicate wings of a butterfly. I'm squirming, I raise my hips up, rotating them – this feels *so* good. All I can think of is him being inside me.

"And who was the first *person* to make you come, hmm? The first to give you extreme pleasure?"

I have never told anyone this. Ever. I lie there silent.

"Hmm? The first to give you that big, mind-blowing O?" he asks.

I say nothing.

"How old were you?"

"Fifteen," I whisper.

"Was she a girl?"

How did he know that? Is he psychic?

"How do you know that?" I ask.

"Because of the way your body is, Pearl. So responsive to the faintest, most delicate touch. Usually only girls know how to caress that way – young boys can be like bulldozers. Girls turn to girls; they explore each other as teenagers. What happened to you is more common than you realize."

How does he know all this?

He moves around to the side of the chaise longue and begins to fondle my breasts with a light touch of his fingers, flicking the nipple softly, and licking me on my navel, then under the arms, tracing his tongue to my nipple, now in his mouth. He sucks it and it hardens. I groan again. I start frantically unbuttoning his jeans and his penis springs up free, hard, erect and *enormous.* I cry out at just the thought of it inside me. But wonder if it's too big for me. *This is hot. He* is hot.

"Keep telling me your story," he entreats.

"We were just taking it in turns to tickle each other's arms and back with a bird's feather. You know how girls do? I felt so relaxed. The feather passed by my genitals a few times and I clenched my thighs tightly together and had an orgasm. It was shocking at the time - such an unexpected surprise. I felt embarrassed as she was my best friend. Soon, I started going steady with her brother. He was my first love, my childhood sweetheart. I trusted him so much. With him it happened – I used to climax. He always took his time. But after we split up when I was twenty-two–"

I can feel tears spilling from my eyes now, the champagne has made me open up, the music is so moving, and the truth, like an uninvited gatecrasher, barges its way through my mouth and into my living room. "I can't come anymore having penetrative sex," I weep. "I'm sorry, it's the way I am, there's nothing I can do about it. There, you know now, Alexandre. I'm sure you'd rather be spending time with another woman, someone young and more malleable - someone more receptive."

"But that's one of the things I love about you, Pearl. You're *very* receptive, and open to adventure. I don't want to spend time with another girl. I want to be with *you*, don't you see that?"

"I mean, I love this," I whisper. "I love everything you've been doing, I think you're gorgeous, you've turned me on more than anyone has for years. You've opened up a secret place that I never knew I had inside me. You're so sexy and everything but–"

"There are no buts, Pearl - it's all in the mind," he interrupts. "Without nerves sending impulses back to the brain, an orgasm wouldn't be possible. It's not just physical - it's a crescendo, an orchestra of emotions. The Big O is just an orchestra, chérie, that needs a conductor for guidance, nothing more. As I say, the biggest sex organ is your brain."

"But I don't want you to be disappointed. Please don't expect too much from me – don't take it personally, Alexandre."

"Oh, I'm going to take this *very* personally. You don't know me so well, Pearl Robinson, but one thing I love more than anything is a challenge."

5

It is the next morning and I'm going over the night before, analyzing every move, every word spoken.

Last night, after I told Alexandre about my inability to come from penetrative sex, he held back. I expected him to want to immediately prove himself, throw me on the bed there and then and hammer me senseless, but he didn't.

Instead, he took me out to an exquisite, outrageously expensive restaurant where all the waiters and staff appeared to be in harmonized sync - administering to your every need or whim without appearing to be there. Alexandre held my hand under the table as we languished over this sublime meal, then he walked me home and kissed me goodnight without coming up to my apartment. It all felt so natural in the moment, so romantic, but now Doubt with a capital D is creeping into my psyche and it has obviously decided to hang out with me like one of those 'friends' you've had for years and you don't have the gumption to tell them to take a walk.

The landline is ringing. Great. Just what I need, it's probably my brother and his Sunday call.

"Hi," he begins.

"Hi Anthony."

"Who are you having brunch with?"

"The usual."

"Your fat friend?"

"Daisy is not fat!"

"She is so."

"You saw her four years ago after she'd given birth, for Christ's sake. Not everyone can be like Madonna and Gwyneth Paltrow, and what's her name who–"

"So did you fuck him yet?"

"If you're going to talk to me please stop munching at the same time."

"It's just an apple."

"Well it's crunching down the receiver, Anthony, and it's very annoying. Anyway, why haven't you set up Skype yet? I'm trying to fold laundry and I have to squeeze the receiver to my ear with my shoulder. It's very irritating not having my hands free."

"Too much of a hassle to set up," he munches. *Crunch, crunch.*

"No, it's not. It's simple. Get Bruce to do it."

"Bruce is hopeless. You haven't answered my question."

"Well for your information, no, we didn't. But we did spend the evening together and we…look, I'm not going to go into details with *you,* Anthony, you're my *brother.*"

"Sounds like he's gay."

"Alexandre is so *not* gay. Why do you assume everyone is gay like you?"

"When was this?"

"Last night."

"And he didn't stay over?"

"No."

"And where is he today?"

"He had to fly to Mumbai," I answer.

"Mumbai like Mumbai as in Bombay, India?"

"Yes."

"On a Sunday?"

"Yes. He's an international business man. Very busy."

"You are so dumb, Pearl."

"What?"

"Do you not see a pattern here?"

"What do you mean?"

"Last Saturday you went rock climbing, right?"

"Yeah."

"And he didn't stay over. And, hello? Pearl? He had a 'business' meeting the next day which was a Sunday and today he's supposedly gone to Mumbai, also a Sunday. Duh! He has a girlfriend or a wife who he has to spend the weekend with. Maybe he can get away with 'hanging out with the guys' during the days every Saturday *day time* and *evening* but by night he's tucked up at home with wifey and hanging out with her and the kid on Sunday."

"He doesn't have a kid or a wife."

"How do you know?"

"Because Haslit Films was thinking about doing a documentary about him and his sister and the phenomenon of HookedUp, so we did some research."

"He has a girlfriend, Pearl."

My heart sinks. *Does Anthony know something I don't?*

"Otherwise a twenty-four year-old guy would have at least fucked your brains out before going home."

"Actually he's twenty-five. He's twenty-five, not twenty-four."

"Ooh, big difference. Unless of course…"

"What?"

"Unless you've gotten all fat and he's turned off by you."

"I am not fat, Anthony! At least that's one area of my life that's in perfect shape. I swim almost every day. I do not eat junk food and slurp down endless sodas like you and Bruce. I take care of my body. Oh yes, Anthony, I forgot to tell you the most important thing of all? Apart from bringing a bottle of *Dom Pérignon* and a massive bunch of roses, he gave me a genuine Art Deco pearl necklace."

"You're kidding."

"So chew on *that*!"

"Pearly you sound real mad at me. I'm sorry, was I being bitchy?"

"Such a mega bitch. So negative."

"Pearleee."

"Listen, I have to go or I'll be late."

I feel as if I'm in *Groundhog Day*. The same conversation with my brother, the same brunch with Daisy. At least the restaurant is different. Today we're having sushi at a place near me on the Upper East Side. And today, Daisy announced at the last minute, she was bringing little Amy along. Sushi is not the best sort of food for a four year-old – I know our meal will be brief.

I have dipped my maki roll in too much wasabi sauce and my nose is on fire. The restaurant has too many mirrors and my reflection is making me uneasy. *Do I have a double chin?*

"Stop inspecting yourself in the mirror - you look perfect," Daisy scolds.

"Do I have a double chin, Amy?"

"Now stop it! Don't answer her Amy, she's being absurd."

"What's absurd, Mommy?"

"When people say silly lies that aren't even *close* to being true, just to get attention."

"I feel so insecure," I grumble.

"He's crazy about you, it's so obvious. He bought you that freakin' necklace - what more do you want? Oh yes, and he lavished you with champagne and roses, too. How many guys do *that*?"

Amy is wriggling in her chair with excitement, swinging her legs back and forth. "Where's your necklace, Pearly? Can I see it?"

"It's at home, honey, but I promise that next time you come over, I'll show it to you."

"Can I play dress-up with it?"

Daisy laughs. "No, darling, it's not a dress-up necklace; it's a grown-up piece of jewelry. Seriously, Pearl, why are you looking so glum? Really, Anthony should be gagged and not allowed to speak. I'm sure Alexandre is telling the truth about his travels. It totally makes sense. He's out there earning money, not text messaging and calling every second. He must have to work bloody hard to keep his mini empire going."

"He told me he was basically a computer programmer."

"Yeah, right. He's being modest. Alexandre is obviously a very shrewd business man, to boot. You don't get that rich just having done some clever coding."

"Why hasn't he called or sent a text?"

"Because he's traveling. He warned you he wasn't going to call. He said that, didn't he?"

"Yes, he explained that he'd be really busy and didn't want to be distracted and he'd call me when he got back."

"Well, there you go."

"I guess so."

"How many days is he going to be away for?"

"Four or five."

"Just stay calm," Daisy tells me sagely. "He'll call."

6

Day four - since the big G spot discovery - and no word from Alexandre.

I am yearning for him. All I've been thinking about is him. Like a dumbstruck teenager, I've let him occupy my thoughts twenty-three hours a day. Even at work, he's there flitting about in my distracted brain, smiling at me or pressing his thumb up inside me, maneuvering me, stroking me. I replay that Big O Over and O-ver in my mind. Me on the chair in the kitchen, crystal glasses in my hand, Alexandre below me, licking me deliciously, bringing me to a fountain of ecstasy deep inside me. Yet *we still haven't made love yet!* Yet. Aye, there's the rub - no pun intended. - *he hasn't contacted me.* He warned me as much, to please not take offense, he'd be extremely busy - that he'd call on his way back. But–

Nothing. No word from him.

I realize, now, that was an excuse. *He's a Latin Lover with a girl in every port*, my brother warned me. He doesn't want some sexually-problematic forty year-old. He's young. His ego would be too bruised by a woman not Orgasm-ing all over the place. Or, more likely - bored as hell by her. *Bored as hell by me.* He doesn't have time for my needs or someone like me. The world is his oyster. Literally. He needs a young woman his age, a twenty-two year-old with tight skin, zero crow's feet. Impressionable.

Damn! I should have kept my mouth shut. I should have dragged him to the bedroom and made love to him; done a *When Harry Met Sally* on him – so easy to do – all those men who think their girlfriends are having multiple orgasms at the drop of a hat – yeah right. I should have done that - not blurted out my sexual shortcomings as if I were sharing my innermost secrets with an agony aunt!

Perhaps a swim will do the trick, a swim at my club to cool off my fury. Fury at myself for getting into such deep water - no pun intended - *who was I kidding?*

I go to my gym. The pool is just what the doctor ordered. They use salt at my gym, not chlorine, so I don't get dry, bleachy skin or green hair. Swimming is what keeps me fit and washes away the tension. I can't run anymore at my age. Pounding the pavement is for women in their twenties. Gravity is not my friend. Swimming is the perfect exercise for me. I can push myself, but not damage tendons; the water holds me up, supports my muscles. I need to keep my bones moving, my spine flexible, my shoulders strong. Ageing is no picnic.

I'll stay in tonight. I'll order in – maybe some Chinese. I love New York. I love the convenience of this city. Its vibrancy too – even with the endless police sirens, the crowded sidewalks. Paris? Who cares about Paris, I tell myself. New York has to be the best city in the world.

When I get home from the gym, I turn on the TV to distract my thoughts, but immediately switch it off again. How many wars can one planet take? How many more starving people, how many more orphans? I feel angry, depressed and, worst of all, helpless. Helpless to save the world, helpless to rescue just the speck of sand that is myself.

Helpless to get this elusive shit of a Frenchman out of my head.

Just then, my iPad rings. Someone is Skyping me. Has Anthony finally got it together? No, It's HIM! I pick it up. When his face comes on the screen my heart starts pounding – the orphans, the wars, the famine – all are momentarily wiped from my brain. I no longer feel sad but am jumping for joy.

"Hi Alexandre." I try to look calm, cool.

"Hello Pearl. How are you doing, beautiful?"

"Oh, I'm fine, just been swimming, Been really busy at work, seeing friends, you know."

I'm a busy, girl-about-town, have not thought about you at all, nooo way.

"You look lovely," he says.

"Thank you. Where are you?"

"In the back of a limo being driven to the airport, I'm on my way home to New York."

"How did the meeting go?"

"Meetings, plural. Lots of meetings. They went fine. We've sewn up an important deal."

"Great."

"Let's see you."

"What?"

"Stand back. Show me what you're wearing."

"Just my office clothes." I balance the iPad so it's standing high up on a chest of drawers so he can take in my whole body.

"Sexy. Open your shirt."

I unbutton my shirt. "Are you alone?" I ask, double-checking that I'm not sharing my image with a third party.

"Of course I am. Show me your tits."

I take off my shirt. I'm wearing a black lacy, push-up bra.

"You're making me hard." He bites his lip and squints his eyes. "Bring them out. Don't take off the bra, just lift them up."

I cup one hand around my left breast and free it from the bra. The nipple is poking over.

"Fuck you're sexy. Now the other one."

I do the same with my other breast.

"Now lick your fingers and fondle your tits."

I do as he says. I lick my fingers slowly, popping each one in my mouth and circle them around each nipple. They turn erect. I can feel a tingling inside me.

"Let me see *you*," I say.

"You want to see my hard cock? It's rock hard, baby, and it can't wait to fuck you. I'm on my way home to fuck you. That's all I've been thinking about. In between this big business deal, is your wet little pearlette. I want it impaled on my cock and to make you come all around it."

He holds his iPhone down by his crotch and I see his huge penis proud in his hand.

"I want to suck that," I tell him. "I want to lick it up and down, circle my lips around its huge head, lick it up and down and then I want to get on top of it and ride it. Ride it hard."

"Fuck you're sexy," he says in a low voice. He's moving his hand up and down, pleasuring himself. It's massive and it's driving me crazy. "Take off your skirt," he commands.

I unzip my skirt and let it drop to the floor. I'm wearing white cotton panties. I can see his face again now. His eyes are half closed – bedroom eyes, eyes of a man who thinks of nothing but sex.

"Wet your fingers," he whispers.

I'm really getting into this and feel like a porn star. I lick my fingers wiggling the tip of my tongue. Exaggerated. Dirty girl style.

"Now put them on your sweet little oyster. I want to see you bend over and press your pussy on the arm of that sofa. I want to see you fuck the sofa, Pearl. Move the iPad so I can see you."

I feel self-conscious but brave. I move the iPad into a better position. "But I won't be able to see *you*," I complain.

"You'll see me soon enough, chérie. Move over to the sofa arm. That's good. Bend over so I can see your sexy butt. Oh yeah, that's good, that's perfect. Keep those white schoolgirl panties on. Bend over. Oh yeah, that's good."

I'm bending over the arm of the sofa which is pressing on my clitoris. The vision of his huge erection is in my mind's eye. I'm feeling really horny now.

His voice continues over the speaker but I can't see him. "Now fuck that as if you were fucking me, as if you were on top of me. I can see how wet you are. I can see that glistening little oyster and the wetness coming through your little white virgin panties."

I start to move my pelvis back and forth. The corner of the sofa is soft but presses beautifully up against me, pushing on my clitoris, pressing at my opening. I can feel my wetness. I'm moving back and forth and it feels great. *Why haven't I thought of this myself?*

"Keep moving, chérie. My cock is so fucking *hard.* All it wants to do is fuck you. Sleep next to you. Wake up. Fuck you again. Keep fucking you." I can hear his fast breathing and I imagine how colossal and stiff he is.

I keep my rhythm going and play with my breasts at the same time. I look down at them, the nipples hard as cherries, and I have a flash of a vision of making love to a woman with big breasts, then I have his thudding great erection in my mind again, then a threesome with him and this sexy, desirable woman. Me kissing her, Alexandre slamming me from behind and I can't hold it any longer. I can feel a rush of emotion gather in a crescendo hot between my legs and I'm coming - my orgasm, powerful like a tsunami wave.

"I'm coming," I moan. "I'm coming."

"Me too," he shouts. "Coming for you, chérie. You're so beautiful, so fucking hot - so sexy."

I lie forward for half a minute groaning with my release, my butt in the air, the throbbing of my orgasm calming itself to a lighter tingle. I collapse on the sofa, laughing with relief.

I can't believe what I've just done! I've had phone sex for the first time in my life.

7

I'm flying again. I'm back at school and soaring high above the room and it's effortless like a trapeze artist but without the trapeze. The freedom is liberating. The history teacher, Mr. Hand, who was hideous before with warts on his face, has morphed into a Greek god. He doesn't have a shirt on and his chest is buff and defined. Why is everyone so rude about him? He's gorgeous. The bell is going - loud in my ear. Time for class.

It's my cell.

I'm groggy. I was dreaming. Damn, so disappointing that I can't fly in real life – it seemed so true.

I pick up.

"I'm outside your apartment building on the street."

"Alexandre?"

"The doorman doesn't seem to be here."

"Sometimes he takes a nap and it's hard to wake him but he's there. What time is it? Never mind, I'll buzz down. See you in a minute."

I call the doorman who is as surprised as I am. It must be before dawn. I frantically rush to the bathroom to brush my teeth, and give my private parts a quick wash. Just in case. Alexandre gets so *intimate.* I splash water on my face and around my eyes. I look at my phone, it's five am.

There's a light tap at my door. My stomach dips with nerves. All I've got on is my crimson silk robe.

I open the door and this vision is standing before me. He's even hotter than I remembered. He's unshaven and messy, his jeans not too loose, not too tight, but all I can see is his mammoth bulge inside as if just talking to me a second earlier has made him hard. Knowing he's lusting after me so much makes adrenaline surge through me - I can feel my juices start to gather – just looking at him makes me moist with desire.

He steps forward and kisses me hungrily. He tastes of apples and mint and smells deliciously of just Alexandre - a smell I wish I could bottle. He pulls off my robe and it shivers to the floor like a pool of red blood. His tongue explores my mouth, my lips – he's kissing my neck, my breasts and he palms my V with his large hand.

"I'm going to have to fuck you – so wet already," he purrs into my ear.

I grapple with the buttons on his Levis and go down on my knees. We are still in the doorway. His jeans fall about his ankles and his erection springs up, this huge arrogant thing, as if it had a life of its own. No underpants. Sexy. I start to lick him the way I described during our phone sex. I hold it in one hand and cup my other underneath his weighty balls. I lick them gently and take one, whole in my mouth, and suck tenderly. I don't want to hurt him or be too rough. I can hear him groaning quietly – his hands are rested gently on my head as he strokes me and runs his fingers through my hair. I lick his shaft slowly, deliberately, up and then down, up and down - then I stand up and bend over because he's tall and I need to position myself right. Still holding him in my hand firmly, I circle my tongue around the head, licking his juices from his one-eyed Jack – wow, he's just as turned on as I am.

"Fuck, Pearl, this is what I've been dreaming of. This is hot. This feels amazing."

My tongue finds its way up to his firm stomach, then back to his hard rod which I take in my mouth as if it were a giant lollipop. It reaches the back of my throat. I tense my lips about it and suck hard, up and down, up and down, up and down, stroking his balls with a feathery touch. I lick my fingers on my right hand, cover them with my spit and trace them slowly up behind in the crack of his buttocks. I press my wet middle finger inside his opening. He's groaning now and I feel powerful. I have this rich, controlling guy in the palm of my hand. Literally. I have him in my mouth. He's all mine and he's groaning with pleasure. I feel strong. Potent, like a queen with her empire. *He* is my empire.

My head is moving fast now, up and down – I'm trying not to gag with his size. Still with my left hand playing with his balls, I press my finger deeper into the crevice of his butt and that's it – a fountain of pleasure spurts hard at the back of my throat. He's calling out my name. He's all mine. I did this.

"Oh Pearl baby, oh Pearl," he rumbles. My eyes look up, my mouth still firmly in place, and observe his face grimacing as if in pain. His release is intense; his body judders.

A moment passes - he's coming down from his orgasm now and I finally take my mouth away.

"That's maybe the best blow job I've ever had," he says, and then laughs.

I feel a wave of jealousy at the thought that other women have done this too. Other women have made him weak with pleasure. But he's *mine.* I don't want any other female laying her hands on him, her mouth. I want Alexandre all to myself.

Minutes later, my power is now diminished. He got what he wanted from me. His release. I am no longer the queen with her empire but a servant that can be tossed aside. Panic sets in as I fear he might leave now - might decide to go home.

But he says, "Come here you gorgeous creature and give me a kiss. It's your turn now, Ms. Robinson. I want to give you what you deserve."

"And what do I deserve?"

"I think you deserve to be made love to, don't you?"

"Yes," I murmur with gratitude. I want him inside me. I notice he's still as hard as he was, still as erect.

"Now bend over and touch your toes," he commands.

My moment of power is over, my reign as empress brief. He holds all the cards now. I bend over. Is he going to spank me? No, he starts licking me delicately around my core. Licking, then sucking. This feels hotly erotic.

"Always so wet, always ready to get fucked by me, aren't you?"

"Yes," I whimper.

"Is it only me? Is it only me you want inside you?" His voice is almost a roar.

"Yes. I don't want anyone else! I can't even look at anyone

else." Except in my dream, I think. *What was my old History teacher, Mr. Hand, doing in my goddam dream??*

"Do you want to kiss anyone else?" he mumbles, now only touching my entrance with the very tip of his tongue. He's teasing me again. My hips start gyrating, trying to push myself closer to his mouth. "Do you want to kiss anyone else?" he asks again savagely.

"I had a little fantasy. When we were Skyping together, I imagined I was kissing another woman while you were fucking me from behind."

"And what was she like? Was she pretty?"

"Stunning. With big, perfectly shaped breasts."

He lifts me up by my shoulders so I'm standing straight and then spins me around; I'm now facing him. He kisses me hard, our mouths hungry for each other.

"You're making me fucking horny," he says. But then his face goes suddenly dark, his eyes fiery. "Who else has been fucking you? Before me?"

"Nobody. I practically feel like a virgin, it's been so long."

He steps away from his jeans which are still pooled about his ankles. "I don't believe that. You're too good. Too expert. Where did you learn all this? Where did you learn to do that?"

"Instinct," I bleat out. "I've never done this before in that way. It's *you*, Alexandre. You make me this way. You make me want to do these things."

"Who else has been making love to my Pearl and her juicy little oyster?" he demands, flicking his tongue on my nipple and then nipping it. A spasm of pleasure shoots directly between my legs.

"Nobody, I swear. I haven't had sex for two years. I haven't had sex since my divorce." *Okay, there was that one terrible time but I keep quiet about that.*

My answer seems to placate him but he stares at me for a second as if to read my face for lies. "Good girl," he whispers in my ear. "I don't want you involved with anyone else, is that clear? I want to keep you for myself. I'm not a jealous man but I am possessive of my treasures."

I'm a treasure?

"This beautiful Pearl and her pearlette are mine, is that clear?"

"Yes." I smile, and feel as if I've won something. Jealous men have always irritated me but this is making me hot. I have made a young, twenty-five year-old possessive of me, and I'm loving it. "What about you? Are you seeing anyone else?" I ask with trepidation. What if he says 'yes' – I'll fall apart.

"I already told you I was unattached."

"Unattached means no girlfriend, no relationship. Are you fucking anyone else?"

"Not now, I won't be. Why go out for hamburger when I have steak at home?"

"Paul Newman said that."

He laughs. "I know - it's a good line. Seriously, Pearl, I really don't want to waste my time with anyone else, now I've found you. You passed both tests one and two, remember?"

I had almost forgotten about that. "Remind me what they were?" I say.

"Test one – you're a dog lover and you care about animals. Test two – you're brave and adventurous; you came rock climbing with me, even though it was obvious you'd never done it before."

"I told a white lie," I admit. "I was worried you wouldn't invite me otherwise. Dogs…" I smile. "Is that the only reason you like me?"

He laughs and adds, "You're the whole package. You're beautiful, smart, sexy, independent, mature, and I still have that little 'challenge' in mind. We still have work to do. Now stop doubting me and get on the bed where you belong."

Did I just hear that right? Where I belong!! Who is this guy with his old-fashioned values? But then I see a glint of humor in his eye and I know he's just kidding.

"When you say 'mature' what do you mean exactly?" I ask. *Is mature a code word for old?*

"Mature. A woman who is mature knows what she wants. Like you. You have a past, you've experienced life. You've borne some knocks and bruises, perhaps. Suffered, had your heart broken maybe. You're a whole person, Pearl. You have a good career. I'm not interested in some young, naive girl hanging on to my every word, my every movement - I'd find that unappealing. I want someone who's my equal. I'm not perfect but I feel comfortable in my own skin and although I'm young I have everything, and I want a woman with substance like *you*," he says, moving close.

I hold him back. "You say mature. How old *am* I?" I ask apprehensively.

Brave move. *What if he thinks I'm older than I am?*

"I don't know and I don't care. I would never ask. But you're beautiful and you have my attention. Now get on the bed."

I lie nude on my four poster bed, lapping up all his compliments and bathing in honeyed words like 'beautiful' and 'you're the whole package.' Pack Age, his accent says – uh, oh, that *age* word again drumming in my ears. But it's my hang-up, not his.

I've got to move on from that.

He straddles me and kisses me softly on my nose, my eyelashes, my lips, my shoulders. I've been waiting for this – waiting to be fucked by him. Whether I have an orgasm or not, I don't care – I want him inside me. My breath is shallow – butterflies are circling my stomach.

His fingers are draped against the full expanse of my vulva like a velvet curtain, cupping me like a glove. What a great fit it is, too. I'm pushing my pelvis against his palm, and his index fingers are making rhythmic upside-down 'come hither' movements along my hot wet entrance, probing into my glistening doorway. He's reaching in and upwards with his smooth finger against my ceiling and hoists me up several inches off the bed. So dominating, so in control – instinctively he knows what my body wants. It feels incredible – my G-spot is hungry for him, hungry for his magic wand.

Still with his fingers inside me, he pulls my groin up towards his face - my back arches off the bed and he presses his still tongue against my vulva. He holds it flat against my clitoris without movement. I'm squirming up against it, gyrating my hips, arching my back more to get closer to him, moaning with pleasure. I'm pushing and grinding and suddenly his tongue, from being quite still, strokes me vertically and diagonally in sudden flashing lashes. He's whipping me with his tongue. I'm tingling with desire, throbbing with longing.

Then he stops. His tongue is still again. My V-8 is humming like the fiery little engine it is. I can feel my juices oozing. I'm so revved-up.

"Please," I beg. "Please fuck me."

"Not yet. All good things come to little girls who wait. Especially neo-virgins – I need to take it slowly with you."

His tongue starts probing deep inside me, in and then out. He stops again. I'm squirming on my back, his head is between my thighs and I grab his hair and try to pull his head up towards my face. I need him inside me. I *need* that huge beast of his phallus deep inside. His tongue starts fucking me, in, out, in out. It feels amazing but I want more, I yearn for all of him to go deep. I miss him so far away from me. I want the intimacy of his entire being, his face on mine, his torso on my breasts. I need him whole. I'm longing for that erection to probe deep inside against my walls.

He gets up and I hear him rummaging about in his jeans pocket. I open my eyes which have been closed in ecstatic reverie and see the condom packet which he is ripping open with his teeth. *Yes, yes, at last!* It's a brand I haven't seen before - XL lambskin. I didn't know they made them extra large but I guess it makes sense for him. He rolls it on to his erection - my V-8 humming away in preparation, throbbing with the thought of him inside me.

He straddles me again – then moves down the bed and circles my clitoris with his tongue, careful not to touch it directly, which makes it more desperate to be fondled. But, he leaves it be. He slowly moves his way higher, his chest now on top of me, my nipples hard beneath his strong torso. I can feel his whopping great cock pressing up against me, about to enter me. I moan with anticipation. I grab it – it is rock hard inside the condom which feels soft, not the usual rubbery texture. I guide it towards my wet opening but he pulls back.

"You cannot have it all, little Pearl. Not yet. Greedy girls have to watch their appetites."

He lets the tip probe my hot entrance but just the tip.

"*Please.*" I am pleading now, whining like a child for candy.

He starts with shallow thrusts, barely penetrating me, his arms enclosing me tightly, his mouth on mine. Then he pauses and lets his erection rest just an inch inside me. He's lingering close but not moving. I'm flexing my hips, desperate to get closer, my hands are like claws on his tight ass, pulling him toward me. *Fuck me all the way. Please,* I beg silently. But he's holding back, his strength and willpower overcoming me.

"So wet, I'm going to have to suck that little oyster later. I'd like that little oyster and its Pearl to come with my mouth around it," he whispers in my ear as he nibbles the lobe.

I groan and tense my buttocks, thrusting myself at him. Only the tip of his huge erection is inside me, then he makes tiny thrusts – and pulls out, each time its soft, huge head pressing up and brushing past my clit. The shaft of it is rubbing against me and he's gently thrusting between my labia without entering me. I'm screaming now. This feels incredible.

"Shush, quiet now. So juicy," he murmurs. "I love your hair, your body, your soft skin, your blue eyes, I love the way you smell. I love the way you're so desperate for me to fuck you." As he says this he plunges his erection deep into me, the whole of him inside, simultaneously pressing his pelvic bone against my clit, holding himself firmly in place before withdrawing again. The tease is driving me crazy. My body is begging for each plunge, the taut fullness of him. I can feel the nerve endings on my clitoris swelling with heat. He pulls out. He's guiding his penis now with his hand – he's slapping it against my clit and I'm moaning.

"I'm going to really fuck you now like you deserve, you greedy little girl. You want my cock? All of it?"

"Please," I cry. "It's so big it scares me, though."

"Too big for you? Too big for your tight little pearlette? It's so tight. Like a virgin. I think it needs to be ripped open by my big cock. I think it needs that."

"Yes," I groan, my buttocks clenched, my pelvis rising higher so I'm pressing deep up against him, his erection poised at my soaked entrance.

"Are you sure you're ready?"

"Yes," I cry. "Please, *please*."

But he starts teasing me with the tip again and, just as I can't take any more, when I think I'm going to come from the rhythmic brushing on my clit, he suddenly slams himself hard into me; his erection swelling inside me, his immense size filling me whole, his pelvic bone pressing hard down on my clitoris. I'm shouting out, my brain concentrated on nothing but my center - my entire universe at this moment. All I care about, all I desire. He takes his cock out again tantalizing me at the entrance, circling me and then slaps my clit with it again. The sensation is so intense. He plunges into me once more, I can feel his pubic bone pressing against that sweet spot and I start coming in a rush of heaven, all my nerve endings in that one area sending my whole body into a quivering spasm. My contractions are tight about his erection, squeezing him as he's holding it there. He pulls away then thrusts it in hard and then goes still. He's moaning quietly now and I can feel his hardness inside me as he explodes. My hands are clawed about his ass, holding him close. My pulse is pounding between my legs…ah…ah…I'm still climaxing and so is he. He's kissing me, his tongue ravenous for mine. My pelvis starts to move up and down. I could keep going with this all day.

"I came with penetrative sex," I gasp.

"I hardly even fucked you, if you noticed. I didn't need to.

This is just getting you warmed up, Pearl. Just getting you used to me inside you. We'll get there. This isn't a race, time is on our side." He pulls out of me slowly and I suddenly feel bereft. His face is inches away, his lips on my cheek but I feel lonely already. I can't get enough of him. This is crazy.

"I want more," I breathe, still feeling tingles from my intense orgasm, craving him inside me again, the intimacy, the deep connection.

"I know you do."

"I want more *now*."

"Well you'll have to wait," he says with a trace of a smirk. "I have work to do. And you do, too." He looks at his watch. "It's seven a.m."

"*Please*."

He starts laughing. I suspect he loves being in control. He is in command of my body as if I were a marionette. I'm writhing on the bed, the sheets deliciously rubbing between my thighs, extending my post orgasm thrill. I swear, if he were to enter me again, I could come once more. But he's standing up putting on his jeans.

"Breakfast time," he barks. "Up, up, lazy girl, get that sweet butt off the bed, move that little Pearlette into action."

"More action - exactly. Give my Pearlette more action. *Please*."

He laughs again. "Let's just say things are going as I hoped they would. I like seeing you hungry for me."

I'm on my stomach, still lying on the bed. I press a cushion in between my thighs and start moving up and down, my buttocks high in the air - trying to tempt him.

"Careful, little girl, or I'll have to fuck you from behind. But really fuck you hard. Till you're ravaged inside."

I start moaning. Begging. "Yes *Please.*" I have no shame. No composure. No dignity.

He approaches the bed and I feel victorious. *He's going to give it to me. Ram it up me. Fill me up. Yes!*

But instead, he lifts me off the mattress and carries me like a baby in his arms to the bathroom. He sets me down. He opens the glass doors of the shower and turns on the faucet. He claps his hands loudly and there's a ringing in the air. He says, "Shower time! In you get, Pearl."

I do as he says. He eyes my naked body up and down and takes his jeans back off. He's stiff again. *Yes!*

We are both in the shower together and I'm still feeling stimulated. I want my power back. I take the shower gel, put some on my fingers and lather it across his back, shoulders and his athletic torso, and I move down his thighs. He's hard as a diamond. I crouch down, feeling the warm water splashing on top of me and take him in my mouth again. I'm hungry - desperate for him, shameless with my voracious appetite. I concentrate hard on making him groan, clinging to his leg as I suck on him.

"You just can't stop, can you?" he says. But I know he likes it, as he flexes his hips towards my mouth.

"No, I can't get enough of you," I pant, and then start licking his shaft as if my life depended on it.

My nipples are erect without him even touching them. The water is splashing on them, arousing me. I stand up and kiss him on his mouth, holding his erection tightly in the grip of my hand. He shoves his thigh between my legs and I gasp. His wet flesh is pushing against my clitoris; he rams it hard against me as I start to writhe on his leg. My hand is moving up and down on his hard-on, faster now to the same rhythm that my pelvis is pushing up and down, pressing against his firm thigh. My hard nipples are smacking against his chest. I keep this up for several minutes until I feel the blood rush along his phallus, and creamy liquid ooze in a gush in between and over my fingers. I push harder on his thigh and hit that divine spot. My orgasm is rising hot between my legs. I'm groaning, kissing his chest, taking his nipples between my teeth. He growls out my name. It's a simultaneous orgasm - both of us pleasuring each other in the same moment.

"Pearl/Alexandre," we cry out at once.

I collapse in his strong arms, the water beating on my head.

Finally, I feel satiated.

Now I can go to work.

8

I have never been this obsessed by sex. Ever. I am akin to a thirteen year-old boy reaching puberty, with sex constantly on the brain. All day, I walk about with fire between my legs.

I am like a zombie at work, an automaton. After this morning's love-making I can't think of anything but Alexandre and his body parts and all the things he has done to me, and will do to me.

I am playing *Under My Thumb* by The Rolling Stones on my iPod – how apt. I have been, literally, under his thumb.

My cell phone wakes me up from my shallow-breathed daydream.

The voice says, "Are you thinking what I'm thinking?" It's HIM.

"What are you thinking?" I ask guardedly, my stomach dipping with excitement and nerves. I've already humiliated myself enough this morning, already demonstrated that I'm like an addict who needs a fix, and that I have no control over myself whatsoever. Not when it comes to him, anyway.

"I'm thinking about you," he tells me, his voice deep and seductive. *Thank God he still wants me.* "And you? Are you thinking the same?"

"No," I reply.

"Oh." I can hear the disappointment in his tone.

"Why would I be thinking about *me*?" I say. "It's *you* my mind is focused on."

He laughs at my silly joke. "I've been planning what I'm going to do to you. Have you thought about that, Pearl? The things I'm going to do?"

"Yes," I whisper. There is someone else in the editing room. "And little else," I add quietly.

"Dinner tonight?"

"I'd love to. Where?"

"At my place. I'll be cooking. Anything you don't eat?"

We both burst out laughing, realizing how apt his question is.

"No red meat. Only free range chicken."

"I'll send a car to pick you up at eight o'clock."

"I'll be ready."

"Oh yes, I know you will."

So arrogant! This man is sure he has me just where he wants me. *Under his thumb.* And what a thumb it is too, zeroing in on my G-spot the way it did the other day. Just thinking about it has me feeling all melty again.

Eight O'clock is going to feel like an eternity.

The exterior of Alexandre's corner-lot, pre-war apartment building is particularly elegant. It is entered on Sixty Second Street under a very high fixed marquee, rather than the ubiquitous green awning seen everywhere else in Manhattan. The doorman lets me in with a flourish. It seems he is expecting me. The lobby is grand and makes my place look humble. This is how the other half live, or rather, not the other half (I am the other half – I have food on the table, right?) This is how the 0.75% lives - the ridiculously wealthy. The old black and white marble floors are polished to a high sheen, set off by large arches. Antique sofas upholstered in silk damask are placed strategically by a vast, marble fireplace overhung with a Louis XIV mirror. I doubt people sit on those sofas very often, as they are pristine. The flower arrangements look as if they were prepared for a wedding or for some charity benefit, towering in old-fashioned copper vases, which gleam so brightly they reflect the room. All this, for just the lobby.

The doorman buzzes open the elevator for me and says, "The Penthouse, Ms. Robinson."

"Thank you."

I walk inside the roomy elevator that smells of roses. Just as the doors are about to close, an elderly lady shuffles forward, shouting, 'wait' but the doors magically reopen, controlled at the entrance by the doorman. The elderly lady steps in. She is draped in jewels, dons oversized dark shades and carries a host of shopping bags from Tiffany and Neiman Marcus.

"Hello," I say and smile.

"Hello dear," she croaks.

The lit-up buttons display our floors, although neither of us has pressed anything.

"You're visiting Alexandre?" she enquires.

"Yes. For dinner."

"How exciting. He's a marvelous cook. I wonder what he'll serve you."

"You've had dinner with him?" I ask, trying not to sound too surprised – I don't want to seem rude.

"Dinner, lunch. He's a lovely boy - everybody in the building just *adores* him. Such a talent at everything he does. He's arranged some soirées for charity with musical quartets and just the best food ever. He's so kind and has time for everyone - even an old lady like myself. Such a honey."

Her door opens at the third floor. "Have a lovely evening, dear."

"Thank you. You too," I call after her.

The elevator is lined in mirrors and has a small bench to sit on, also upholstered in silk damask. I inspect myself. I'm wearing a black dress, a beautiful, vintage Jean Muir which I picked up for a song somewhere in The Village. It is silk knit and hangs like a dream. Simple, elegant, understated. It fits like a glove, perfect around my bust and breasts, demanding no bra. I have a small back which means a lot of tops and dresses swim about me, but it's also a blessing as it means I can pick up things from the sixties and seventies that don't fit today's modern woman.

I left my apartment looking as if vandals had ripped my bedroom apart. Every single item of my wardrobe is lying in chaotic piles on the bed, strewn over chairs, on the floor. They have even found their way into the bathroom. Decisions, decisions. I was going to wear a slinky, long, red dress but thought it was too 'sex siren' - not the message I want to advertise. I think Alexandre has got the point. I don't want overkill. I tried on a beautiful cream dress with rosebuds but I looked too 'little girl'. Then I decided that I *must* wear the pearls. Not something I can put on for work, and where else can I wear them if not for dinner with Alexandre? So then the dress became all about, 'what will go with the pearls?' Thank goodness I left work early and gave myself time. I finally settled on this old favorite, the Jean Muir. Classic. Timeless. It reaches just below my knees, is tight about the bust but flares in two layers so if I spin about it almost makes a circle around me. I put on some simple pearl studs but would you know it? The pearls of the earrings did not match – did not pick up even one of the forty shades of the choker. So I tried some diamond studs which my mother gave me for my twenty-first birthday, which match the clasp of the necklace - just about. The faithful, high, nude pumps complete the outfit. Nude pumps with a black dress? Yes, they lengthen the legs. A tip I picked up from Vogue.

Hair loose, mascara, a little eyeliner and some lip gloss. My eyes don't look good with a lot of make-up, and I'm so bad at blending foundation that I pass on that.

My bag is a simple black clutch (that's a first) and I just have a pale blue cashmere wrap, in case I get chilly, but right now it's pretty hot outside.

The elevator doors open directly at the Penthouse on the thirteenth floor (lucky for some) and I walk inside the apartment. There is no corridor. It seems that there are no other apartments on this floor – Alexandre has it all to himself.

He welcomes me. He looks even more informal than usual in just his Levis and a T-shirt. He's barefoot and I catch a glimpse of those elegant toes.

"Good evening, Pearl, you look quite beautiful." More *Beauty Full* than *Beauty Fool,* his accent says. Let's hope I can keep going with the Beauty Full and not slip into the Fool which I fear I did this morning with my needy begging for sex. He said himself he likes me because I am 'mature' – I need to act like a grown-up, not a spoiled brat screaming for more candy.

He kisses me softly but not passionately, as if to say, *let's try not jumping each other's bones in the first few seconds.*

I keep my shoulders back (thanks for that tip, Mom, it has served me well) to try to give the gliding, poised look. It seems to work. I feel tall in my heels.

"You look so elegant in the necklace," he says. "I appreciate that you're wearing it for me."

"Not as much as I appreciate the gift. Every time I look at it, I'm bowled over."

"I have another gift for you."

"Oh no! Alexandre, please. You're cooking me dinner, that's already special. And this choker was beyond generous. You really don't have to give me anything else."

"Don't worry, it's very simple. I'll show you in a minute. Now what can I offer you to drink? Champagne? A cocktail?"

"A cocktail sounds tempting but I think I'll go with champagne, please."

"As lovely as you look in those shoes why don't you kick them off - you'll be way more comfortable – I'll show you around my abode."

His *abode*? His palace, more like.

He's right. I'm tottering about and feel self-conscious with Alexandre being so informal. I sit on a chair and slip my shoes off my newly buffed and pedicured feet. My toenail polish is ice blue. I look in awe about me. Like the main lobby, the floors are marble, not black and white but a pale gray. Up here the feeling is more Bohemian chic than in the lobby. Nothing is too polished, nothing flashy or overdone. It gives the air of an eighteenth century Parisian house that you might read about in a novel or see in a period movie. Everywhere there is wood paneling, even hiding the elevator when it closes. There are paintings on the walls, mostly figurative - an eclectic mix of modern and old, and a worn priceless-looking tapestry – a medieval scene of unicorns and ladies picking apples from trees.

Just this hallway is practically the size of my whole apartment.

Alexandre takes my hand. "Come, I'll give you a tour."

He leads me into the first room. The floors are now parquet, the wood buffed to a warm glow. The room is also completely paneled.

He stands there, his legs astride, and tells me, "This walnut *boiserie* is original 1930s when the building was constructed. None of the other apartments have this paneling. See how the era's ribbon-edge wood motifs are intact?"

I notice how it adds a kind of rococo accent to the place, adorning the doorframes, and the cabinetry and bookshelves which are integrated within the paneling. They run along one side, and on the other are picture windows looking across Central Park to the West side, letting in beams of evening light. The massive room has two fireplaces and a double-aspect - from the south windows there are views to the Plaza and Fifth Avenue. In the middle of the room are two enormous sofas facing each other with a coffee table in between, and at one end of this striking living room cum library is a black, grand piano.

"Do you play?" I ask.

"No, but my sister does."

"Where is she now?"

"In Paris. But she always stays here when she's in New York."

"How often does she come?"

"Once a month, or so."

"What's it like having a business partnership with a member of family?" I pry.

"Put it this way, I couldn't have done it without her. We're a team. She's savvy, smart and has a good head on her shoulders when it comes to deals. She's a tough negotiator."

"Did she go to Mumbai, too?"

"Oh yes. I don't make deals without her present. She got a scholarship to Harvard Business School – she's very well versed when it comes to corporate, multinational stuff."

I lean against the Steinway and run my fingers along its smooth lines. "I used to play," I say. "If only we'd had room for a piano like this in our small apartment, maybe I would have continued more seriously."

"Really? Be my guest. Play something now."

"Oh, I'm very rusty."

"No, you're not," he replies with a wry smile, and I roll my eyes at his innuendo. "Go on, play something," he entreats.

I sit at the piano stool and shake out my fingers and wrists. "It's been a while."

He leans languidly against the grand, waiting. I take a deep breath and begin one of my favorite tunes.

"Erik Satie," he says with a knowing smile. "*Gymnopedie number 1* – so haunting. You play beautifully, Pearl."

When I finish he claps and I feel pleased that I didn't make any mistakes. It makes me remember why I chose the instrument in the first place. I would give anything to have a piano like this.

"Some champagne," he remembers, opening a hidden bar, camouflaged by the walnut paneling. He looks into a small refrigerator. "For some reason there doesn't seem to be any in here. Let's go to the kitchen."

We make our way down a wide corridor and I find myself in - not a normal kitchen - but a sort of show-room. The ice-box alone would fit a regular-sized bathroom inside it. There is an island in the middle of the room, a big round table at one side, and wall to wall cabinets reaching to the high ceiling. All is white, the counter-tops marble, the floor marble. Light is pouring into the room as the windows are massive. There is a gas-burning stove, wider than an elephant, from which is emanating a delicious aroma of something roasting quietly in the oven.

"That smells wonderful," I comment.

"Well, let's hope it tastes as good as it smells." He walks over to the refrigerator and takes out a bottle of Dom Pérignon rosé champagne and pops open the cork.

"The lady from the third floor was raving about your cooking," I tell him.

"My grandfather was a chef – I picked up a few tricks."

"I guess you have the best food in the world in France."

"Oh, I don't know, lots of other countries have caught up with us in many ways. I had the most exquisite dish near San Sebastian in Spain a couple of weeks ago, and some of the pizzas here in America rival Italy."

"Pizza doesn't count," I exclaim, "as world-class cooking."

"Never underestimate the culinary importance of pizza, Pearl," he tells me with a sardonic smile. "If you were on Death Row you probably wouldn't ask for *haute cuisine*."

"I'd ask for my mother's macaroni and cheese."

"Exactly, there you go. It's the Italians that have us all hooked on their food." He pours us both some chilled champagne. It's crisp and aromatic. Champagne, an unbeatable French export.

I raise my eyebrows. "Do you sometimes think about that? Imagine being on Death Row?"

"We don't have the death penalty in France but since I've lived here in The States I do question the possibility sometimes." He says this with a serious look on his face. Is he kidding? I can never quite tell with him.

"Do you think you'd be capable of murder, then?" I ask, half teasing.

But his answer is serious. "We're all capable of murder, aren't we, Pearl? Given the right - or rather the wrong - circumstances."

I stare at him. I can't read his expression. He's a dark horse - an enigma, that's for sure. I return to the more comfortable topic of food. "You're probably the only European I've met who hasn't touted his country's cuisine as the best in the world."

He laughs. "Oh, I never said we weren't the best. We take our cooking very seriously. The lunch hour in France is sacrosanct. Everybody sits down for a three-course meal. The point is, we *want* to be the best – our reputation matters to us. We want to create gastronomic fantasies – so that our guests beg for a second helping."

The way he says this speaks volumes. That *double entendre* again. He's got me begging for a second helping, that's for sure.

"Follow me." He leads me by the hand to another room with a flat screen TV splayed across one wall – the room peppered with opulent sofas and chairs. There's a wrought-iron, spiral staircase and he leads me to it, guiding me as I climb the steps in front of him. At the top, we arrive in a Victorian-style conservatory, spilling over with tropical plants and trees. "I have several species of rare plants here. My sister could be arrested by Customs. She transports cuttings from all over the world in her suitcase."

"Don't the plants die in transit?"

"The secret is to wrap the cuttings in kitchen paper towel first, and then plastic. The paper towel is important or the cuttings sweat to death with too much moisture. This way they can survive a good twenty-four hours."

"Your sister sounds like quite a character."

"Yes, Sophie can be formidable. Not someone to have on the wrong side of you."

The more I hear about his sister, the more wary I am, although she seemed perfectly friendly when we met in the coffee shop.

I look about this conservatory which is full of small orange trees, purple bougainvillea and towering palms. It has a sweet aroma of jasmine which I notice climbing on trellises, wild and free.

There is a table in the middle, and elegant garden furniture composed of wrought iron, topped with sumptuous cushions, and double French doors which lead out on to a garden.

"You have a *garden* on the roof? In New York City?" I squeal in delight, running outside.

"I told you I was organizing my life around my dog. Rex should be quite content here, don't you think?" His lips curve into a mischievous grin.

The garden has real grass running across the length of the roof and small trees which are swaying in the evening breeze. The view across Central Park is spectacular – a sea of green reaching across the park to the Dakota on the Upper West Side, and I can even spot the Empire State.

"Now, where would you like to eat? Up here in the conservatory or in the dining room downstairs?"

"I don't know, I haven't seen the dining room yet."

"Well, I'll show you."

The dining room is perfectly round and a work of art. *Tromp l'Oeil* murals adorn the walls, making everything look three dimensional. Looking up, there is a painted blue sky around a dome with puffy wisps of clouds and a hawk flying through the air. It looks so real! There are double-doors opening onto a lake with swans, the view reaching to a far away horizon. The effect is extraordinary. I feel as if I am in an Italian palace centuries ago.

I catch my breath. "I'm in awe"

"So which is it to be, the fake view or the real, rooftop view?"

"I don't know which to choose. Both are unique. Which one would you suggest?"

"Let's toss for it." He reaches into his jeans' pocket and pulls out an odd silver coin.

"That doesn't look like a quarter," I remark.

"It's my lucky coin. I carry it with me everywhere. It's a silver stater from ancient Greece." He shows me a wonky coin, almost the shape of a small pebble – more oval than round with an image of a sea turtle. On the other side are triangular notches.

"Heads for upstairs, tails for down here, okay?"

"Okay, which side is heads?"

"The turtle side."

He throws the old coin in the air and catches it between his palms. *Those palms that cupped me and pressed against my sweet spot only this morning.* A shiver rushes through me. He slaps the coin on the back of his hand.

"How d'you know that stater is real?" I ask, foolishly forgetting for a minute that Alexandre is so wealthy he can buy anything he wishes, even museum relics.

"Because I had it checked out by an expert at the Met. She said one of the earliest and busiest Greek mints was on the island of Aegina, off the north-eastern coast of the Peloponnese. It's probably from around 550 BC. It comes everywhere with me. Nice to have a slice of history traveling about in my pocket wherever I go. Tails it is."

Before I can ask him where he got the coin from, he takes his cell from his other pocket and says something to somebody in French. He then turns to me. "Let's go back on the terrace, Pearl, and watch the sunset."

After we spend a good twenty minutes watching the sky turn from hues of deep oranges and shades of purple to spotting the first star (which happens to be Venus), we go back down to the round dining room. I do not see or hear a person anywhere. It is as if invisible fairies have swept about and organized everything: the table is set for two with a white damask tablecloth, crystal glasses and silver candlestick holders. There are just the candles lighting the room – those on the table and others in sconces on the walls.

The mood is romantic; a warm, golden glow flickers about the room. Etta James is singing *At Last* softly in the background – mirroring my frame of mind exactly – that's how I feel right now…*at last.* At last I have met someone I feel so strongly for. At last I feel passion again.

I look about the room. "Where did those magic hands come

from? The noiseless ones that laid the table?"

"You'll soon see. You sit and I'll bring you a little *amuse bouche*."

"What's that?"

"Literal translation: something to titillate your taste buds. A bite-sized *hors d'oeuvre*."

I sit in a daze studying the room, letting my eyes stray to landscapes of lakes and trees. I can hear low mumblings in the kitchen. He has help but obviously likes to keep that low-key. Soon, he comes in carrying two small glass dishes and sets one before me.

"This is a little Carpaccio de Dorade - sea bream - with Gelée de Poivrons – peppers. Sorbet Poivron et Piment d'Espelette. Special peppers from the French Pays Basque region right next to the Spanish border."

He pours me a glass of chilled white wine and I notice three glasses in front of me – this is sure to be quite a culinary experience to be paired with different wines.

He sits down and we begin. I pop the little roulade into my mouth and feel it melt. The chilled creaminess melds beautifully with the delicate flavor of lightly spiced fish. Sublime.

"So do you ever get tired of traveling so much?"

"You know, Pearl, even if I had the budget of a student, I think I'd be getting away whenever I could, maybe backpacking about the globe. You learn so much by visiting other parts of the world, immersing yourself in other cultures - the music, the language and customs. And it makes me grateful for what I have in life when I return home. I work hard but still, I'm not unaware of my luck. Every time I come home I think, look, look at everything I have."

"And where do you consider your home is? Here or Paris?"

"Good question. More and more I feel rooted to New York but I suppose there'll always be a place in my heart for Paris. Rex is there, of course. When he gets here, I'll find it harder to leave."

"When's he coming?" I ask with too much eagerness in my voice. Selfishly speaking, I want that dog to arrive ASAP.

"Soon. I have some more business meetings overseas and when a few more deals are tied up, I'll go and pick him up by private jet." He is not smiling when he says this.

"Really?"

"It was your suggestion, Pearl, and what a good one it was, too."

"I never said–"

"You sowed the seed in my mind - asked me the other day if I flew about by private jet. Why should poor Rex be subjected to a travel crate in the hold of a commercial plane – the air conditioning blasted up too high, or worse, none at all?"

A young girl in a shift dress appears from nowhere. She looks no more than eighteen. The smile on my face drops with consternation because she's extremely pretty with long dark hair, a neat little figure and rosebud lips. She silently clears away our plates. He takes her by the wrist. *A sexy little maid he sleeps with on the side?* My heart races with envy and suspicion.

"Elodie, meet Pearl. Pearl, this is Elodie, my niece from Paris - Sophie's daughter. She's working for me this summer. Learning a few tricks of the trade."

"How do you do?" I say, wanting to shake her hand but she's holding the plates.

She smiles awkwardly. "Bonsoir," and slips away, faster than a stream of water - back to the kitchen.

"She's very shy. She comes with me to the office every day – she's quite a wiz at programming but she's a loner, she keeps to herself. Her English is appalling so I'm trying to get her to go out and about more to meet people. She refuses. I thought I'd make use of her this evening so she's been working as my sous chef and helper."

Elodie brings in two more plates and exits as quickly as she entered.

"This is my version of one of Paris's great chefs, Guy Savoy's signature dishes. It's Artichoke and Black Truffle Velouté. You are meant to dunk the brioche into it. Usually the soup is served hot but as it's summer, I thought it would be good chilled. I baked the brioche – everything here is made by me from scratch."

The soup is rich, silky and earthy, and the accompanying toasted brioche flaky, with a smear of black truffle butter on top. I dip it into the creamy soup, garnished with fresh black truffle and shaved Parmesan. It's mouth-watering. "This is delicious," I gush.

"Thank you."

The whole evening has a surreal quality to it. It feels formal and now I know his sister's daughter is milling about the apartment, I feel uneasy and self-conscious. I expected Alexandre to have a sleek, modern home full of leather and chrome and Italian furniture, but I see he lives in a wacky sort of museum. He drives classic cars, one of which looks like the Bat Mobile, and he plans to travel, not by private jet himself for business, no, but to accommodate his dog. Are all French men like him?

We have two more dishes, both served to us by the bashful Elodie. Razor Clams from Galicia, garnished with Seaweed Butter and Ginger, and then, for a second course, Roasted Pigeon with Tomato Chutney and Tiny New Potatoes. That was what I smelled wafting from the oven earlier. All this Alexandre has concocted himself. It rivals the best restaurants I have ever been to.

Last comes home-made vanilla ice-cream (made with real Cornish cream from England, no less) topped with his own Rose Jelly made by him.

"I collected the rose petals from my garden," he says, his eyes bright.

"In Paris?"

"Didn't I tell you? I have a place in Provence?"

My stomach churns. I went to Provence when I was a child and remember fields of lavender, vineyards and clear blue skies, but not much else, except a yearning to return one day to a place that captured a young girl's heart.

"You have a house there, *too*?" I ask him.

"Yes. I believe in putting my money in bricks and mortar in preference to the stock market. If things go wrong, at least I'll have a roof over my head – that's how I see it. You must think me very greedy owning all these properties."

"Not greedy, just lucky."

"I told you I was lucky. The house in Provence was a ruin when I bought it. It's an old stone farmhouse, a *mas*. It's very rustic and I never go in winter so it doesn't even have central heating. I have a few vineyards and some lavender fields."

Every word that comes out of Alexandre's mouth makes me want to weep. With joy. With fear. Fear that he won't want to be with me anymore – that all this could be over. That I'll never be invited to Provence. My dream is to run through lavender fields, taste the sun on my skin, be loved forever and ever by this man's side; this man who has seduced me with his quirky sense of humor, with sex, and now his home-made food, and hints of what could be in the future. I find myself speechless. Lavender fields. Vineyards. *A man who makes his own Rose Jelly? Really?* Am I in a dream? A fantasy in some romance novel? I pinch myself because I seriously wonder if I am. Surely this is all a figment of my overactive imagination?

To make matters worse, he adds, "If you play your cards right, I'll take you there."

That has done it. My cards? *What are my cards?* My hand is shaky, at best. If I only knew the secret ingredient to capture Alexandre forever, I'd bottle it and sprinkle it on his food when he wasn't looking.

I laugh uneasily. "I went to Provence once when I was about five. With my parents before they split. It was magical. I remember the scent of lavender."

"I have something to show you," he says, taking me by the hand, "that might invoke those sweet memories."

He leads me to a large bathroom tiled with white mosaic. At one end is an Art Deco bathtub, and at the other a shower, also covered in mosaic. There is a floor to ceiling Italian-looking gilt mirror - antique, of course. On a table are two bottles filled with clear liquid. He pops off the top of one and presses it to my nose. The sweet odor hits the back of my throat as I breathe the delectable scent into my lungs and fill them as wide as they will go. I'm in a trance of memory, of desire. Now I think about it, is that what has hooked me? *That is what his skin smells of…. Lavender!!*

"That smells out of this world," I say.

"I bring vats of it back. If I ever feel down or stressed I breathe in the lavender oil and all my troubles melt away in seconds." He starts to run the bath pouring the liquid in. "It makes your skin really soft, too, and has great healing properties, gets the circulation going." He gives me a mischievous smile.

Circulation. I think of the blood pumping through his veins, of his rock-hard erections. It causes a pool of nerves to gather deep in my solar plexus.

"So that was the smell I couldn't quite fathom," I reply, remembering reading somewhere that lavender oil is an aphrodisiac.

"They say people are attracted to each other mainly by scent-based chemistry. Now you know my secret," he tells me with a grin.

"It's true. I've read that some researchers think scent could be the astrophysical secret in the sexual universe, the key factor that explains who we end up with."

"So if I didn't happen to have a few drops of this lavender up my proverbial sleeve, perhaps you would have ignored me when we met in the coffee shop," he jokes.

"Maybe - who knows?" I tease. "But more likely, it was those subtle olfactory messages operating below the level of conscious awareness emanating from your pheromones, or whatever they're called."

I know this is true. The faint fragrance of Alexandre's sweat when we made love sent me into a frenzy. He smells delicious, never mind the lavender. I'd marry that smell.

We strip naked and lower our bodies into the water. Alexandre takes off my pearl choker - perhaps it would melt, after all. The bath is big and he positions himself at one end and I, in between his legs, my back pressed up against his chest.

"What about Elodie?" I ask suddenly, feeling as if she could burst in on us any moment, even though the size of his apartment means we can't hear her at all.

"Don't worry, she's going on a date tonight. Someone from work is taking her to a club. I made her say yes. She's in New York City, for God's sake, she has to learn to be more social."

"I didn't know your sister had a daughter."

"Elodie's her step-daughter. Same thing."

Feeling more at ease now, I relax back into his arms. He kisses my hair. "You smell great," he remarks.

"It's the lavender."

"No, it's you."

He starts to massage my shoulders and I feel myself unwind and my body slacken. "That feels wonderful."

"You have such beautiful shoulders."

"It's all the swimming I do."

"Some women's shoulders slope - not yours. But they're not broad, either, they're elegant, poised, you have a great posture. And your waist - so pretty, so hourglass."

His hands slip around my hips, massaging the oil into my skin. He kisses the nape of my neck and a quiver shimmies along my spine. All of a sudden, I hear some pages flicker and his voice, deep and melodic, begins to read to me in French. I don't understand, but it's beautiful. No man has ever read poetry to me before, let alone in French.

"Who's the poet?" I ask when he pauses for breath.

"Baudelaire." He continues reading and I close my eyes, listening to the pleasing rhythm, the cadence of the lines, but just as he is saying:

Avec ses vêtements ondoyants et nacrés,
Même quand elle marche on croirait qu'elle danse –

my backside slips beneath me and I go sliding under the water, my head knocking the book into the bath, splashing lavender-scented water all over the floor. When I come up - my hair soaked, water up my nose, I see the sinking poetry book and I gasp. It's an old leather edition. *What have I done?*

But Alexandre bursts out laughing, takes the sodden book and puts it aside. "What am I doing? I'm being absurd – reading you poetry when I have poetry right here in my arms, poetry in your lips, in between your thighs."

He guides my body around so I am facing him. He runs his finger across my Cupid's bow, holds my chin in one hand and then kisses me, first by letting the tip of his tongue part my lips, pushing it into my ready mouth, longing for him, waiting. I've been controlling myself all evening and now I let myself go, responding with heat and aching desire. I can hear myself moan which makes him react with increased ardor. He's kissing me hard now, his tongue probing deep – he's growling like an animal, forcing me closer to him by cupping his hands under my ass and grabbing me tight, holding me up with the strength of his muscular arms. He's licking me all over, my chin is in his mouth - he's moving down to my throat, my shoulders, and in a circular motion around my breasts, grazing just the edge of his teeth gently against each nipple until they harden. He catches one in his mouth, sucking lightly. It's as if a golden thread links them directly to my groin - I can feel that deep tingle inside me. His rigid erection is above the water, pressing up against my stomach. I feel myself wetting up, even though I am already in a bath I can feel myself oozing with excitement. His fingers are exploring in between my thighs and his index finger slips its way inside me.

"So welcoming, Pearl."

I take his erection in my hands and massage him with the oily water. Ooh, he's big. How did I forget that? It was only this morning and yet it's as if I'm feeling him fresh for the first time again. I can't get enough of him. He's making soft little nips around my shoulders now and I shiver even though the water is still warm.

"It's too small in here, let's move to the bedroom," he suggests.

Like a true gentleman, he lifts me up from the tub so I don't slip, takes a warm towel from a heated rail above, and pats it about my body. We get out, and my legs still dripping, he scoops me up and carries me in his arms, the towel still wrapped about me. I can smell the lavender oil sweet on my skin and in my hair. When we get to the bedroom he throws me onto the bed, literally, I land on the soft mattress with a bounce. I open up my towel, my nipples still erect, my body shiny with droplets of oily water.

"Spread your legs," he demands.

I do as he bids. He doesn't have to speak, I can see his huge erection flex so I know how much he wants me and all I can think is how much I want to covet that organ – the centerpiece of his beautiful body.

He's standing there above me naked, running his eyes over me. "Look at you," he says, "you're beautiful. All I could think about all through dinner was fucking you. Making you come, making you cry out my name. What have you done to me, Pearl Robinson?"

I smile, feeling triumphant inside but not wanting to gush.

"Oh yes, I almost forgot - the gift I have for you. Wait there, don't disappear on me now," he jokes.

He leaves the room and what he said gives me an idea. I'll hide! I look about and wonder where. The room is huge, grand. It could be at the Ritz in Paris or anywhere opulent. There is even a mini-bar next to the bed. There are sweeping silk drapes pooling on the floors in front of enormous windows. I could hide there. No - too obvious. Under the big brass bed? Too uncomfortable. I make a dash for his walk-in closet. So childish - but why not? I hide behind rows and rows of laundry-fresh shirts. Behind them are suits. Suits? I've never seen him wear one. I ease my naked body behind a row of jackets. My breathing is heavy and I hear him bluster into the room.

"Pearl? Pearl? Where are you?"

He walks out again, probably thinking I've gone to the bathroom, or something. This goes on. I almost come out but decide to stay put. His footsteps fade as he walks about the vast labyrinth of his home. I hear doors opening and closing and then he's gone. Has he gone up to the roof terrace? This game is silly, I realize, and am about to come out, when he enters the room again. For some reason my heart is pounding, the way it does when you play Hide and Seek as a child. I hear the closet door open and light floods in. There are neat rows of shoes and trilby hats on shelves above. I see silk ties and color-coordinated sweaters and T-shirts.

"I think a naughty little girl is playing games with me and she could be in here. I think there's a naked creature in here who's asking to be punished for her naughtiness."

I feel genuinely frightened now. What if he's some crazy that wants to beat me up? His tone is serious. I push my way back further but the movement makes a shirt fall on the floor.

"Caught you, you minx. I can smell you in here. I can smell lavender and little girl, and I think she needs a good beating."

I swallow a glug of air and see his hands come through the suits and land on my wrists. He pulls me out of the closet his face harsh - no smile.

"I'm not kidding, Pearl, you've been disrespectful and I'm going to have to teach you a lesson you'll never forget." I notice his jeans are back on but he's topless. He grabs a couple of silk ties from his closet. He lifts me up again and carries me like a child and dumps me on the bed. "Lie on your back."

"What are you going to do to me?"

"You've been a bad girl."

"I was just kidding."

"I'm French, I don't share your sense of humor." He binds each leg so I am straddled on the bed on my back, legs wide open, each ankle attached securely with an ice blue silk tie to the brass bedstead. I want to thrash myself out of this position but curiosity is impelling me to stay. A little voice flashes through my brain saying, *Idiot, what if he's like that American Psycho character? All charming, at first, but who'll stab you in a hundred places and chop you up – too rich to be caught, so clever he gets away with it all. He said himself he was capable of murder.*

Please help me God, I hardly know this man.

He's scanning my body with his eyes. "Okay that will work. Now, these pearls will do nicely for your wrists." He takes the pearl choker from his pocket. "I'm going to tie your wrists together with this. Now, you know how valuable this is, don't you?"

I nod. God knows what he paid.

"Any struggling, and you'll break it, and we wouldn't want that now, would we?" He fiddles about with it, his expression severe. No kissing – his look is tough. I sense he is genuinely annoyed with me. He wraps the pearl choker around my wrists and guides my tied hands above my head. "I was going," he continues, "to let you open the box with your gift inside, but now you've spoilt things. Now you won't get to see it, only feel it - because I'm going to blindfold you."

"Please don't hurt me, Alexandre."

"But you've been bad, and as I said, you need to be punished, Pearl. Haven't you ever heard about a Frenchman's pride? I'm going to have to teach you a lesson in good manners."

From his other pocket he produces a blindfold. It's big, somewhat padded or something.

I feel so vulnerable lying on my back, my hands tied together above my head with the pearl choker, my legs wide open, each ankle bound.

"Please don't hurt me," I repeat. I think back to our conversation in the Corvette on our way to rock climbing, and remember how horrified he seemed to be by bondage, and yet here he is about to do something cruel. Will he bring out a whip?

He leaves my side for a moment and is doing something - putting on a record – it's an old-fashioned record player. Music begins. I recognize it - Chopin – I used to play it on the piano – *Prelude in E minor*. He puts the eye mask around my head. It's heavy on my eyes as if it's been weighted down with something and it smells of heavenly lavender.

His voice is low. "I had this eye mask made for me. It's stuffed with lavender from my fields in Provence, together with grain to make it weighty. I've put on a record as the sound is always crisper than a CD – I love Chopin - isn't this beautiful?"

I feel more relaxed with the soft music and fragrance of lavender all about me, heavy in my nose, but I'm still nervous - thinking about what he's going to do to me as I can't see a thing. *Why did I stupidly hide in his closet? It was all going so well!*

"I'm going to open up your gift now. If you hadn't been so disobedient, Pearl, you could have done it yourself."

"What is it?" I ask with trepidation.

"You'll soon find out."

I hear the ribbons being untied and the lid of the box being pushed off, as it lands on the sheets beside me.

"I'm going to start now, okay, Pearl? Your punishment will begin after I count to three. Are you ready?"

I brace myself for something horrible. Tense my legs and stomach and scrunch up my face in preparation.

"One."

His voice is low, forbidding. My heart is pounding with dread.

"Two."

I can hear his heavy breathing – he's really concentrating, and adrenaline is pulsing through my veins.

"Two and a half."

I'm really scared now.

"Three."

Yet….Nothing.

Then I feel something so light I know he can't have started the punishment. There's a tickling on my toes and then above my ankles. It is brushing me weightlessly along my calf. It is not his finger, what is it? A paintbrush?

"Can you feel what it is?" he asks in a soft voice.

"It feels good. Really good."

"Remember that little story you told me? About your first time?"

I'm focusing now. It's on my other leg, trailing up my thigh. It is indescribably erotic. Not being able to see or move, I still feel fearful, but the sensation is radiant, wispy. I am aware of my pelvis moving, wanting whatever it is to move higher between my legs.

"You still can't guess, Pearl?"

"It's a feather."

"A Kingfisher feather. It's blue and orange at the tip. Can you imagine how pretty?"

He's tracing it up my body, onto my belly and circling it around my breasts. It's barely credible how such a light, helpless object can have this sensual effect. It's under my arm now and it tickles. Now on my throat, my lips, and now back on my throat, my shoulders, flicking with such delicacy on my nipples. I'm tingling all over.

"It's glistening like a little pearl."

"What is?" I ask.

"A part of you I want to put my lips around and then fuck."

I groan with anticipation. I'm feeling ready.

"It's wet and shiny and inside it's like a velvet glove, welcoming me, encompassing me whole - pulling me in, grabbing me all around in a tight embrace."

"What does it feel like?" I ask. "Making love to a woman? To me, I mean?"

"Oh, Jesus, you have no idea how good. It's warm and wet and delicious. It tastes sweet and salty and it wants me so much.

It's greedy for me like a comforting house inviting me in where I belong and offering me comfort - but with hot, hot sex at the same time. Do you want me inside you, Pearl? Deep inside?"

"Oh yes," I say, wriggling beneath the touch of the kingfisher feather. "I can't think of anything else. All day long I get moist and throb with desire, just imagining that huge great erection of yours - your sexy lips kissing me, your eyes - that tongue darting in and out of my secret places."

I'm trusting him now, my fear has left me and I'm opening up. *This feels amazing.* The feather is now brushing past my clitoris and I sense his thumb enter inside me as he makes slow circles with it, engulfed by my juices. Then he takes it out and I can hear him pop it into his mouth and suck it.

"So tasty, but I think we need a few extras to sweeten you up even more."

It's dark behind my blindfold. I hear him open the mini-bar door beside the bed. *What's he doing? Having a drink?*

After much rustling about, I feel something cold oozing onto my navel. It shocks me for a second. What is it? It's thick and gooey, not too runny. It smells sweet. So sweet but the lavender is making me confused.

"What is it?" I ask.

But he doesn't respond. Then I feel something cold being pressed inside me. Maybe round. Something fruity. One, two - three of them. *Wait a minute! All this was already in the mini-bar – did he plan this?*

"I smell fruit," I say.

"And what else?"

"Honey?"

"Big, black cherries and honey. But Pearl, I'm going to untie your ankles now – I think your punishment has gone far enough."

"No! *Please,* Alexandre. Please punish me some more."

"More punishment? Really? Don't you think you already paid the price for your disobedience?"

"No, I was a bad girl and I need to be disciplined."

"Okay then. I'm going to add another ingredient. Something very French. Something I used to eat for breakfast as a boy."

I'm waiting. Eager. I can feel the cherries inside me like little balls – so sensual - and suddenly he smears something creamy on my breasts. There is a whiff of chocolate. Do I smell Nutella?

My hands are still above me, clasped into the Art Deco choker, which I'm scared of breaking, so I hold still. He starts licking my stomach, his tongue lapping up the honey. His mouth heads up to my breasts and he sucks each one greedily, flipping his tongue back and forth on my nipples. I'm moaning and writhing about like a snake. The large cherries feel so good inside me. The pleasure is intense.

"Your breasts are like fruits. They fit perfectly in my mouth, not too big, not too small. I'm going to have to fuck those tits."

His hard penis laps against my stomach and then in between my breasts. His hands are cupping them, clamping his erection between them. When he moves up I try to catch it with my tongue.

"I want it in my mouth," I beg.

"I thought those avaricious lips might want my cock."

"*Please.*"

It's in my mouth now, dripping with honey and Nutella. I'm licking him, ringing my tongue around the head of his shank, sucking. He rises higher and I catch his balls and I suck each one individually, each one whole inside like enormous balls of candy, as he guides his penis over my face stroking my nose, my forehead with it. He moves away now, his tongue trailing south down my body, parting my lips, holding my inner thighs with his thumbs as he starts to suck out the cherries inside me – vacuuming them out. His tongue is wild, slapping against my entrance – then he lets just the very tip touch my throbbing clitoris and then holds his tongue down still on it, pressing hard. I start thrusting myself up and down on his flat, motionless tongue, pressing against it and I start coming. It's in hot waves rushing through me. I still can't see, can hardly move, my body a vessel of pure pleasure. Behind my blindfolded eyes I see flashes of color and I go into a tunnel of black and red and gold, still climaxing, still pressing myself against his tongue as my body ripples and tremors.

"Ahh…ah…ah…aaaaa."

Then he starts licking again, sucking out all my tastes from my opening but careful not to touch my tender clit. It makes the climax all the more intense.

Then slowly, slowly, I come down, the spasms gentler now, the tingling in tiny bursts but still on a plateau. Such a surprise, this has never happened before. The myth has come true – *I'm having an orgasm from oral sex!*

He begins to remove the ties on my ankles and then unclasps the choker around my wrists. He kisses me softly on the lips and I taste the mélange of flavors; honey, cherries, my salty turned-on self and Nutella. He lies beside me on the bed. I shake my hands free and bring them about his arms and shoulders. Finally, I can touch him. I unravel my fingers, stretch out my palms and stroke his smooth back. I'm still wearing the blindfold and don't take it off. I can hear him fiddling about with something and more music comes on.

"This is for you, chérie. The song's called *Black Cherry*."

I grin. "Very apt. That was amazing but what about you?"

"You think I haven't enjoyed this? I nearly came just giving you so much pleasure. I had to count to ten to stop myself. And another ten to stop myself from plunging into you."

"Why didn't you?"

"This isn't about me, Pearl, it's about you."

"It's about us both, isn't it?"

"I want you coming," he says in a low voice, "all around me when I'm deep, deep inside you."

"But you've already hit the jackpot."

"I want to make sure it wasn't just luck, though. I was just skimming the surface. The most important erotic muscle you have is your mind. I have to get to know your mind better, get inside you, metaphorically as well as physically."

The way he says that frightens me. He's already got me free and clear, can't he see that? *Is he trying to give me pleasure or control me?* I want to say something, put up a fight but my body lies there exhausted, and the only expression on my face is a contented, I've-had-the-first-and-best-oral-sex-orgasm-of-my-life smile.

He strokes my head. "Sleep now, princess. At least for a while."

The chill-out music is making me relaxed, heavy-eyed. I run my hands over my body, assuming I must be a sticky mess, but find myself quite clean. Licked new. He did a good job.

A very good job indeed.

9

I don't know how long I've been sleeping, but when I awake he's sitting on the bed next to me, watching - his eyes resting on me, transfixed.

"I wasn't snoring, was I?"

He laughs. "No."

"Not dribbling or anything horrible, or talking in my sleep?"

"No, not at all. You look beautiful and serene. You had a sort of Mona Lisa smile set on your lips, so you must have been dreaming about something very pleasant."

"How long have I been asleep?"

"All night. It's time to rise and shine."

I sit up and see faint light coming through gaps in the heavy drapes. "You're kidding? It felt like I was asleep for ten minutes."

I can't believe I wasted that precious time with him merely sleeping. *What a fool!*

"Sorry, I must have really taken it out of you," he apologizes.

"You took cherries out of me," I joke. "And there I was, terrified, thinking you were going to thrash me with a whip or something." *Even kill me.*

"I'm sorry, Pearl. Did I really frighten you that much?"

"I was nervous when you tied my ankles."

"But you could have escaped any time – the knots were very loose, the necklace you could have snapped open at the clasp."

"At the peril of destroying an original Art Deco piece of jewelry? Never."

"I'm sorry, seriously, if I scared you. I would never, ever, hurt a woman. Not even kidding around." After he says this his lips are tight, pressed together, all humor wiped from his usually open face.

"Whenever you mention women and beating you look as if you're talking from past experience. Did something happen once?" I ask. "Are you trying to chase away personal demons?"

"Unfortunately, you can't chase away something that lives inside you."

"You have a violent past?"

"Yes."

Uh oh. I look at his face and wonder what he did that was so violent – he's fighting against his dark side. "Can I ask what happened?"

"I'm not so keen to discuss it."

"Surely you need to talk about it with someone?"

"I hardly know you, Pearl."

"You know me well enough to have tied me up, to have bought me an outrageously expensive gift, to have delved, literally, into my private places. You think I've ever let anyone that close to me before?" I bark. "You think I go round opening my legs up with abandon like that, opening my heart up like that to any man?"

"I'm sorry, I didn't mean to sound dismissive."

I start to get out of bed, hurt that he is choosing to close himself off from me, and fearful I am falling for a man who has a violent side. I've heard that men like him do that; ply you with gifts, win your confidence, make you fall in love, and then, when it's too late, they show their true colors.

"My father used to beat the shit out of my mother," he suddenly says, his eyes on the floor as if he were ashamed.

I observe the grim expression on his usually happy face. "How awful. Are you violent, too?" I ask nervously.

"I have been."

"With women?"

"Christ no."

"When?"

"In certain situations. I have triggers that set me off which I try to keep under control."

"What happened with your father, then?"

"We nearly killed him."

"We?"

"My sister and I wanted him dead."

"Well, it must have been your sister more than you, she being so much older." *So much older? She's still five years younger than I am. Wish I hadn't said that.* I look at him hard, trying to read his face but he's staring into the distance as if not focusing – a memory stirred up of something better forgotten.

"Because I assumed you were young," I continue, "when your father left. I mean, how could a little boy have hurt a grown man?"

"I was seven."

"Only seven." I don't comment more but cannot imagine what a seven year-old could have done.

"My sister was seventeen. But it was my idea, not hers. I was mixing rat poison with his food. Amongst other things."

"Wow, that was imaginative."

"My sister stabbed him in the groin when he was sleeping."

I try to picture the scene. Worse than any movie. "What had he done…" I inquire tentatively, "to deserve that?"

"He was a monster. The shit really hit the fan when that happened. The stabbing. He threatened to put Sophie in a juvenile delinquent home for offenders – we had to get away from him at any cost. The only reason Sophie stuck around was because of me, otherwise she would have left home a lot sooner. By the way, this is private information, Pearl. I have never told a soul any of this."

"You can trust me. I would never say a word to anyone. I swear. So you all left?"

"Sophie and I packed and told our mother we were leaving. Told her that if she ever wanted to see us again, she'd better come with us."

"And?"

"She stayed behind with him."

"You're kidding. Why? She was your *mother*? You were so young."

"She wasn't Sophie's mother. Her mother died when she was ten – our father remarried my mother."

"But she was *your* mother. Mom to a seven year-old boy! I'm sorry, but I find that outrageous that she stayed with him after everything."

"She was terrified. That's what can happen in abusive relationships. One partner gets worn down so much, they lose all self-confidence. It can happen in subtle ways at first, until the dominant one has all the power. It defies common sense, transcends reason. She was too weak – we tried to protect her, but failed."

"You did not fail! You were only children. *She* failed," I exclaim, as I angrily run my fingers through my hair.

"Anyway, we left home. She joined us a year later."

"One whole year later? She chose her violent husband over her seven year-old *son*? Ouch."

"My sister was like a mother to me."

I let out a heavy sigh. "I find this really hard to comprehend. I thought you said you called yourselves The Three Musketeers."

"Sophie and I were The *Two* Musketeers for ages. My mother couldn't contact us. We didn't trust her not to tell him where we were, so we remained invisible. My sister got cash jobs, waitressing and other things, and we had alias names. Sophie pretended to everyone that she was my mother – lied about her age, said she was older."

He is staring into space now, locked in this memory. The way he is spilling all this out to me makes me feel as if he hasn't shared this with anyone for a long time. Maybe never.

"Later," he continues, now glancing at me, "Sophie called my mother and met up with her, but kept me hidden just in case. But my mother had learnt her lesson by that point and swore she'd leave him. She did, and never looked back."

"How can you forgive your mom for not coming with you in the first place? For not denouncing your father?"

"You forgave your father, didn't you? For abandoning you?"

"Yes, but my brothers and I weren't in *danger*."

"Brothers? I thought you only had *one* brother."

"Well, no. I had another brother," I admit. "John - who died of an overdose."

"Shit. I'm sorry."

"My life hasn't been such a picnic, either."

Looking at me, Alexandre asks, "What made your brother do that?"

"He was an alcoholic. I don't know, he was really messed-up about my father leaving, and was always disturbed as a young boy. He was a sensitive soul who took on too many burdens of the world. Then, one night, just over ten years ago, he had a lethal cocktail of drink, prescription medication and cocaine. He died."

Alexandre holds my hand and squeezes it a little. "Shit."

"Yeah, it was a shock. I still miss him."

"Yeah, I bet. People do strange things. Not a day goes by when my mother doesn't hate herself for what she did. Your brother, Pearl, was powerless against his addiction."

"Was your mother using drugs, too? Or drinking?"

"*He* was her drug. He was her poison."

I notice he can't bear to use the word *father*.

"Was he your step-father or your real father?" I ask.

"When you say, 'real,' do you mean biological?"

"Yes."

His normally sumptuous mouth sets into a thin line. "Good - because he was never a real father to us. His seed produced us, but he was not our father."

"I'm so sorry. I thought I had a sob story, but yours - well it must have been awful."

"You can't even begin to imagine."

"I could try."

"Pearl, what he did to us is *beyond* anyone's imagination."

"He abused you? Sexually?"

"Let's get something to eat. I'm hungry. They do a great breakfast at The Carlyle."

"Isn't it a bit early?"

"They know me there, it'll be fine."

I shower and put my Jean Muir dress back on. Alexandre offers to lend me something of Sophie's to wear but I decline. There's no way I'd feel comfortable dressed in anything of hers without her permission. Men don't get that - how women are about their clothing.

Alexandre puts on a dark gray suit, one of *the* ice blue silk ties, and shoes polished to a high shine. He looks so different, I'm stunned.

"You look highly sophisticated," I marvel, "very handsome indeed."

"Thank you, Pearl. I have a lunch meeting with an elderly gentleman, the type who wouldn't appreciate my usual attire."

I feel very 'morning after the night before' in my dress and heels, but when we arrive at The Carlyle by cab - I couldn't walk more than a block in those heels - I don't feel out of place. Plus, Alexandre looks so dapper in his suit; I'd feel ashamed to stand beside him in something more casual. I realize when we sit down for breakfast that I have left my gifts behind; the kingfisher feather and the pearl choker.

The hotel's dining room is elegant like an English country manor house, with plush chintz-covered banquettes, rugs adorning the floor, and mirrored alcoves set off by a towering floral arrangement of lilies in the center of the room. This is a first – doing breakfast. I'm a grabber, a black coffee guzzler, running and eating at the same time. When I tell Alexandre this, he laughs.

"Food on the go," he exclaims. "Very American. In France, people are discussing what they'll be having for lunch while they're still eating breakfast, and while they're eating lunch, what they should make for dinner. People want a hot lunch, even in summer. Especially people who live outside big cities - everything closes at noon sharp until two o'clock."

"You can't go shopping during those hours?"

"No way! Everyone's having lunch. And on Sundays? Forget it. Sunday is family day. Walking in the park et cetera. You can shop on Sunday mornings for food - the supermarkets will be open - but little else. The afternoons are for relaxation only."

We sit down at a table with a white tablecloth and I feel as if I'm on a date, although it can't be more than seven a.m.

"What else is different about the French culture?" I want to know, smoothing out my dress.

"Let me see. Oh yes, your drinking laws. In France, teenagers are expected to try a little wine with their food."

"They must go wild."

"Not really. Because it's available, it's less of a big deal."

"What else?" I ask, fascinated.

"Well, I think I explained to you why Sophie and I have made our business more of a success here in the States than in France. Being an entrepreneur in the U.S is respected – something many people aspire to. Being an entrepreneur in France is what you do if you're unemployable or cannot get a 'real' job. Things are changing, but slowly. People have to stand on their own two feet more than before – 'jobs for life' are hard to get these days."

"Something you and Sophie had to do – fend for yourselves, stand on your own two feet."

"Exactly, we had training." He laughs – the somber look has been replaced again by his happy-go-lucky demeanor. Thank God. I see touching on his past can cause demons to re-visit. I would have liked to have delved more into who his father was, and what became of him, but the look on Alexandre's face, back at his apartment earlier, told me to shut right up.

The waiter comes over to ask for our order. I like to think that he imagines that Alexandre and I are married - a well-dressed couple at breakfast together. The fantasy of wedding this Frenchman is now taking hold of me like a child clutching a lollipop. *Pearl, get a grip,* I say to myself with wry humor. Clutching onto a dream, a fantasy – not wanting to let go of the lollipop.

"What would you like, Pearl?" Alexandre asks, putting his hand on mine. I feel all melty and warm. *We are together having breakfast. We have spent the night together.*

"I'll have poached eggs and smoked salmon with Hollandaise, please."

"Could you just bring me a big bowl of blueberries?" he asks the waiter. "I don't see it on the menu but–"

"Of course, sir, anything else? The waiter sounds deferential. The smart suit is working wonders.

"Shall we get coffee?" Alexandre turns to me.

"Sure," I reply. "And maybe some orange juice?"

"And some freshly squeezed juice, please," he says. "Oh yes, and a little yoghurt, perhaps."

"That's all you're eating?"

"I'm crazy about blueberries and stuff my face with them

whenever I can. You see that? How accommodating the waiter was? Blueberries not on the menu - but *no problem*. That's what I love about this country, people want to make you happy and there's no shame in the service industry – you guys go out of your way to smile. Americans have different values and one of those key values concerns the customer."

"Anything you don't like about us?" I ask.

Someone is leaving him a message on his cell. It buzzes on the table. He ignores it and also ignores my question.

"You Americans also value innovation," he carries on, back to his topic, "and individualism. Standing out is a good thing here, but in France, people can be suspicious if it's not done in the 'right' way. Don't get me wrong. At school I learned philosophy - and this wasn't a private school, even. We're educated very well in France - cheaply too. If you have a big family, the youngest get to go for free, even in a private school. But you aren't encouraged to think for yourself, nor operate by instinct or gut feeling, nor come up with original ideas – nor think too much 'outside the box.' It's drummed into you to only debate something if you have well, *thought out* opinions and arguments that can be backed up with a host of proven examples. And certain things are expected from us in society in France. The American dream still exists here. In France, people are discouraged to dream - it's not practical."

I'm in my element listening to him spout forth; his melodic voice spurting off opinions, his defined jaw raised, almost haughtily, with his beliefs. *Please, God, if you care about me, let Alexandre take me to Paris, to Provence.*

"And what," I press on, "about the positive side? The things you really *miss* about your country?"

"Well, leisure is a necessity in France, not a luxury," he says, loosening his tie. "We live to eat not eat to live, and the same goes for relaxation. We spend time with family, have longer, paid vacations – we value our free time and don't feel guilty about it. In America, if you tell someone they're a workaholic, they take it as a compliment. In France, a person would be horrified if you said that to them. All these are sweeping generalizations, of course. There are exceptions to the rule in both countries. But this is what I've experienced with my limited understanding of this cross-culture."

"And what drives you nuts about France?" I ask, noticing his cell buzzing on the table yet again.

"Zero customer service. People can't get fired easily so they behave any way they feel like, especially with government paid jobs. The cockiness is something to be believed. In America, a company *earns* its clientele – in France the customer is not the king, that's for sure."

"Wow, it sounds both fascinating and frustrating."

"It is. It is."

"What about French women? Do you see a difference there?" *This is the question I have been longing to ask from the beginning – translation – are you and I serious? Or will you end up with a French woman because Americans just can't compete?*

He ponders this. "Not so much the women themselves, but people's attitudes towards them. In America, youth is worshipped. In France we love *women.* Girls are for boys. Women are for men. At least, I speak for myself. I am attracted to women, not girls." He looks hard at me and then smiles.

I know my days of being a girl are long since gone but I still find it hard to accept that I am 'mature' – I still hanker after being mistaken for a girl when I walk down the street. When you are a mature woman, the wolf-whistles from construction workers stop, and that's a scary thing.

The cell is vibrating, almost moving across the table of its own volition. Whoever is calling is desperate to speak to him. *At seven fifteen in the morning?*

"Excuse me, I obviously need to listen to these messages." He looks at his cell. "It's Sophie, it must be urgent."

Mess…. Ages, his accent says, as if in warning.

As he listens to his messages, I study the expression on his face which changes from animated and delighted to concerned, and then visibly upset. He makes a call. Calling Sophie back, no doubt. I watch him in as discreet a way as possible. I don't want to appear nosey. I pretend to look about the room. I fumble in my clutch bag, while all the time keeping my peripheral vision honed in on him. He is saying, "*oui, non, incroyable*" and words to that effect. At one point, he looks at me and then away. *Has somebody died?* He puts his cell on the table, sighs and brings his hand to his face, cupping his chin, half covering his mouth. Something is very, very wrong. His eyes are stony and just his expression is making me want to sink through the floor.

"Pearl. Oh, Pearl,"

I say nothing. He gives me a look that I can't quite fathom. He is not happy.

"Why didn't you tell me, Pearl?"

"What?" I ask innocently. I have a horrible feeling I know where this conversation is heading.

"Who you were?" he asks in a quiet, disbelieving voice.

Help! He thinks I'm a monster, I can see it now, written all over his face. His lips are tight - the way they were when he talked about his father. *I am now in the father category.*

"What do you mean?" I ask like a fool. I should just blurt out, 'I'm sorry' but I'm feeling defensive. *Really, I am not a bad person!*

"Is this what all this is to you?" he asks with disgust, waving his hand in the air. "This breakfast - spending time with me? Jesus - even making love to me. All this so you can glean information for your bloody *documentary*? Get me to open up to you, the way I did about my intimate *private* affairs? You asked me if there was something I didn't like about Americans – for all the good about your country, you lot would sell your souls, wouldn't you? Sell your own grandmothers if it meant advancing your careers in some way?"

A minute ago he loved America and Americans. Now, because of me, we are all slung like soiled underwear into the laundry bag.

"Alexandre, let me explain, let me–"

"Explain what? That you basically lied to me? Oh yes, very clever, not *lied*, exactly, no - just *omitted* to mention the fact that you were hunting me and my sister down. Why didn't you just come out with it? We're not ogres. Who knows? With some persuasion we might have even said, yes. Why weren't you honest and simply tell us that you wanted to do a documentary about us?"

"Because I–" I'm all tongue-twisted, I can't speak, my breathing is shallow and fast, my heart is racing and my eyes are welling up. "Because–"

"Don't fucking cry on me now. I'm not falling for that."

"I love you, Alexandre." It plops out of my mouth – I can't help myself.

"Yeah, right. That, I really believe."

The tears are flowing now – I'm mopping my face with my linen napkin and see the couple at the table next to us staring with curiosity. I don't care – I blabber on, "When I met you at that coffee shop - it was a mistake - I didn't even know you were there - I'd given up - I'd missed your talk." It's all coming out garbled, my lips stuttering as I swallow air in great gulps - "I don't care about the documentary. I want to do a film about arms dealing, *I don't care*."

"That's clear. You don't care. Well you know what? I *did* care. I thought we had something special. I thought you were different, but all along, I see you wanted to get to know me for ulterior reasons! Not because you were having fun with me, not because you felt for me, but because you had a fucking film to make and I, along with my sister, were your targets. Why the hell didn't you just *say* that that was what you wanted? Be straightforward - not sneak about like some snake in the grass." He's standing now, not even looking at me anymore. He gets out a couple of hundred dollar bills from his suit pocket and slaps them on the table. "I don't know what the check will be," he snaps. "Please deal with it, keep any change."

Keep the change – what am I, a whore?

"Please Alexandre - my boss was away - I never even let her know I'd met you. I wasn't even going to tell her so she'd forget about that silly documentary—"

"There you go again, Pearl. Not being straight with people. Not telling your boss you met me? Hiding stuff. What are you - ten years old?"

"I'm sorry, Alexandre. I'm so sorry. I lo—" the rest of the sentence doesn't even get a chance to come out.

"Bye Pearl. I'll get your necklace delivered to your door. And that other ridiculous gift."

"I love that gift," I mumble pathetically.

I want to tell him he's the best thing that ever happened to me, that I'm besotted with him, but he's leaving now, not looking behind. I see the jacket of his sharp suit swish away as he walks with steely purpose out of the dining room. Mortification does not do justice to how I feel. I brought this upon myself. I dug my own grave. Nobody but my sorry-ass self can be blamed. There I was, fantasizing that I was like Rachel from *Friends, a* cute-charmer-character lost in a silly little sitcom predicament. But Rachel and I are worlds apart - I can't laugh over it with a mug of coffee. No. This is real.

I have blown everything.

10

"Don't you see how childish that sounds, Pearl?"

Like a real glutton for extra punishment, I have called Anthony. *Why, why did I do this?* I'm in my bedroom, throwing off the Jean Muir dress, while climbing into something more casual. If I don't hurry, I'll be late for work. Sinead O' Connor's *Nothing Compares 2U* is blaring on my music system, a reminder that Alexandre is irreplaceable. Unique. And I've lost him.

"Pearl? Are you there?"

"Yes, I'm here, I'm just battling with my dress."

"Rachel from *Friends*? Seriously? You're likening yourself to a ditzy TV character? I mean, maybe you are that way but you don't want others to perceive you so. Do you know how lame that sounds? Not to mention *dated*. So 1990s. It really shows your age, too."

"I happen to love Rachel. And you make it sound as if being

forty is some sort of disease."

"It is when you're dating someone from kindergarten."

"Okay, I'm hanging up now."

"Don't hang up…did you mention that to Frenchie – that you are still hung up – excuse the pun – on Rachel from *Friends*?"

"His name is Alexandre. No, I did not mention Rachel from *Friends* to him. Maybe I did tell him I liked *I Love Lucy* and *Bewitched* and *I Dream of Jeannie*."

"Forty years old going on seven. Honestly. Interesting how all those characters tell fibs. I guess you must identify with them."

"Well I love them all and I still laugh when I watch re-runs."

"Honey, you're not going to get a chance to re-run this little episode, don't you get that? And I don't hear you laughing now, sweet pea. Do you know anything about French men? Do you not realize they are the proudest people on the face of this earth? You messed with his pride, girlfriend, you ain't never gonna get another chance."

"Stop that 'girlfriend' lingo, Anthony."

I imagine Anthony swanning about San Francisco 'girlfriend-ing' everyone and giving high fives, and for some reason it makes my blood boil. I yell, "Anthony, what is all this, 'French people do this and Americans do that?' We are human *beings*, not stereotypes from some 1960's Berlitz travel guide."

"Do you remember that Mexican travel guide of Mom's?" he cackles. "How we'd roar with laughter?"

"Listen, Anthony, I'll call you later, I'm running late. Thanks for listening to my woes. *And* being an ass."

"Laters, baby sis. Take care now, don't do anything rash, ya hear?"

When I arrive at work, I nearly have a heart attack. Natalie is sitting quietly at her desk.

"Natalie, why are you back so early?" I ask, dumping my monster handbag on the floor. It's back with full vengeance now – everything is packed inside – just in case. As in *suitcase*, it's so heavy.

"Good morning to you, too, Pearl."

"I'm sorry – just - I thought you were in Hawaii until Monday."

"I tossed up whether to stay and check into a hotel or come home early. In the end it made sense to get back."

"Hotel? What happened at Dad's?"

"Your dad didn't seem to want me there anymore."

"What? But he's crazy about you!"

"Was. Seems he got bored."

"No, Natalie, you just read him wrong. That's his style. He's a loner, a surfer dude – just been used to being independent."

"Selfish is what he is."

"Okay, you know what? You are my boss and I love and respect you but I spent my whole life hating my father and finally, finally we became friends. I know he's selfish, I know he is a terrible husband, boyfriend whatever, but I do not want to know all the details of what an asshole he is. Especially, not right now."

I find myself in tears again, and Natalie takes me in her arms. I begin to howl like some sort of wolf. The fact that she says, 'there, there, let it all out,' makes it worse. I let it all flow freely. I am like a dam suddenly being unblocked. My whole life is being spilled into her bosom. In between sobs I tell her my Alexandre story, minus the mind-blowing sex. That is my precious secret - too beautiful to share with anyone.

"She listens carefully and then says, "Yes, I had his sister, Sophie Dumas, on the line this morning cross-questioning me."

"*What*?"

"I mean, it was pot-luck I was at my desk so early. I came here directly from the airport – took the Red-eye. I guess they're five or six hours ahead of us in France. She was pretty pissed."

"What did she say?" I ask - my heart on the floor.

"She wanted confirmation of your name. She had the e-mails in front of her, the ones I had sent her asking for a meeting and confirming your presence at the conference. She couldn't understand why you hadn't approached her honestly when you met them at that coffee shop after their talk at InterWorld. And, of course, she was aware that you've been dating her brother – he must have spoken to her about you."

Natalie is looking at me in a way that says, 'Yes Pearl, why *didn't* you just do things the way you were meant to? You have let us all down.' But no words come from her lips – just *that* look.

"I know. I know, Natalie. I screwed up. She and Alexandre were standing there in line. Very friendly. Very amenable. I just kind of froze with…I don't know…with what. Fear? Excitement? All I know is the second Alexandre spoke to me I turned to Jell-O. I thought he may think I was a stalker. I wanted to be the beautiful girl he met in a coffee shop, not someone…someone *wanting* something from him. I'm so sorry, Natalie."

"You would have still been that beautiful girl at the coffee shop, Pearl, no matter what."

"I'm sorry," I say again.

"They wouldn't have gone for it anyway," she says in a soothing tone. "At least, not Sophie. She sounded pretty fierce. It's just a shame it has all gone so horribly wrong with you and Alexandre."

So horribly wrong. Her words are like clanging cymbals, or nails on a blackboard.

"Were you planning on telling me?" Natalie asks, looking me in the eye.

"Of course. But you asked me not to disturb you on vacation," I stutter, telling a half-truth.

The day drags on. I can hardly concentrate. I do research, catch up with important calls and e-mails, but I can't picture anything but the shadow of disappointment on Alexandre's face. I don't mention the pearl necklace to Natalie. And hope he doesn't send it back to me, after all, as he promised. A reminder of what *could have been* if I wasn't such a dunce.

I reflect on all the dumb things I've said, the way I have behaved like a child when I'm almost a middle-aged woman. I loathe, loathe, loathe that word, 'middle-aged' and cannot bear to let it sneak its pushy way into my vocabulary, but as Anthony reminded me – 'how long, exactly, do you expect to *live*, Pearl? *Of course* you are heading into middle-age – you can't deny it.'

After hours of beating myself up, I start remembering the sex between Alexandre and me, and can actually hear low whimpers coming from my very being, the way when you have a fever and groan quietly. I think of his worked-out torso, his strong thighs pressed hard between my legs, how the water gushed down on us, swirling about our pleasured bodies. I think of his tongue meeting mine and how it licked me, pressed me on my sweet spot until I came, my body writhing in spasms of bliss. I think of him inside me - and my belly churns upside down.

I have to call him, or at least send a text – I can bear it no longer. Even if he thinks I'm a despicable human being who lies, surely he can at least have sex with me? I pick up my cell and begin to write him a message:

Dearest Alexandre - no, scrap the 'dearest,' that sounds ridiculous.

Alexandre, please forgive me. Can we meet up? Just to talk?

No, that gives him a chance to say no. I erase and start again.

Alexandre – I need to see you – please come over.

I can hear Anthony's voice, 'Helloooo, Pearl? *Desperate*!'

My cell rings and my heart practically pops out of my skin - it gives me such a jump. Alexandre? No, it's Daisy.

"Hi Daisy."

"You called me four times, is everything okay?"

"I've really screwed up, Daisy."

I tell her the whole drama in whispers. I don't want anyone in the office to think I'm a hopeless wreck (which, of course, I am).

"Okay, Pearl, listen to me. DO NOT send him a message or speak to him. Wait for me. How soon can you leave work?"

"In an hour," I murmur.

"Meet me in the park - no, better still, I'll pick you up from work and we can walk there together. I repeat, do not send any messages or call him, okay?"

I don't reply.

"Okay?" she repeats in a stern voice. "Promise me."

"Okay, I promise."

"What do you promise?"

"I promise not to send Alexandre any messages, nor call him."

I can hear her sigh with relief. "Good. See you in a jiffy."

Just knowing that Daisy's one-woman rescue team is on its way, I find myself (after a couple more black coffees) getting a ton of work done. I do more in an hour than I have all week. I need to get a grip. I listen to Julie London croon *Black Coffee* and identify with the lyrics as if the song were made just for me. I too, am feeling as low as the ground.

If I work really hard perhaps I can get Alexandre's smile, sex with Alexandre, and Alexandre's very being - which has bored its way into my very psyche - out of my one-track mind.

I am a successful documentary producer, not a teenager. I am a woman, not a girl.

I am in control of my life.

I thought Daisy would be bringing Amy along, as she suggested Central Park, but no, she is alone. I am delighted (selfish me) that I have her and her undivided attention all to myself. She is in her tough-love mode.

It's a relief to get away from the sounds of horns and the ebb and flow of traffic, from the hot dog vendors and the bustling streets, and enter Central Park. We sit down on a patch of lawn and Daisy lets out a stream of wise advice, enunciated slowly from her heart-shaped lips. Her red hair is wilder and curlier than usual today, which makes her particularly animated – the humidity has gotten to us both – curls for her - for me, hot and bothered between my legs, caused by a too-young Frenchman who is no longer interested in seeing me.

"Okay," Daisy begins, sounding more British than ever, the aay of the okay drawn out languidly like a yawn. "This is not a foregone conclusion. You still have hope."

"I do?" I shout out. "Really?" Music is playing in my ears. Operas, symphonies.

"IF you play your cards right. If you don't, you don't have a chance."

"What are my cards?" I ask desperately.

"To do nothing."

"But Daisy I need to apologize, I need–"

"You have already apologized. Worse, you blurted out to him that you loved him. Twice."

"One and a half times. The second sentence he cut short. And the first time, he didn't even believe me."

"He'll be clocking what you said, trust me. Men are not so far removed from us, you know. They *also* dissect conversations and do post-mortems, even if it's just privately in their own heads."

"Not to the extent we do, surely?" I ask.

"They do care. Remember, I'm married. I see their human side."

"Yes, but you've forgotten about the rest of it," I grumble, thinking about her sweet, kind husband who adores her - and knowing she could never truly understand.

"Pearl, you have no choice. You have to save your dignity.

You cannot go running after him in guise of 'apologizing' or 'discussing' things. Firstly, men do not like to discuss. What's done is done. Men are more forgiving than we are, too. He'll forget what you've done soon enough and start remembering the good times he had with you."

"There's no way, Daisy. He was furious. He hates me now. He thinks I'm scheming and dishonest. And if I don't tell him that I'm sorry, he'll think I'm even worse."

"He'll think you're a bore. Let it go. Leave it be. If you do not, not, *not* contact him, he could call you, - he *could* want to see you again. He'll wonder why you haven't got in touch – it will pique his curiosity."

"But he was livid. Really angry–"

"Good, that means he likes you. You touched a nerve," Daisy expounds.

I say nothing and digest everything she has said. Then I come out with, "Daisy…the truth is I'm hooked on him. I want more sex."

"That's only because you hadn't had it for a couple of years so you're obsessed. Quite normal."

"No, really. He was like *a god* in bed."

"Even more reason, then, you need to listen to me. Even more reason you need to control yourself."

"What if I dress up really sexily, go somewhere I know he'll be, say hello so I don't seem rude, and then ignore him?"

"Pearl, how old are you?"

"That's what he said to me, that I was acting like a ten year-old."

"I can see you're not listening to a word I'm saying and you're going to do something really foolish, really humiliating that you'll regret later. And then don't come crying to me afterwards." She's standing up now, brushing down her dress and looking about the park. She's irritated by me, her pursed lips say it all.

"Daisy, where are you going?"

"To get an ice-cream, or something. I'm hot."

"I *am* listening to you, I swear." I stand up, too, and breathe in the smell of freshly mown grass. There's a baseball game in the distance and a dog chasing squirrels.

"Someone could get a ticket," I observe. "Aren't dogs meant to be on leashes at this hour?"

"As if you care, Pearl."

"I care for the owner and the dog. Of *course* dogs should be able to run free, as long as its owner picks up after it. Everything's gotten so regimented these days – so many rules." I can feel Daisy is bored by me so I try to win back a star. "What you're saying is really sound advice, Daisy. I'm going to try my hardest to follow it to the letter."

"Good!"

"I just need to keep busy."

"Normally, I can't even get you on the phone at all, Pearl. Your job has been everything to you. The fact that this Alexandre business is taking up all your energy just goes to show how you've lost the plot. This is not like you at all."

"I know."

"Remember when I went out with that Argentinean? Latin men like a chase. All men like to chase but that lot more than most. I have never dated a Frenchman but I'm sure if you come over as all keen, he'll run a mile."

"I guess you're right."

"Do you remember that little book that came out in the 90's?

The one with rules for dating? That told you what and what not to do? How to get them to be crazy about you?"

"I'd forgotten about that – it was a bestseller."

"Do not ask a guy on a date. Do not accept a date at the last minute. Always end the conversation first–"

"Do not say 'I love you' until the guy has said it first," I interrupt. "I broke that one already."

"Well," Daisy says hopefully, "it isn't too late to repair the damage. Don't call. Don't get in touch. And if he rings you, don't go all gushy and pathetic. Stay cool, calm and collected. You are a busy woman. You have plans, places to go, people to see, deals to make. You are not some pathetic, whimpering, sex-craving fool."

"Do you think I can pull it off, Daisy?"

"I *know* you can pull it off."

11

A whole week of agony has passed. Work has consumed me – what choice do I have? I call Daisy when I'm feeling weak, when I need to be reminded to not humiliate myself, to keep my resolve.

I got my period and I cried. I had a fleeting fantasy that by some fluke the lambskin condom was faulty and I would magically be pregnant - carrying Alexandre's child. That when he met his baby, he'd fall in love with me, and we'd live happily ever after.

Dream on, Pearl.

I have a great new contact at the UN who is willing to talk covertly - things are looking up career-wise. But the second I let my mind wander, I re-live moments with Alexandre; the image of his body, the things he did to me - and a mixture of longing, lust and sadness surges through my body. I have had a few crying-on-the-bathroom-floor moments, but each day gets a little easier.

He hasn't called nor even left a message. I am being strong

and have resisted the temptation. I even went out on a date with an old friend from college who used to have a crush on me. Yawn, yawn. We saw a movie and had dinner, and then I told him I had period pains in order to end the evening early. It was a half truth. The only pain I had was his pain-in-the-butt-you're-boring-me pain. Poor guy. I tried to disguise my feelings as well as I could. I smiled sweetly and told him I'd be so busy at work there was no way we could see each other for at least a month.

It will be hard to keep Alexandre off my mind as today is Friday and I won't have work to keep me distracted this weekend. But I have an idea….

When I arrive home I go online - I have to erase him from my brain. Perhaps it is a physical need that I've awoken and I can cure myself with a simple remedy.

My search online is for 'sex toys'. I have never in my life resorted to them, but hey, why not? Couples do it all the time. It's a good way to get to know your own body, apparently.

I had always thought using them was kind of like cheating. I have had a vague notion all this time - completely unfounded of course - that pleasure has to emanate from another person and anything else would be a sort of 'fraud.' *Ridiculous!*

I look at the range before me, the variety of colors and shapes. One is made from stainless steel. Ouch. Although it promises to heat up once inside - from your own body temperature. Others are neat things that look almost like cell phones and others, regular dildo shapes.

I read the reviews of one. **'YES,YES, YES! A great vibrator. Def worth the extra bucks. As soft or powerful as you want it to be.'** Hmm, sounds good.... I read on.... **'Not had solo use with it as it is so great with my partner.'** *Partner.* Good while it lasted with Alexandre, I think. Now I am partner-LESS. A dildo is a poor second choice, though, and could I even go through with it? All I want is *him* not some plastic substitute. As Alexandre said himself, the biggest sex organ is your brain. How much of a mental turn-on is a fake penis? I want to smell his skin on mine, taste his tongue.

No, Pearl. Stop! Don't torture yourself anymore.

I put some music on and start dancing to *Sex Machine* by James Brown. It happens to come up on random play. What are the odds of that? Not the most distracting thing to listen to while I'm trying to get my mind off Alexandre, but at least I get so into the song - I let loose, and forget for a while. I'm dancing wildly.....gyrating, grinding my hips.

I hear my landline go. Anthony calling to check up on me? Or the doorman? Maybe the pearl necklace has arrived, although surely Alexandre would have already sent it by now? If it is the necklace, I should really send it back - let him know, loud and clear, that I'm not somebody who is after *things*. There is also a pounding at the back door to the kitchen where the service elevator is. The trash. Did I forget to put it out? No, I did put the trash out. Why is the superintendent knocking at the back door? I go to answer.

My mouth hangs open when, what I see standing before me, is none other than HIM. As if my fantasies have materialized. Am I dreaming? He looks sexier than ever, beads of faint sweat on his brow, his dark hair ruffled.

"I came up the stairs," he pants.

"So I see."

"That'll be the doorman calling now to warn you that a rapist is trying to enter your apartment from the back door." He's not smiling. He's standing there, legs astride in *that* suit. No, it's a different suit, a shade darker – smart, elegant. I can feel my knees wanting to buckle beneath me but I take a deep breath and thrust my shoulders back. Daisy's words are echoing in my ear: *'Stay cool, calm and collected.'*

"Aren't you going to invite me in?" His foot is now planted firmly against the door so I can't close it on him, his tongue licks his upper lip for a split second. He's running his eyes up and down my body with a look of lust on his face. I can feel the familiar tingle in my groin.

"I don't know."

"Fuck it. I'll invite myself in," he says. Still no smile. He heaves himself forward, his body close to mine as I step backwards into the kitchen. His lips are centimeters from my face and he's breathing heavily. "I have to fuck you Pearl."

Before I have time to answer, he grabs me and pins me against the wall. He's kissing me hard, his hands in my hair. Gone is the sensitive man with the kingfisher feather. He's all animal and seems tremendously tall, like some sort of dark-haired Viking, but dressed in this chic, tailored suit. His tongue is licking my lips. He's hungry for me but seems full of anger. He cups my breasts and pulls my shirt off over my head. Forcing me. Forcing me to raise my arms, his fingers all over me, needy – stroking my navel, nibbling my nipples between his teeth. Then he's sucking my breasts greedily, and shoving his hands up my skirt pulling my thighs apart, palming me, pressing hard, then letting his middle finger slip inside me. I can hear myself moaning.

"You want to get fucked, Pearl? The way you fucked *me* over? Using me like some commodity to advance your career?" He's got his thumb inside me now and he's circling it. "Oh yes, Pearl, I can see you want to get fucked – really asking for it, aren't you? So wet. So tender."

Sex Machine is thumping loud. Alexandre has unzipped my skirt and I'm standing now in nothing but heels and panties, which happen to be red. I didn't put on a bra this morning; it was too hot. He grasps my hair and holds back my head, licking me on the tongue like a wolf preying on a bitch in heat. I want to push him off but I can feel the moisture between my hot, humming V-8 – it's beckoning – it wants only one thing. I fling back my head and groan, flex my pelvis forward. He's parting my panties now to one side. He hasn't even bothered to take them off. Then he goes down on his knees - peeling my panties aside with his teeth, licking me, shoving his tongue up inside my opening.

"You wanna fuck, Pearl? That's what you do in this country, isn't it? Fuck each other over, like the ambitious career whores you are."

He's still furious with me and the whole of the USA and something about his rage, coupled with his accent, wants to make me laugh and tell him to leave – take my control back. But the sweetness of his tongue, his soft hair brushing against my clit, his mouth making me wetter by the second, has me moaning in response.

He unbuttons the opening to his pants and his huge erection springs free like a beast. It's smooth, irresistible. I'm like a bitch in heat, a veritable she-wolf, and I grab it with both hands. He's fumbling now – putting on a condom.

"I shouldn't be using this," he growls. "I should just fuck you hard until my seed catapults its way inside you and makes you pregnant."

His words are Latin passion nonsense but they still turn me on, even though I know they can't be true. Yes, this man could make me pregnant – I'd welcome his baby. *Pearl, shut up!*

I'm still standing in my heels and can feel him slide into me and ram me hard, pressing my butt back against the wall. I cry out. This is hot. I shouldn't say it, but it is. He's pumping hard to the rhythm of *Sex Machine* and with every thrust I feel the muscles of my core clinging to him, not wanting to let him go.

"I. Love. Fucking. You." His voice is raspy. He's like a rock. It almost hurts but I can't resist. His tongue is on my neck, his hands clasping around each of my buttocks, pulling me close to him, sealing me against his groin. He's slamming me deep, his fingers clawed into the flesh of my ass.

"You like being used, Pearl? Or you just like using." The second statement is not a question.

"I'm sorry. I was just interested in *you,* not your company. I wanted to get to know you for *you.*"

"Is this what you wanted to get to know?" he says, slamming into me so hard it bruises me inside.

"Yes," I whimper. He sees me as a manipulative bitch and all I can do is moan with pleasure. I am being used by him and I love it.

"So tight!" he cries. "This. Tight. Velvet. Glove. Clenching. My. Hard. Cock….Your tight little pussy doesn't want to let me go. Don't tell me you don't want this." He's pounding hard, really cramming me full with his size, pounding into me with no mercy.

"I don't want it," I gasp. "Please release me, you're too big for me, it hurts." But my body is telling a different story - I'm driving my hips forward, meeting him with every thrust and I'm crying out with gratification. "I love you...fucking me," I pant. "I love you.... inside me."

"You love me Pearl? Is that what you're trying to say?"

I don't reply but moan even more. I tighten my fingers, like talons around his ass, and pull him closer. I can feel him thicken and harden even more, filling me up with his expansion and then burst inside me. He growls, literally - his release is like an animal in the wild. He's still fully dressed, jacket unfastened, only the opening in his pants from where his huge erection meets me, parting my panties to one side, his thick cock forcing my pussy lips wide open like the wake of a vast barge on a river.

I'm dreading the minutes ahead. He's got what he wanted and now he'll pull out and leave. Like a punishment. To teach me a lesson. This will be the last time I'll see him. I should have told him to go. Kept my dignity. I should have resisted but I dissolved, as I always do with him, like melting vanilla ice-cream.

All his. Wanton and lusty, letting sex rule my brain. Sensibility, not sense. Why does he have this hold over me?

He does pull out, but to my surprise, he isn't done yet. He's still stiff as if he hadn't had an orgasm at all. He spins me around, his hands forceful on my hips and shoves my ass against the corner of the kitchen table. He pushes me down, bends me over till my crotch is pinned against the corner.

"I'm not finished with you yet," he snarls, his body pressed flush behind me, holding me sandwiched between his crotch and the table. I can't move. I can hear no smile in his voice. No charm. He's pissed as hell.

I didn't climax, so I'm feeling hot and ready for another round even though I'm sore.

From my peripheral vision, I see him knot up the sperm-filled condom and put on another. Fast. I don't even need to suck or fondle him, he's ready all right, his huge member proud as the Washington Monument. I can feel it against my buttocks. He grabs a cushion from one of the kitchen chairs and wedges it between my groin and the table corner.

"Fuck the table," he commands.

I feel uneasy. Self-conscious. This is what he asked me to do with the arm of the sofa when we had phone sex. Furniture has a whole new meaning now.

He rips down my moist red panties with one hand and grabs my butt - I feel the soft hardness of his erection pressed up against my behind. I start gyrating in anticipation. I'm wet and I want him inside me.

"Good girl. Push harder against that cushion. That's right, just like that. Seeing that peachy ass moving, and pressing that hot little pussy against furniture gets my cock so fucking hard."

I'm moving my ass back and forth and sense the glorious head of his erection ease itself inside my rumbling V-8. He's taunting me with just the tip. I'm grinding back and forth, his tip teasing my opening and the cushion rubbing on my clit, which makes me wet and hot. Really hot. My nipples are erect. My skin is tingling all over.

"Gotta love this pussy," he murmurs in a rumbling voice. "It's warm and welcoming. So sweet and glistening."

I feel demeaned. He keeps using the word, *Pussy*. But something about feeling like a whore turns me on. I keep moving. I can feel my juices oozing, tempting the head of his thick shaft.

I'm bent over almost double, my ass high in the air, as I press hard against the table corner, the cushion acting as a soft buffer. He's rimming the wet slits of my opening from behind, controlling his penis with his hand. Round and round – all my nerve-endings are alert and begging. Begging for him to thrust it all the way in. Every now and then he unexpectedly changes the rhythm and does plunge deep inside, pulls back, and then continues with the tease. I'm moaning, "Please Alexandre, *please*."

My forearms are flat on the table, my body in an L shape, my panties around my ankles, my nipples like bullets. I can feel his suit pants rubbing against my thighs, his big balls are slapping slowly against my pulsating opening – it feels so sensual. Three places are being stimulated at once, all zoned like targets in between my legs. There is a whole empire going on there. Aah! I press backwards with each thrust to meet him - each and every time he eases into me and then nearly all the way out. Then he starts pumping hard, really fucking me, and I can feel an expansion of sensation building up, blood is rushing up inside me – one more thrust, any more friction on my clit against the pillow - one more thrust inside me and I know it's coming, it's coming….ah…AH!

My body is a convulsing, quivering nerve-mass. He's pumping rhythmically, but slower now, as I'm climaxing around him - I can feel his penis thickening even more. I'm still enjoying the intensity of my orgasm when he cries out my name and I feel a throbbing against my insides. He's coming too, simultaneously - he's emptying himself into my depths, expanding against my inner walls. My muscles contract and open, contract and open, clenching tightly around him. *I'm still coming – it hasn't finished - wow this is great. So intense.* I'm crying out.

"What am I going to do, baby?" His voice is almost a whisper. "What can I do, I can't keep away from you. I have to fuck you. I just have to." He sounds anguished, almost tormented.

I feel mini after-waves undulating inside me, less like a tsunami now but the sensation of fluttering butterflies. I'm groaning softly. He's kissing my back, the nape of my neck and cupping my buttocks with his strong hands like he owns my ass. I collapse on the table, my chest flat down, my legs still splayed wide open on either side of the table corner, and I release a sigh. I want to tell him I'm crazy about him but I bite my tongue.

Cool calm and collected.

That's me.

12

"Pack your suitcase." He's doing up his pants.

"What?"

"It just occurred to me now. I'm taking you away for a long weekend."

"Well, I don't think I can go just like–" I click my fingers–"*that.*"

"Yes, you can. Don't argue, just get some stuff together."

I'm standing there, naked, in nothing but high heels. Who does he think he is? He barges through my back door unannounced, fucks me like I'm a whore, and is now demanding I go away for the weekend with him? Then my faux irritation relents. *Isn't this exactly what you fantasized about, Pearl?*

He looks at his watch. "We don't have time for procrastination. Hurry up, get your essentials and a change of clothes together. A friend of mine will be taking off soon – if we hurry we can get there in time, we can't miss the slot."

The slot? In a daze, I wander into my bedroom, find a suitcase at the back of my closet and start to throw a few things in. He follows me, watching to make sure I'm doing as I'm told - meanwhile speaking on his cell. He's talking to someone in French so I don't understand a word except 'jet' and 'passport'. Then he orders a cab.

"Passport?"

"It's in my handbag," I say.

"That giant ogre of a thing?"

"Yes."

"We'll have to do something about that." His eyes narrow, then he runs them up and down my body like he wants to fuck me once more. *Not again! How potent can his libido be?*

He claps his hands together. "Okay, done. Let's go."

"Wait, my toothbrush and stuff."

"We don't have time – I can buy you anything you need."

"That's a cute offer, but I usually buy my own things, thanks."

"Yes, of course you do. Hurry up," he orders, slapping my nude backside.

I scramble into the bathroom and run some water over a washcloth and wipe in between my legs, then race back into the bedroom and grab the first dress I see from my closet and toss it over my head. It's an old 1950's flowery thing with a dirndl skirt, cinched at the waist, full-skirted with a tight bodice and low neck. It's the last thing I want to wear but Alexandre is tapping his polished shoe on the floor with impatience.

"Perfect. You look like a little girl." He drags me from the room by my wrist and grabs my suitcase.

"Wait! I haven't put any underwear on."

"No time."

"Where are we going?"

For the first time today he smiles. "Surprise."

It was a race to get here, but now we are ensconced in the swanky private plane, luxuriating on beige leather seats, while each of us is being offered an *apéritif* by the hostess cum flight attendant.

His 'friend' turns out to be some high-ranking, government official, next in line, it seems, to the French president himself. The man is on his way back from a secret, unofficial meeting - in other words, he is using the jet for his own personal use.

He and Alexandre spoke to one another in their native tongue and it was translated to me that the politician didn't want to seem rude but he had a ton of work to do before we landed, so did we mind if he kept to himself during the flight? Thank goodness. My pidgin French would have been an embarrassment, coupled with the fact that, while we were walking up the ramp to embark, a breeze of air blew the skirt of my dress up above my thighs, and I was sure this high-ranking government man saw my bare, private parts. Alexandre laughed – the man he decided, was too ugly to pose a threat. "I don't know," I teased, "I could be the next Carla Bruni."

"Socialism in action for you!" Alexandre says now with a wry grin. "Our government is probably paying for his mistress somewhere, maybe a private apartment here or in Paris – don't you just love the double standards?"

"And what about us? Is this flight a freebie, courtesy of the poor French tax payers?" I ask.

"Let's just say the French government owes me a couple of big favors. I'm sorry to say, I have no control, whatsoever, with how they manage their budget. We're coming along for the ride, Pearl, that's all."

"We're taking advantage of a dishonest situation. That could be construed as immoral."

"I'm an opportunist, Pearl." His smile is bad-boy. "Just like you."

"I…" I stammer.

"You knew what you wanted and you came after it."

"What do you mean?"

"The way you sucked your iced cappuccino through that straw when we first met at the coffee shop. Flicking your tongue around your lips."

"It was *you! You* were doing that – licking your lips, staring into me with those startling eyes of yours, getting me all hot and bothered."

"I wanted to fuck you there and then."

"Well, why didn't you?" I demand. "What took you so long?"

"Because I was hoping you'd be - how can I say this?"

"Begging for it."

He laughs. "You said it, not me."

I stare out the window as we take off. I love that dip in my stomach the plane makes – it reminds me how I have felt these past few weeks. Alive. On the edge. I watch the twinkling city of New York gradually fade below - the lights of matchbox cars turn to tiny dots. Alexandre has one hand on my bare thigh and the other tapping on his iPad, writing notes.

"Sorry, just doing a list," he explains, "of things I need to get done."

"You're a list writer then?"

"That way, the problems are no longer swirling about in my head, but committed to paper, or these days, my iPad. That way they have less power over me, I don't have to think about them anymore – at least not until I look at my list and systematically knock each thing off when the time is right. It ensures a good night's sleep." He shoots me a sly glance. "One of my secrets of success."

"Like Madonna."

He knots his brow. "Madonna?"

"She also writes lists of things to get done."

"How do you know that?"

"Because my brother is obsessed by her. He also informed me that Beyoncé wears four pairs of pantyhose on stage to keep it all in place."

"She must get very hot."

"To use your expression - tricks of the trade. Secrets of success."

"And what's your secret of success?"

I raise my eyebrows. "Ah, that would be telling."

Alexandre nods over to the direction of his highfaluting friend. "So much for him getting important work done – he's already fast asleep. Look, he's snoring."

We are at one end of – I would like to say - 'room' - it's so spacious – and this man, wearing old-style spectacles, is at the other. He looks like a schoolteacher, not a politician. If I knew anything about French politics I suppose I'd be impressed but I do not have a clue who he is.

"Are you a member of the Mile High Club?" Alexandre suddenly asks.

I roll my eyes. "That is such a cliché."

Secretly, though, I have always wondered what it would be like to make love thousands of feet in the air. Probably uncomfortable – don't people always do it in the bathroom?

"In all seriousness, Pearl, are you a member of the Mile High Club?"

"No."

"Me neither. Should we join?"

"The membership comes at a price."

"I can afford it."

I give him a lopsided smile. "Maybe you can, but me? I'm not so sure."

"What kind of price are we talking about?"

"The price of discomfort."

He laughs. "Oh, you assume we'd have to do it in the toilet?"

"Well, yes, isn't that par for the course?"

"No, it certainly is not. There's no way I'm scrunching myself up double in some toilet," he exclaims with a look of mock outrage, smoothing his tailored suit pants with his hands.

"Well, where then?"

"Right here, baby. Right here, on these luxuriously comfortable seats. They've been very thoughtful – even made them of leather for us – easy to wipe down," and he mumbles in my ear, "because I know how wet you get." He slips his hand higher up my thigh.

"Shush, stop that dirty talk! The politician will wake up. Or the flight attendant will see us."

"No, he's out for the count – I doubt very much he'll stir for several hours. And the flight attendant – well I'm sure she'll make herself invisible. The staff isn't meant to hang about with the VIPs in private jets - unless they're needed."

"Are we Very Important People?"

He laughs. "Hell, yes."

"You're just kidding," I say, "about doing it in public."

"Don't be so sure. Haven't you ever had sex in public before?"

"No, I certainly have not. You?"

He temples his fingers and brings them up to his face as if in great thought. "Let's see. On a beach in the Bahamas once, on a yacht, in a swimming pool, on a ski slope just off *piste*, in the Bois de Vincennes, in a–"

"Okay, I think I've heard enough. I get the picture." I'm in a jealous sulk for a second, furious at the ex-girlfriend(s) who have dared to be so brave with him in all those places, but – then, I ask, "By the way, where's the Bois de Vincennes?"

"It's a huge park in Paris on the eastern side. The lungs of the city."

I say nothing. Back to my silent, jealous ravings.

"You're beautiful, Pearl, especially when you're green-eyed."

An unwanted smile steals itself across my face. *How did he know?* I pummel him, my mock angry fists coming up against his hard abs.

"I've never done it on a plane though," he tells me. "Promise."

"No. Forget it, Alexandre. I won't be part of one of your *lists.* Crossed off as something '*done.*' " I stick my tongue out at him like a seven year-old.

He's laughing again. "Touched a nerve, have I?"

"You've touched several nerves, actually. Did you know that" and I lower my voice to a murmur, "—the clitoris has over eight thousand nerve endings?" I squeeze my thighs tightly together so he can't get his hand any further. "Not here, Alexandre. Stop it."

"Well you *are* a mine of information - Madonna, Beyoncé, now this. No, I had no idea, but it does make sense. I'll remember," he whispers in my ear, "all those sensitive little nerve endings when I've got my tongue up there." He's trying to force my thighs apart and, although I desire his hands all over me, I cross my legs rigid and clench my thighs super-tight like closed scissors.

He's nibbling my lobe now and a frisson runs down my spine. "Careful now, we know what happens when you do that, little girl, when you cross your legs too tight. Especially with no panties on."

It's true. The pressure is turning me on and I start squirming in my seat, even though I have my seatbelt on. He eases his hands underneath me, cupping both his palms below my buttocks, lifting me a few inches off my seat. His fingers are slipping into me from behind, then tracing up the crack of my ass and back down. His thumb is inside me now – that magic thumb which seems to know where my G-spot is. I start moaning quietly. I have my eye on the flight attendant, still strapped into her seat. She's reading a magazine and the seats between us almost block her view. Almost.

"Haven't you had enough of me for one day?" I ask in a whisper, conscious that we could be seen.

"Don't forget, you're still being punished for being an ambitious little American brat." He punctuates the 'brat' with pressure from his thumb on that elusive spot. It feels amazing.

"What kind of punishment?" I ask softly - the throb more

intense as his thumb circles inside me.

"I think a bit of slow torture, don't you? I think you need to be taught a real lesson."

"What kind of lesson?" I breathe.

"I'm sure I can think of something."

"Oh yeah? Like some more whipping me with your tongue? Or beating me again with the feather?" The idea of it makes me shudder with anticipation.

"No. Not that."

I can feel my breath quicken. "What?"

"You'll see."

My legs are still crossed tight. The full skirt of my pink flowery dress covers his hand, but the plane has leveled out now… oh no! The flight attendant is un-strapping herself from her seat and is making her way in this direction.

I wriggle in my seat, "Alexandre take your hand *away*," I hiss at him, but he's laughing and he won't move it. His thumb is pressing harder on that sweet spot now. Ah…panic - she's meandering towards us – smiling at us. This is the most embarrassing thing that has ever happened to me. Oh my God! I cross my legs tighter, my thighs acting as clamps to try and force his hand away out from in between my legs. She's upon us now. I can feel it building up. At the last second he takes his hand from out beneath me but it's too late because seconds before he releases it, he pushes hard with his thumb and I feel a volt surge through me and explode in a massive spasm…the fear of being caught, the excitement, the shame, all merge into one thundering orgasm, pounding like an adrenaline-rushed heartbeat shooting right up my V-8. My legs are still crossed. I keep the pressure up and squeeze my muscles together even tighter and a second rush is upon me. Boy oh boy, this is gloriously intense. But very embarrassing.

"Can I get anything for you both?" she asks sweetly.

My body is shuddering with delicious contractions. Every nerve is concentrated between my legs as if the rest of me was a rag doll. I'm coming in both places: Alexandre's thumb's final press on my G-spot, coupled with the clench of my thigh muscles putting pressure on my clit, has sent me over the edge.

Alexandre is laughing. My eyes are half closed, my mouth hanging open, my breath caught in what seems like a seizure. My stomach muscles are juddering. I'm shaking all over.

"Are you okay, *madame*?" she asks in a French accent with a look of great consternation. She is bending over me frowning - her eyes worried.

"She gets a little queasy," Alexandre replies, and then bursts out laughing again.

"Is she going to be sick?"

"No, she'll recover," he utters with an ironic smirk. "If you could bring us some champagne that would be great."

The hostess looks shocked. She must be thinking he's crazy to ask for champagne when I seem as if I'm about to barf, or worse, have a heart attack. "Are you sure?" she double-checks.

"Quite sure – champagne is good for her, eases up the muscles a bit. Don't worry, I know what her body needs."

Oh yes, I think, still shuddering. *You know my body better than I do.*

The flight attendant moves off. Thank God. I am aware that he could have said all this to her in French but he obviously wanted me to experience full humiliation. His punishment.

"Are you having fun, Pearl?" He chuckles again.

I can't speak – the mini aftershocks of that 9.1 earthquake on the Richter scale are still giving me ripples of intense pleasure – tremors like bells inside my body have every part of me shimmering and quivering.

"Such a disrespectful little hussy, aren't you? Have you no decorum at all?" He breaks into another grin.

I finally uncross my legs. "You bastard." Then a smile forces its way onto my lips.

"Well I did say we were '*coming* along for the ride.' But to be honest, I wasn't expecting it to happen so soon."

"*Coming* along for the ride. Really, Alexandre," and then I joke, "don't rub it in."

We both laugh. "Don't think you're off the hook yet, Ms. Robinson, we still have to fill in our membership form. I'd like to *come* along for the ride too, don't forget."

"Fill in – very funny. Forget it. I refuse to be a member of this silly Mile High Club. Won't do it. Just won't. You can put a giant tick against the 'Pearl - Public Humiliation' box on your goddam list and leave me alone in peace for the rest of the flight."

The chilled champagne arrives. I look up at the flight attendant from under my lashes and smile furtively, sheepishly - then keep my gaze down, mortified that she can guess what has just happened. Perhaps it's part of her job – to pretend she doesn't know what's going on.

Egged on by thirst and a sense of shame, I find myself glugging down my beverage like water, wondering what else could be on Alexandre's proverbial (or actual) list of things to 'encourage' me to do. He's clever – it all appears as if it is coming (no pun intended) from my own free will - and it is – yet-

Why do I feel I'm being controlled by him?

I curl up against his strong shoulders and the next thing I know, my body collapses into an exhausted, profound sleep.

When I wake up all the lights are dimmed and it's pitch dark outside the plane windows. I find myself - not curled up next to him anymore - but stretched out, the seat down like a bed. He must have moved me when I was asleep. I glance over and he's working on something – charts or graphs – it looks extremely mathematical.

"Hey, baby, you're finally awake," he says, winking at me. I'm glad to see the gentle Alexandre has returned.

"How long have I been sleeping?"

"About four hours."

"You still haven't told me where we're going."

"Haven't I," he says distracted, still concentrated on his task.

"No."

"Hang on - I'll be all yours in a minute - just have to finish this."

I get up, grab my handbag and go to the bathroom. Even though it's a private jet, the toilet lights are disconcertingly bright. Yuk. It shows up every wrinkle, every blemish. I have to stop myself from launching into a full facial there and then. I pee, then wash my hands and face, underarms and private parts and brush my teeth. I notice panda rings around my eyes – how did that happen? I clean them up and re-apply my mascara, brush out my hair and dot myself with my perfume, which happens to be French, a heady but fresh scent of figs that always makes me feel invigorated. I dab some under my arms and a teensy bit on my mound of Venus. I look in the mirror. That's better, I'm ready. *Ready for what?* I ask myself.

Ready for anything.

When I get back to my seat, Alexandre has Bob Marley's *Is This Love?* playing softly on his iPad. A good sign, I think. He welcomes me with a grin.

"Sexy woman," he comments, and he then unwittingly bites his lower lip. Uh, oh.

"Alexandre, we need to talk."

He looks me up and down. "I'm listening." But he's not listening - his eyes are roving all over me. I'm standing – a trick I learned about self-empowerment; when you have something important to say, take the high ground.

"We haven't had a chance to discuss what happened – the way I behaved, my reasons."

"It's in the past now," he answers, running his gaze to my cleavage.

"Well, it's not. You were so angry with me. You didn't call me for a week."

"You received your little punishment, it's over now."

"It's just - before I met you, I expected you to be some kind of geek. I'd only seen one photo of you–"

"I don't do photos or interviews, nor red carpet."

"I know - you took me by surprise. I didn't want you to think I only wanted to get to know you just because of what you did – your job. I wanted to–"

"You wanted," he clarifies, "to fuck me the second you saw me and you worried that if we were involved professionally it would spoil things. That you might blow your chance with me."

"You are so arrogant!"

"I'm French, what do you expect?" But he's laughing in a self-depreciating way, so I begin to laugh, too.

"What am I going to do with you?" I say, waving my finger at him. I'm still standing.

He angles his seat into a flat bed and then grabs my legs. He's pulling me onto his knee. "You're going to ride me."

"No way, we've been through this. I won't."

"Oh yes, you will."

I look about the cabin. It's quiet and the politician is fast asleep. The flight attendant is nowhere to be seen. "No, Alexandre. And after your 'rape' earlier today in my apartment, to tell you the truth, I'm a little bit sore."

"You're right. I behaved like a thug. It was just that….all I could think about was you. All week. I was going crazy. Just picturing your ass in my mind made me hard. All I could think about was your ass, your tits, your face. Relax now, Pearl - sit on my knee for a bit and I'll tell you about where we're going."

I sit on his lap, feeling all warm with the knowledge that he was obsessing about me as much as I was about him. "I'm so excited about this trip. Paris?"

"No."

"Provence?"

"That's right, baby." He pulls out the kingfisher feather from his pants pocket and blows on it.

"I never got a chance to see this," I remark.

"Pretty, isn't it?" He brushes it lightly across my brow. "Close your eyes," he whispers.

I close them and feel the lightest touch. He strokes my nose with it, my lips. "Hold up your hair," he says in a soft voice. "And bend your neck down." I do, and he traces the feather along the nape of my neck. I purr with pleasure. "The lavender fields should be in bloom," he tells me. "There are wonderful markets everywhere with fresh produce sold directly by local farmers. Hundreds of cheeses to choose from - and olives and pastries. Pretty hats. Delicious treats to eat. Thousands of wines. Chilled rosé at lunch, pale as rainwater - *tapenade* on home-made bread."

His beautiful voice is distant as I'm in a zone all of my own, enjoying the sensation of the feather on my neck. He draws it up behind my ears and I shiver. Then around to my front. It's on my cleavage now – my body with a mind of its own doing its tingling. I wanted to say no – I did say no, but I find myself silently willing him to unzip my dress at the back. He does. I wiggle on his thighs pushing my panty-free ass into his groin and feel that familiar hardness. I start throbbing. *Groundhog Day* all over again - but in the best possible way. I want to keep doing this forever. He's kissing the back of my neck so gently, and running the feather around my breasts, circling them, grazing the feather over my nipples.

"Oh Pearl," he whispers in my ear. "Sweet, delicious Pearl – so addictive." I can feel his hands pull his erection free from his pants and he lifts my skirt so it is flesh on flesh. His hardness against the soft pad of my butt. "I love you….so close. I love you….near me."

"Are you trying to tell me you love me, Alexandre?" I smile.

He lifts my leg over so I am in a straddling position facing him. He kisses me on the mouth. There's no turning back now. I simply don't have the willpower. He's pulled the top part of my dress down from my shoulders and his tongue is flipping and rolling over one nipple. He lies back flat, pulls me down and eases me on top of him by maneuvering my hips.

"So wet, baby," he coos as I slip right onto him. "Oh yeah,

that's good. Soo good. Oh yeah. So ready. Now what I'm going to do is just lie here and you ride me as you see fit. You have the reins, okay?"

I nod. I'm loving this horse. This stud. Something about knowing we could be caught mid-act turns me on even more. He feels incredible. I straighten my legs so we are flush - flat body to flat body.

"Here," he says, popping a little cushion under his tight buns. This way I'm closer to you, you'll feel me more. Remember, go as slow or as fast as you want. You dictate the rhythm, chérie."

The cushion under him has his pubic bone pushing on my clitoris every time I come back down. I'm pulling out almost completely so that only his tip is at my entrance. My clit brushes against his taut stomach, the hard points of my nipples graze against the muscles on his pecs. I take another pillow and push it under his head so he's closer. He starts sucking my tits like they were fruits, rimming his tongue around them, nibbling them. I launch back down again so I'm all filled up, swollen and hot with his size. Then I pull up, slowly. Aah, this is bliss. I'm squirming about on him making little circles and then coming hard back down. It's making him groan and he grabs my hips so I can't move.

"I thought you said I was in charge," I scold, lightly biting his neck.

"Baby, if you do that one more time I'm going to come. Easy, you sexy rider."

I'm loving this; even more, knowing that it is just me and my movements that are turning him on so much.

"Suck my tits again," I whisper. He does.

I lie there languidly on top, his throbbing cock only an inch inside me. The pleasure from his nibbling and sucking is immense. I start moving now, just a little bit, and can feel myself building up to it. I circle some more and he's got his hands tight on my ass.

Now he's moving closer, lifting up his hips with each thrust and doing his mantra… "I…. Love…You….Fucking….Me."

His pubic bone is rising to meet my clit like a secret weapon, his whopping great shaft inside pressing my sweet places, his abs, the sweat beading on his muscular chest, his lips, his hair mussed about his face, the biceps of his lean arms…it's all too much of an irresistible cocktail of pleasure and beauty….

A thunderous bolt pushes up through me, shudders roll over my body - I can feel the hot center of us united as one - I'm coming all around him – I start to moan, kissing his lips hard, then closing my eyes in concentration as I'm still fucking him. His penis is widening now - the spasms, his and mine together, are intense as I feel him spurting inside me, more than ever before.

"I'm coming Pearl – you sweet, sexy goddess."

"Me too," I gasp. I'm moving hard now. Slamming up and down on him - almost in tears with the power of my deep orgasm which I'm still savoring.

I feel like there's liquid honey down there. I keep moving, gently now, letting the tingles and ripples fade, until I collapse on his chest. I put my finger down below and feel a sticky pool leaking out everywhere. Then suddenly it clicks. Duh, he didn't put a condom on! He's come inside me!

I am not on the pill.

"Welcome to the Mile High Club." He grins. "We're fully-fledged members now."

13

Not even my childhood memories can compete with this. I look out the wide open French doors in my bedroom, which lead onto a Juliet balcony. I see rows and rows of deep blue lavender fields buzzing with activity - bees perhaps? Beyond, are pine trees, bright, deep green, and in the shape of giant parasols. The sky is like crystal, a pale morning blue which I know will brighten up as the sun gets higher. It's already hot but there's a small breeze shimmering through the doors, enough to blow a tendril of hair off my face. The smell of lavender is rich and heady; the faint air wafting the perfume towards me. It's so divine it knocks me back and I lie on the bed, looking up at the ceiling in a daze. I didn't see any of this last night in the dark, nor on the way here, as I fell asleep for most of the journey. The politician was also coming to his summer house. We landed in Avignon and his government limo picked us up and deposited us here, at Alexandre's house, en route. I still hardly know where I am - nor where the nearest village is. I guess I'll soon find out.

Alexandre must be downstairs, or even outside. I heard quiet activity earlier, voices chatting in French. I sit up amongst the fresh linen sheets and ease myself against the plumped-up pillows, thinking, *I am in Provence at Alexandre's beautiful house!* The bed is four-poster yet with no cloth, just the tall wooden posts reaching high. The room is like something out of Interiors Magazine – eclectic, yet somehow luxurious. The walls are white-washed and with dips and crevices – I could practically climb them if I had those rock climbing shoes. There is a vast fireplace of ancient stone with an antique gold mirror hanging over it. The floors are oak, I think, with different sized and shaped floor-boards which creak as you step on them. Everything creaks here. Everything is crooked and topsy-turvy. There are paintings on the walls but the best painting of all, of course, is the view. There are massive wardrobes, the old-fashioned kind which you could walk inside and if you kept going you might end up in Narnia or some fabulous kingdom.

There is someone at the door. I sit up and fasten another button of a big white shirt I'm wearing which I found strewn across the end of the bed. The footsteps are not his, but light – a lady's footsteps.

"Bonjour?" I call out.

A slim woman enters, carrying a tray. She's wearing an apron and is petite the way only Europeans can be petite, with fragile bones like a bird. The tray swamps her and I immediately jump off the bed to help.

"Ah no, madame," she protests. "I put Break Fast on bed. You eat."

The way she says breakfast is split in two and reminds me about the origins of the word. She is smiling and gestures for me to get right back into bed. I do. She sets the tray before me, laying it carefully on the bedspread – it is replete with a variety of goodies that smell of oven baked freshness.

I breathe in. Heaven. Fresh-baked brioche and croissants, home-made jellies and jams of three or four different fruits, a mound of yellow butter, a pot of steaming coffee with hot milk in a jug. Melon dripping with honey and sprinkled with cinnamon, and some little mousse-like cakes which must be from the patisserie. All this combined with the view, the perfume of lavender blossom. Did somebody plunk me in Paradise?

She is shy and trots out of the room as soon as she is done. I begin to delve into the feast. Breakfast in bed. I can't remember the last time this happened – maybe only in some hotel when I've been on business. But the experience has never rivaled this. I spread the croissants with butter and it melts – naughty, I know. They probably don't need butter at all. You couldn't do this every day of the week. Or could you? I saw a book called, *French Women Don't Get Fat*, about dieting and food which says you can have it all, but in moderation. Is this moderation? I plunge the croissant into my mouth-watering jaws and feel the butter, the freshness of the pastry, mix with the home-made cherry jam, melting into one happy symphony on my tongue. The coffee is also delicious. French women might not get fat but this American sure as hell would - if she lived in this country!

As I'm chewing and savoring all the calories, I think of the possible consequences of what happened on the plane with Alexandre. I could get pregnant. The idea sends shivers of excitement through my body, but then my sensible, *don't be an idiot you hardly know him*, voice makes me stop chewing for a minute. When I pointed out what he'd done, he just laughed and said, "And what's so terrible about you getting pregnant? I think a baby would be a wonderful addition, don't you?" I was so stunned - I didn't know what to say except, "you're not HIV positive, are you?" He laughed again and said that no, he'd had a test only six months ago and that the last person he'd had relations with was a recently widowed woman who hadn't even done it with her husband for the two years previously, let alone anyone else. Then I told him that the chances of getting pregnant at my age were very slim and that even if I did manage, I'd probably have a miscarriage, as that is what happened to me before with my ex. He looked pensive when I said that, squinted his eyes as if he needed to find some sort of solution and then said, "no, we can't have that, a miscarriage won't do at all." Is this the Latin man-must-sow-his-seed thing, I wonder? Or does he seriously want my baby? I can't believe a man so young would consider getting tied in with a family. Certainly American men aren't keen for that at age twenty-five - most are commitment phobes.

Perhaps he doesn't want a family at all, but various replicas of himself running about the world – a woman, as my brother reminded me, in every port. Children in every port, too? He can afford child maintenance, so why ever not?

I'm so wrapped up in this train of thought and am beginning to feel furious at him when he enters the room. His charming smile soon makes all wrathful thoughts dissipate and, within seconds, I'm back to wanting his offspring again. Did I rush into the airplane toilet yesterday and frantically rinse off the sticky mess of the lovemaking aftermath inside me? No, I have to admit, I did not. Instead, I lay back on my beige leather seat with my legs up – a trick I read about when trying to conceive. I am as guilty as he is, if he is to be condemned for fantastical castle-in-the-air desires. Yet he started the ball rolling, not me.

Alexandre is standing before me now, his legs astride – a pose he often assumes. Very masculine. It's all Alain Delon again, and I'm melting all over just looking at his face and body. He's wearing loose black swim trunks and is all wet, his hair slicked back off his handsome face, his green eyes gleaming.

"Enjoying your breakfast?" he asks, kissing me and stroking my cheek.

"Dee-licious. Have you just been for a swim?"

"Yes, the pool's very inviting. Come down, I'll show you the garden."

The garden is more lavender, and paths meandering through secret entrances and archways, all divided naturally by hedges and plants. It is like a formal garden in a chateau, yet more rustic, matching this pretty stone house which he keeps referring to as a 'farmhouse' yet seems far too grand for that.

"You know why you can see the stone on my house and it isn't covered up?" he asks.

"Because it's so pretty? Why would anyone want to cover it?" I ask, my eyes distracted by white butterflies - like snowflakes everywhere.

"True, but in those days, the peasants who once owned houses like mine couldn't afford the *crepi*, the plaster rendering, so the stones remained bare. Each and every stone was collected by hand from the fields. Can you imagine the labor? They built their own houses in the past, maybe getting their friends and neighbors to help. Little by little, carrying sacks on their backs, or with mules and horses if they could afford them."

"And now it's some of the most expensive real estate in the world," I comment.

"I know. Sad in a way. A shame the billionaires have moved in and all the summer vacationers have pushed up the prices even more."

The billionaires…he's one of them, I think to myself. "I thought the English were the guilty ones. I read that book, *A Year in Provence*. Didn't that start it all?" I ask him.

"Well, it didn't help. But the British did us a favor, in a way. They went about restoring houses back to their original condition, ruins that were falling apart - things we French didn't even want at the time. Okay, they put in tennis courts sometimes, or pools, but they showed us how important our *patrimoine* was. They genuinely loved the land and all the quirkiness of the damp, crooked houses. But now, some people only want to live here to bolster up their status symbol. Still, I have an interesting bunch of friends around - some film directors, artists and such. It gets quite busy in summer."

"So who looks after everything when you're not here?"

"As you can see, even when I *am* here, I have people. You met Madame Menager this morning. She and her husband run the place, and a couple of others, too, who come and go. It may look quite rustic but a lot of care goes into this garden and house."

"Yes, I can see," I reply, looking around. The pool is now in view, the water rippling with a myriad of colors reflecting the blue of the lavender and the sky. It is bordered with real stone and has grass surrounding it, and trees shading one end. No Hollywood blue here. It's discreet. "I love the color of the water," I say.

"I had it rendered with a gun-metal gray – keeps the temperature up and gives off that natural, been-here-forever sort of impression. Come for a swim, the water's warm."

Like a schoolgirl desperate to impress her older brother and his friends, I do a back dive into the deep end, careful to keep my legs straight and my toes as pointed as a ballerina. I come up for air and then start the crawl – fingers out in a torpedo point, legs smacking the water with a fiery, rhythmical kick, and breathing only to one side. I clear a few lengths but realize my breakfast has hardly settled – my showing off has got the better of me. When I spring up with a splash, his eyes are fixed on me. Thank God. What if I'd done that show for nothing?

"Very impressive," he claps. "I can tell what country *you* come from. You really are a Star-Spangled girl, aren't you?"

I feel self-conscious. *Is that an insult or a compliment?*

"Most Europeans don't know how to swim like that," he explains.

"I swim a lot."

"I bet you were competitive at sports and games," he jibes.

I was. Ridiculously so. I always wanted to ace everything.

"What do you mean by that?" I ask. "Are you taunting me for being an American?"

"Being number one is important to you lot, isn't it? Winning?"

"What's wrong with winning?"

"It's partaking in the game that counts," he tut-tuts. "Not just the result."

"You can talk, Mr. Winner Takes All," I tease.

"Haven't taken all yet. Not quite. Still working on it." He narrows his eyes.

"What more can you ask for?"

"You. I want you."

You've got me, buddy, I want to scream out. But I don't. Let him think I'm a challenge. Let him believe I'm special. I'll play along with that.

Cool, calm and collected. That's me.

We spend the day lolling about the house and garden and meandering through the lavender fields. Madame Menager prepares a delicious lunch outside, under a canopy of vines, which shades us from the hot sun. The crickets are chirping a high song, and there is a gentle crooning from a pair of doves in a pine tree. We drink a pale, pale pink rosé wine, so chilled, so refreshing, that I find myself flopping onto one of the living room sofas, unable to do anything.

Oh, this is the life.

The living room has a terracotta floor as old as the hills, and like hills, it undulates and buckles with a life of its own. The fireplace is at least eight feet wide and inside is a vast wrought iron fire-back of a dragon – iron to reflect the heat of the fire, I suspect. The room is lined with bookshelves and, amidst plays by Voltaire, Jean-Paul Sartre, Camus, I notice a lot of English titles of novels - smart sets printed by a publisher called The Folio Society. I inspect some. Several have stunning, color plate illustrations. He has The Wind in the Willows! I open it up and read an inscription: *Darling Alexandre, this was my childhood favourite, hope you enjoy. All my love, Laura.* Favorite spelled the British way. My heart starts pounding with an unfathomable jealousy. How dare she know about *The Wind in the Willows*? Who is this Laura? Laura, who must have been lining his shelves with classics in the English language! There is *Doctor Zhivago, The Greek Myths I and II, The Grapes of Wrath, Vanity Fair, Madame Bovary* - not in French but *Madame Bovary* in English!

Alexandre comes into the room. "Ah, there you are, I thought you'd done a runner."

"Where did you learn expressions like that?" I demand in a ridiculous way, my eyes turning from blue to emerald green.

He laughs. "Ah, I see, you've been having a look at my English books."

"Yes, I have. Who's Laura?"

"A friend."

"A friend?"

"She's a friend now. She was my girlfriend. From London. You'd like her."

I'd hate her, I think to myself, but say, "Oh yes? She has good taste in books. She must have been a great reader."

"Somewhat."

"Somewhat? There are piles of them here. Did she *live* here?"

"She comes in the summertime."

'She comes,' not 'she came,' Oh my God – he's still seeing her!

He says casually, "Why d'you think my English is so colloquial? It was Laura who taught me. She was ruthless - she'd correct all my mistakes."

"How long did you date her for?" I ask nonchalantly, trying not to show my envy.

"We didn't date, we lived together."

"Oh." *It gets worse!*

"We were engaged."

I feel as if I've been stabbed. "What happened?"

"She left me for someone else."

Was she nuts? "She dumped you?" I ask with disbelief.

"I don't like the sound of that word, but yes, I suppose she did 'dump' me."

"Are you still in love with her?"

"No, but I still care for her. A great deal."

I need to stop this conversation now. I feel whoozy. *Stay cool, calm and collected, Pearl. Don't be a bunny boiler.*

"That's nice that you're still friends," I say, and then smile sweetly at him.

"Hey, tonight there's a party and I said we'd go."

"Where?"

"A few kilometers away. At Ridley's house."

"Ridley?"

"He's a film director. You'll like him."

"I have a feeling I know exactly who you're talking about."

"All sorts will be there, it should be fun," he says with enthusiasm.

"Okay, great. Actually no - not great."

"Why?"

"Because I have nothing to wear. I was in such a rush I threw the worst outfits into my suitcase."

"Pearl, you could wear a potato sack and you'd look amazing."

"Thanks for the vote of confidence but I don't see myself in such a positive light."

"Alright then, let's go shopping."

"It's okay, Alexandre, I'll make something work." I say this because I don't want him buying me things. Ridiculous, but I'm not used to shopping with a man. "The truth is," I add, "it's so beautiful here, I'm loath to go anywhere."

"That's how I always feel when I'm here; it's hard to get away. But let's go for a drive and you can see some of the surrounding countryside. The party doesn't start till about eight – we have a few hours."

Alexandre's garage is a low stone building covered in pink, climbing roses. Perhaps they are the roses he uses for his homemade rose jelly. The garage blends in beautifully with his house. Madame and Monsieur live in a small guest house next door, and behind is a walled-in garden bursting with rows of organically-grown vegetables, dominated by tomatoes which are a dazzling sunny red – and other produce like cucumbers, onions and even strawberries. The garage houses a host of shiny vehicles, even a Deux Chevaux, the quintessential French car. Batman's car is there, too, in its full glory, the Murciélago, proud and intimidating but Alexandre opts for a royal blue, vintage Porsche.

"She's a 1964 356SC Coupé with an electric sunroof. I had to have her the moment I laid eyes on her," and he looks at me, his gaze roving from my toes up to my face where he fixes his stare. I catch my breath. I'm just wearing shorts, a thin cotton top, and flip-flops – nothing special, and am amazed how desirable Alexandre makes me feel. Each time he looks at me like that, his green eyes piercing me, my solar-plexus leaps and circles around itself. I feel like a teenager inside.

"She's adorable," I say, stroking her smooth lines. "So cute. I've always dreamed about having a car like this."

"Would you like to drive her, see how she feels beneath

you?"

"You make it all sound so sensual, Alexandre, so naughty."

"She is naughty. She likes to be driven fast, likes to grip the road around corners. This baby likes to have fun."

"Speaking of babies," I say guardedly. "What you did on the plane? It's a slim chance but....I could get pregnant - a slim chance, as I say, but still possible. This isn't something you can treat cavalierly like it's all a game."

He takes my hand and holds it in his. "Pearl, you make me happy. I'm crazy for you - can't you see that? I want to be with you, and stay with you. I'm a monogamous type. Once I find someone special I don't play the field. Look," he emphasizes, locking his eyes with mine, "if you were twenty-something – which you wouldn't be because I'm not into young ingénues – but if you were, then you'd be on the pill or something. But we don't have time."

"You mean my biological clock?"

"I hate that expression - it sounds like some sort of time bomb, but yes. It's unfair for women and God was being pretty sexist when he designed that one, but there it is. Let's just see what happens, shall we?"

"You're acting as if I have no say in the matter. You're just assuming I want children. You never asked me. I have a demanding career - maybe I don't even want a family."

He looks shocked. "You're right - I never even brought the subject up with you. I did just assume—"

"But your instincts were spot on. I do want a baby. It's just....I'd given up. I didn't imagine I'd meet anyone special enough. You're the only person I've slept with since my divorce."

"I know. I was lucky to catch you before somebody else

snapped you up."

I take a big intake of breath and ask him the question that has been on the tip of my tongue all day. "Why did you split with Laura? Did you want to have her baby, too?"

"Laura…how can I explain Laura….I'll show you some photos of her when we get home and some letters she wrote me. When you see the pictures, you'll understand why she left me."

"Was she a supermodel, or something?"

"She was beautiful both inside and out. And yes, she did do some modeling."

I feel a painful stab at my heart. Obviously, I am the rebound and this Laura was some sort of goddess who I'll never match up to. I need to be more upbeat, not let jealousy consume me. He says he wants me and wants my baby – what more could I ask for? Marriage? I don't know if I believe in marriage, anyway. One divorce was enough - I couldn't risk that again. I need to change the conversation. I blurt out in a jolly voice:

"I always think cars have faces, don't you? This car has excited round eyes and the elongated Porsche badge looks like a funny nose. The way the hood is made looks like she's smiling."

He opens the driver door for me. "Slip inside. Doesn't she smell good?"

I ease myself behind the steering wheel onto the old black seats and breathe in the odor of vintage car. "She smells divine."

"Start her up."

Nervously, I do, and back the car out of the garage onto the driveway. It is a stick-shift and although I learned driving one, living in New York City doesn't give me the chance to practice very often, and I have certainly never been at the wheel of a car like this before. It is low, as he said, I can feel the ground beneath me – the idea of taking on something with so much personality and chutzpah is exciting. He jumps into the passenger seat – he's wearing a grin, thrilled, no doubt, that I'm taking an interest in his passion for cars.

We meander along country lanes, flanked by stunning views on either side of us. *What a Wonderful World* by Louis Armstrong is playing loudly and I think, yes, Alexandre couldn't have picked a better song – it really is a wonderful world. I mull over our baby conversation. It has been my secret fantasy, kept close to my heart; something I never share with anyone. Pearl, the career woman - the one who supports herself both financially, and in every other way. Pearl, who relies on nobody – that's what I have told myself for the past two years. There is no such thing as a knight in shining armor, I convinced myself – nobody is going to come along and wave a magic wand.

Then I met Alexandre. Is he waving a magic wand? Or is all this romance he is offering going to turn horribly pear-shaped?

I have been self-reliant and had even considered adoption but realized how tough it would be being a single parent and raising a child in New York City alone. Does Alexandre really *mean* what he says about starting a family? Or is he just so young he hasn't thought it through properly?

My thoughts now turn to the moving view – more of his magic, bringing me to this fairytale land. As well as lavender, there are vineyards and stretches of golden wheat everywhere. Now and then, there is a tiny stone building plunked right in the middle of a field – so picturesque, it looks like a postcard.

"Don't be afraid, Pearl, to really give it to her. She likes to be pushed harder. You don't need to change gears so soon – keep her in third for longer. I know what she needs."

"You know a lot about what females need, don't you?" I tease. "You like to keep me in third for longer, don't you? And sometimes, when I'm begging you for fourth, or even fifth, you put me back into second. Sometimes even first."

He laughs joyously, his right arm relaxed against the sill, the wind whipping his hair from the wide open windows. "I love that analogy. Yes, women are like cars – they need to be controlled."

"You're so sexist!"

"They like to have their limits pushed - but not too much - and then be brought back on track. They like to be managed but at the same time experience freedom."

"You are quite something, Alexandre Chevalier. Quite a secret macho control freak, aren't you?"

He laughs. "Not so secret."

"And there I was, mistaking you for this humble gentleman!" I rev up and speed along a straighter road, gaining more confidence. I'm in my element driving this car!

"There, you see how happy she is? She likes to show you what she's capable of," he shouts above the vroom, vroom of the engine.

"She likes me?"

"She loves you, Pearl."

"Does that make her gay?" I joke, brushing my hand on his leg as I change gear.

"I think she's bi," he says, winking at me. "And if your sexual fantasies during phone sex are anything to go by, you'll get along together just fine."

"Shush, that's a secret."

I think about what Alexandre said earlier, "Pearl, you make me happy, I'm crazy for you…" and I hum Madonna's *Crazy For*

You to myself. Does he really mean those words?

Before long, we stop at his nearest village, Ménerbes, which is perched on top of a hill.

"You know, Ménerbes," Alexandre begins in a serious tour guide voice, "has been inhabited since prehistoric times. Archaeological excavations have uncovered the remains of villas and an ancient cemetery dating back to Roman times. These villages were built on hilltops to protect them from invasion," he informs me, "particularly during the religious wars. Picasso had a house here and Peter Mayle who wrote, *A Year in Provence*."

"So this is where he lived," I murmur.

We enter through a large arch into the small central square, and potter about the tiny village which, from certain points, offers striking views of lush, rolling hills below, dotted with farmhouses and hamlets making a patchwork of colors like a quilt.

"This place is famous for its truffle market," Alexandre tells me. "They use dogs mostly, these days, for digging truffles, the pigs got a little greedy. Truffles are so expensive, they can't afford to lose even one."

Our next stop is Gordes, marked with a sign as one of the most beautiful villages in France, *Les Plus Beaux Villages de France.* It, like Ménerbes, is perched on a hill with breathtaking views below. We park the car and wind our way through the narrow cobbled streets where no vehicles are allowed, and look up at tall houses of honey-colored stone, many of them built right into the rock itself. Natural and man-made beauty rolled into one supreme medieval mélange. There is a castle in the middle of the village where we wander about watching tourists pass by, oohing and aahing at the history of the place. We sit in a café and relax our legs. I order an iced tea and Alexandre a Pastis, an aniseed drink that, when mixed with water and ice, turns milky - a drink favored by the people of Provence, he says.

On the way back, he drives. Way faster than I did, I may add. Even though it's past seven, the sun is creating a magical, golden dusk light and there's a cooler breeze now.

"So tell me, Pearl Robinson, did you grow up in New York City?"

"I still haven't grown up," I quip.

He laughs. "Alright, were you 'raised' in New York?"

"Yes, in Brooklyn. We moved to Manhattan when I was twelve because I got a scholarship to a private school on the Upper East Side."

"You must have been a good student."

"I worked hard. I was keen to prove myself, get top grades. I had to show them I earned the scholarship. I didn't want to let anybody down. What about you? Did you do well at school?"

"No, I was a disaster. I experimented with drugs, you know, smoked weed, dropped some acid. I was a bad boy. A high school dropout. But I did have a passion and that was IT - all self-taught, and bit by bit I cleaned up my act. I got into an excellent school in Paris for graphics and communication but only stayed a few weeks – the fees were too high. My sister tried to help, but when I realized the kind of work she was doing, there was no way I could accept, so I left to get a job."

"Why, what was she doing?"

"Just something that wasn't good for her soul."

"What?"

"Never mind."

He's whetted my curiosity, that's for sure. What could Sophie have been working at that was so bad for her soul?

When we get back, I busy myself with getting ready for the party. I take a shower and put on a pair of high, platform sandals and a short, slinky dress that's red. Too much? Maybe. I look in the mirror and dissect myself. My hair is looking pretty good and I caught quite a tan today, just walking around and being in the pool. Those crow's feet though, they're a drag. I put on another layer of mascara to open my eyes up wider and I see the reflection of Alexandre standing behind me. He's back to his casual self, in a black T-shirt and jeans. His chest muscles are prominent, even though the T-shirt is quite loose. His hair is wet from the shower. His eyes rove over my body and I immediately feel self-conscious.

"Too much?" I ask. "The red?"

"No, not too much. Perfect. Sexy. You look stunning."

"Is it too skimpy, though? Too femme fatale?"

"Well if it is, I love it. You've got the body so flaunt it."

He comes behind me and cups my buttocks with his palms. "Great ass."

"It's the swimming, I guess."

He lets his hands wander up the small of my back and around to my stomach - then strokes the curves of my bare breasts. "Great tits, too."

For the first time ever, I push his hands away. I should feel complimented but a clutch of anxiety takes hold as I imagine his ex, Laura, to be so much more than me. She broke up with him –

she must be something else. "You said you'd show me photos of Laura," I say, turning to face him.

"What, now?"

"Why not?"

"We should really be leaving."

"Just a quick glance. I'm curious about her."

"She's a special woman."

"Yes, so you keep saying." *What is this? Is he trying to keep me on my toes by making me jealous?*

We go downstairs to the living room where the giant fireplace and all the English books are. Madame Menager has left a tray on the table with a bottle of chilled champagne and some tasty-looking canapés. He pours me a glass. I sip the refreshing drink, savoring the bubbly taste, and I nestle onto the sofa, while Alexandre gets out a photo album.

"This is typical Laura," he tells me. "I don't have any printed photos myself – everything is on my computer and iPad but she used to make albums – very English that." He's holding a large, blue leather-bound book in his hands. My heart is beating with trepidation – why do I want to torture myself?

He puts the book on my lap and sits next to me. I start carefully turning the stiff pages. There, before me, is a young woman who can't be more than thirty, smiling into the camera, jumping in the air. She is tall, blonde, with a body like a swimwear model and a smile that takes up her whole face. She is gorgeous. On the page next to it is Alexandre looking really young, thinner and more boyish. I turn the page. Another set of pictures – them sailing at sea, soaked through – it looks like it's a wet day with clouds in the sky. They are both laughing their heads off.

"That was in Cornwall, the south of England. We called ourselves the Salty Sea Dogs. It was always raining, or so it seemed. We sailed a lot, Laura was practically Olympic level."

Now I understand. She was an all-rounder. Stunningly beautiful, smart (all those books), and sporty. She looks older than he does, perhaps she went off with someone more age appropriate. I turn more pages. A birthday party, she blowing out candles, her lips luscious, her eyes as big as saucers - she makes me look like Plain Jane.

"She's beautiful," is all I can muster.

More of Laura and him. Now they are in India riding elephants painted with flowers on their wrinkly skin. There are temples in the background. I feel envious – the love between them is so evident. I turn more pages and a jolt of shock arrests me.

"Who's that?" I ask, pointing at a blonde woman in a wheelchair. It looks like Laura. She must have broken her leg or something.

"It's Laura," he confirms, covering his face with his palms. He looks as if tears could well in his eyes.

I turn more pages. She's still in the wheelchair here. "What happened?"

"We lived in a basement flat in London. One night we came home late and the next door neighbor's child had left one of his toys on the steps. Laura tripped and fell. I couldn't catch her in time. She tumbled down the concrete steps and landed really badly. It was one of those freak accidents with a terrible consequence."

"Oh no. Was she really hurt?"

"Paralyzed from the waist down. Luckily, no damage to her head."

"Oh my God." I have tears in my eyes as he tells me this. "But she was a sportswoman and so active."

"I know. Life's unfair, isn't it?"

"And now?"

"She's a lot better now. She's walking with a cane. Limping, but the doctors had told her, originally, that she would probably be paralyzed for the rest of her life, so what she's achieved is a miracle. Her husband has been incredible, too. He's been by her side every step of the way."

"Husband?"

"The man she left me for. I was broken-hearted. He'd been her childhood boyfriend and had always been in love with her. I felt, at the time, as if she was dismissing me as useless, as if I wouldn't know how to care for her, or didn't care enough. But I would never have deserted her. Never. She knew what she wanted, though, and it was him. James. She was right, in hindsight. He's been fantastic. I couldn't have been there for her the way he has been."

"Had you started your business by that point?"

"Just. Of course, when she left me, I threw myself headlong into work to keep my mind off her. I moved back to Paris and did nothing else but get HookedUp off the ground. I didn't see daylight for weeks, holed up in my dark basement office, coding and working out formulas and ways to make it successful. Meanwhile, my sister was having meetings and getting backers."

"You said your stepfather helped you."

"He lent us fifteen thousand Euros and some of his friends pitched in, too. They've made their money back several thousand percent, I'm glad to say. They took a risk."

"And you and Laura are still friends?"

"Of course. She and James are coming here in a couple of weeks. I won't be here, though. I lend them the house every summer. We'd better get a move on, Pearl, or we'll be late."

I now see Alexandre in a whole new light. He is not the philandering, 'woman in every port' type, at all. He's loyal and a good friend. He was prepared to stick by Laura even when she was crippled, not out of a sense of duty but for love. He's a kind person who cares about people.

I want this man and his baby - more than ever.

14

We roll up to the party in the Murciélago, black as night. I would have felt self-conscious in such an outrageously flashy car, were it not matched by vehicles almost - but not quite - as impressive, lining the driveway. I can already spot some movie stars – I feel as if I'm in Hollywood at an Oscar party, not a place in the middle of the French countryside.

Alexandre walks over to the passenger side and opens the door for me. I ease myself out, careful not to expose my panties to the world. Who knows, there might be paparazzi here – they could be interested in Alexandre Chevalier's love interest. *Love interest? What am I painting myself as, an actress in a movie? I am his girlfriend, am I not?*

My insecurities are assuaged when he introduces me to the host and his friends, saying, "This is my girlfriend, Pearl."

The house is slicker than Alexandre's; more luxurious, but

that's to be expected of Hollywood royalty. Is that Charlize Theron I see over there? Beyond stunning. And is that Susan Sarandon, looking so elegant in a black sequined dress? The candlelit rooms are milling with the bold and the beautiful, spilling into the garden. Alexandre is holding my hand, leading me around.

Once in the swing of things, and after a few glasses of champagne, I feel completely at ease. After all, my main job as producer is communication. Chatting with people is easy for me and we've had a few stars doing voice-over work for us at Haslit Films. I'm not intimidated by fame.

After a while, we meander our separate ways. I get chatting to a woman from LA – shop talk, really, and Alexandre gets distracted by one of his neighbors – they're talking about their vines and lavender production. Before I know it, someone who looks oddly familiar has joined us and he soon overtakes the conversation. Who is he? That's the problem with actors - you think one is your neighbor or even your old friend, because you feel you've known that person all your life and then you realize you've seen them on TV or in a movie and you are a total stranger to them. Who *is* this man? Anyway, the woman has slipped out of sight now and I find myself discussing Haslit Films with him and my next, hopeful project. He's smiling away and I'm smiling away, too. Finally, he asks my name and I tell him.

"And your name is?" I ask. He looks surprised as if I should know and then says, "Ryan." He's thirty-something - blond, blue eyes. Handsome in a classic way although not my type. Funnily enough, he reminds me somewhat of my ex.

We are just beginning a conversation when I feel Alexandre grab my wrist from behind. "We have to leave," he says briskly.

"What, already? I feel as if we just got here."

The movie star is looking awkward so I introduce him to Alexandre. Alexandre nods and murmurs in a husky tone, "Pearl, we have to go."

"Bye," I say. "Nice meeting you."

"I was having a good time," I hiss at Alexandre. "Why are we leaving?" *Is he jealous?*

As we are walking out the front door, an elegantly dressed woman gives me a look of disgust like a dagger being thrown into my face. I recognize her but I can't place her. What is wrong with me tonight? As I pass her I hear, "fucking cougar," and wonder if the insult was directed at me.

Alexandre bundles me into the car and screeches out of the driveway. I feel like Batwoman in this thing. He's no longer in a happy mood and I fear that I've upset him by unwittingly flirting with that famous actor, although what he's famous for, I have no idea. Alexandre is silent, staring ahead at the road.

"You were right about your dress," he says in a cold voice. "It drew too much attention to you. It was too garish."

"I wasn't flirting. At least I wasn't conscious of doing so."

But he doesn't say a word. Twenty minutes go by and I'm aware that he doesn't take a turning I noticed earlier on our way here. Half an hour later and we are still not home. He's driving fast now, really fast. I can feel angry vibes emanating from every pore in his body. Jesus, if chatting with another man makes him jealous, this relationship of ours is not going to work.

"Are we going somewhere?" I ask.

"I'll get Madame Menager to send your things on. We aren't going back to my house."

Oh my God! I am being dumped! He's breaking up with me for some harmless flirting. That's my job! I have to be charming, have meetings, lunches and sometimes, yes, they happen to be with attractive men. I'm looking over at him and see the rage on his face. Uh, oh. I'm feeling scared. Maybe it's best to break up with him, anyway, if he's going to be like this. I don't want some possessive psycho as my boyfriend.

"Alexandre, what's going on?"

"I don't like seeing you treated like that. Fuck, just because you were wearing a short red dress doesn't give people a license to be so judgmental."

"That guy, Ryan, was being perfectly friendly. He wasn't being lecherous or rude in any way at all."

"We are not talking about him, for fuck's sake," he shouts. He has never spoken to me with that tone before and it shocks me. "We're talking about you," he adds, ominously.

I can feel myself well up. "I was just being friendly. Discussing my work. I didn't even find him attractive."

But he doesn't reply, just mumbles, "fucking bitch," under his breath.

I want to sink through the floor of his car. If this really was the Batmobile I could press a button and be shot out into the sky or something. Tears are now spilling onto my dress. The dress, I realize that is causing all this turmoil. I knew I shouldn't have worn it. Too short. Too red. It's screaming out 'slut'. I feel humiliated and small. He's racing around corners now like some Formula One driver. He seems to have control but the speed and the way his temper is flaring has me crumbling into a wreck. I'm sobbing now, I have nothing to wipe away my tears but this vulgar dress. It's smeared with mascara which is also, no doubt, half way down my panda-eyed face. He looks over at me.

"Are you crying, baby?" he asks, his voice suddenly soft.

"Of course I am," I heave between sobs. *What the hell does he expect?*

He pulls the car over in a dark lay-by and turns off the engine.

"Oh, Pearl, I'm so sorry."

"This goddam dress."

"Well, I love that dress," he says, unclipping his seatbelt and mine. He takes me in his arms and draws me close. "You think I was angry at *you*?" he asks tenderly.

"You called me a 'fucking bitch.' "

He let out a small laugh. "Oh shit. No, Pearl. Not *you*, chérie. I was talking about my sister."

"Sophie?"

"She turned up at the party," he explains.

Duh, I click. That woman I saw was *Sophie*. Sophie, who shot me that look loaded with poison daggers.

"She called me a cougar," I tell him.

"In my book, that's a compliment. Cougars are beautiful, streamline, elegant and intelligent creatures."

"I don't think she meant it as a compliment."

"Why," he slams his hand on the dashboard, "can't she mind her own fucking business." He strokes my hair and kisses me on the forehead, then his mouth presses gently on my salty cheeks. "I'm sorry, baby. I'm sorry. That's why we're getting out of here – I'm really not in the mood for a scene. She'll be staying at my house. You don't want to be around."

"Why does she hate me? What have I ever done to her?"

"She's just jealous, that's all. She feels you're distracting me from my work."

"But you're still working your ass off, despite seeing me!"

"I know, but lately, she's right, my heart and soul are not in it. Since I met you I've been reminded that there is more to life than HookedUp. Besides, my work there is done. All the creative bit has finished, it's only about deals now and making more money. That's not what I'm about. Yeah, the money's great. I mean, look at this car, my properties and stuff, but...." he trails off, deep in thought as if an idea had just struck him.

"Where are you taking me now?" I ask.

"I'm taking *us* to Cap d'Antibes. I thought you should see a little of the French Riviera, the Côte d'Azur. I'll get our passports and anything important biked over to us tomorrow and then we'll fly to Paris from Nice the following day." He's now putting my seat back so I am reclining, the seat almost making a bed. "Let's just forget this episode, shall we? I'll sort things out with Sophie next week. I won't have her ruining things between you and me."

I take a deep breath and am placated, at least for now. No more tears.

He's running his eyes along my body and says, "You look amazing in that little red dress. Did you see how you were like a magnet? Everyone was looking at you. The best looking men in the room couldn't keep their eyes off you." His hand has moved its way between my legs and he pushes them apart gently. "And you know what turns me on? They want you - but you're mine. All mine." The next thing I know, he brings out the feather from his pocket. "It's had a bit of wear and tear," he says, "but it might make you feel more relaxed. Close your eyes, chérie. Think of lavender and rolling waves and just relax."

I lie back and he begins to trace the feather around my ankles and along my calves, and he tweaks my nipples with his fingers, rolling them between his thumb and forefinger. I can feel the pulse between my legs and I splay them open. He leans over and kisses me, flicking his tongue on mine and then kissing me hard on the mouth. I moan and start jiggling about in my seat. He traces his finger down my navel, around my belly-button and down to my panties. He presses the palm of his whole hand over my core, holding it there, still. I can almost hear the throb of it like a heartbeat.

"Are you feeling better now," he asks. "More relaxed?"

"Yes."

He presses my clit ever so lightly through my panties and holds it down for a second. I start pushing up against on his firm hand. But then he takes it away and starts the engine.

"What are you doing?" I gasp, longing for him to take me right here in the car.

"I'm hungry. It's a good hour away, yet, and I want to get us there in time for dinner."

"So French," I moan. "Your belly comes before anything else, even sex."

He laughs. "I know how to handle you, Pearl Robinson. I may be greedy for food but you are greedy in other ways. I'm just whetting your appetite - just making sure my chick is still clucking."

I'm clucking alright. "You bastard," I exclaim, pounding his thigh with my fist. "You can't leave me here like this, moist between the legs, tingling all over." I see the huge bulge in his jeans and it makes me catch my breath. *Why does he insist on this torture?*

He has a knowing smirk on his face as he drives off, the car noisy like a racing car. "You just sleep now, baby, we'll be there soon. Dream of me, and remember - be prepared, because I'm going to get you to ride me later. See how hard I am? That's all for you."

15

I've done it again. I've wasted a night sleeping! Last night, after a mouth-watering dinner, which was accompanied by both vintage red and white wines (so delicious, I drained every glass), I conked out on the sofa in our suite. Alexandre carried me, woozily drunk as I was, to bed, and here I am the following morning in the most beautiful place in the world with the most beautiful man in the world, nursing a hangover. What a fool. Except, right now, I appear to be alone in our sumptuous suite, which is decorated with pristine antique furniture.

I go to one of the two bathrooms, a marble affair, beyond luxurious, and look in the mirror. Uh, oh. My hair is wildly messed up and I have dark makeup around my eyes. Did he wake up to that unsightly mess? Poor guy. I splash water on my face and glug down some mineral water to clear my foggy head. I wander back into the bedroom and living room. Alexandre is definitely not around. I have a memory of last night's dream, quite Freudian, perhaps, that I was making love to a black horse. Well, not with his actual wiener, but riding his foreleg which was pressed in tightly between my legs, holding me up. I was worried I was too heavy for his leg as he was supporting all my weight, and I asked him if it hurt (of course, animals speak in dreams). The horse replied, 'no, it's fine - keep riding.' I was meant to ride Alexandre but ended up dreaming about a horse instead! I think I had an orgasm in my sleep. Well, in the dream I did, but does that make it really happen? I have always wondered that – when you come in your sleep are you actually climaxing, or just dreaming you are? For men it's obvious, they wake up with a sticky mess on the sheets, but for women it is more of a mystery. Sometimes, I still have my hands between my legs, still tingling and hot so I know it happened. But today, I'm not sure.

Alexandre has awoken my sensibility, my sexuality. To think that less than a month ago, I had resigned myself to a sexless, passionless life, centered around work, and little else. Yet, I am only forty – too young to give up so soon. Forty. Not long ago that seemed a lifetime away for me, and then the number crept up - and here it is. Four O. Four Oh! Like the pearls, I am made of forty shades, a different tone for every year I've been alive. Forty. For some that seems old, that I am a preying cougar, that I have no right to be with a man fifteen years younger than me. Yet, for centuries it has been accepted when the roles are reversed. How many people even blink when they see a man fifteen years older than his partner? Princess Diana was only nineteen when she met Prince Charles who was thirteen years her senior, and the whole world thought it marvelously romantic. Yet she was still just a teenager.

But I am seen as a Cougar with a capital C.

Cougar - Sophie's one word, spat at me like venom, is echoing in my ears. I should ignore her spite, but I can't. I feel I am being judged, and that eyes are upon me, not just Sophie's, but others, too. Will people be observing me here, thinking, 'how did she get that young guy?' *Shut up, Pearl!* He wants to be with you, just accept It. Be happy, stop doubting yourself all the time.

But I do doubt myself. I can't help it.

I gaze out the window from my balcony at the view, and tears well in my eyes. Tears of happiness, tears of despair. Have I ever witnessed anything so perfect? I look across the century-old grove of pine trees to the sea before me - a blue more profound than I thought possible. Even Hawaii cannot match this. I have heard all my life about the Mediterranean and here I am at the Hotel du Cap-Eden-Roc on the southern tip of the Cap d'Antibes, the pearl of the Côte d'Azur - no pun intended - where the glamorous and great have been coming for a hundred and forty years.

Here I am, me, Pearl, in this place that holds such mythical status, standing on my balcony listening to the sound of nature's summer music - the cicadas chirping in my ears - and breathing in the scent of jasmine, or something delicious, mixed with pine. Perhaps the great playwright, Bernard Shaw, stood right here, or the Hollywood legends, Tyrone Power and Rita Hayworth.

The turquoise water is shimmering with the morning sun and there is a sailing boat in the distance, its white sails like fairy wings edging on the deep horizon. The deep green of the pine trees compliment the glistening blue - his eyes and mine – green and blue. I think back to when I was a little girl putting my green and blue crayons side by side together – my two favorite colors, so pretty, peaceful, pleasing. Now those colors are part of my soul.

Only yesterday I was a little girl.

Today, I am a 'cougar'.

I take a shower to freshen up, wash my hair, but once dry, I realize I have nothing to wear but the fated red dress. There is no way I'm strutting about this hotel in that, garnering stares from the glamorous guests. I heard a rumor last night that Madonna is staying here. Eat your heart out, Anthony!

I call reception and order a blue and white bikini, a tennis skirt and T-shirt from the hotel boutique – something, for now, to make me blend in. Then I ask for breakfast to be brought to the room. It is ten o'clock – where is Alexandre? I don't want to go looking for him. I have my iPhone but my battery has run out and the charger is back at his house. I open the mini bar and drain a whole bottle of orange juice. Already I feel more alive and am grateful I have had this last hour to myself alone. No more drinking alcohol.

Famous last words, I know.

When Alexandre returns, he finds me in my little tennis outfit. He stands at the doorway and gives me a wolf whistle. I laugh.

"Hi Pearl, love the look. But isn't it a bit hot to play right now?"

"I have no intention of playing tennis," I reply. "All I want to do is get into that crystalline sea. I had to wear something so I got this tennis gear, and look," I say, flashing the bikini underneath. "Ready for a swim?"

He saunters up to me, kisses me on the mouth and lays his hand on my butt. "Absolutely."

"Where have you been, by the way?"

"Making some calls." By the look on his face I know who he

has been speaking to.

"You talked to your sister?"

"I needed to get a few things straight with her."

"What's her problem, anyway?"

"She's possessive." He leads me to the sofa and sits me down. He obviously wants to explain things. Explain why his sister is such a tough cookie. Why she dislikes me. "Look, she was the same with Laura. Laura was never good enough for me. Until we split up, of course. Then, suddenly, the sun shone out of Laura's ass and she could do no wrong."

"Even when Laura was already married to the other guy - to James?"

"Exactly. Once safely ensconced with another man, Laura became the perfect woman for me. They're great friends now. For some reason, my sister feels that if I am in love with someone, she'll lose me."

I bask in his words. Does that mean he's *in love* with me?

"But Sophie has a step-daughter," I argue, "and a husband - she has a life outside HookedUp. You're not a seven year-old boy anymore. She doesn't need to play mommy to you any longer."

He's shaking his head solemnly. "She can't let go."

"And what about you?" I ask. I'm beginning to see his sister as a major obstacle to our relationship. Like a wicked, jealous mother-in-law with whom you'll never see eye to eye.

"She's had a tough life," he answers, as if by way of explanation.

"So have you, but it hasn't made you aggressive."

"Oh, I can be, Pearl. When crossed. Sophie's the same."

"But I haven't crossed her! I met her once for five minutes." I put my hand on his knee and soften my voice. "Something you said yesterday has been haunting me. You told me she did a job that wasn't good for her soul - to help you with tuition fees. What was it?"

"I really don't want to go into that."

"Was it dealing drugs?"

"No, she's never had a drug problem. She's pretty straight. In fact, she was furious when I was loafing about smoking weed and playing video games when I was a teenager. She was the one who insisted I get my act together."

"So what was she doing that was so awful?"

"Pearl, I don't want to judge people, least of all my sister. What she did was just her way of trying to make ends meet. It was hard for her at age seventeen when she had to support me. She had to endure stuff she wasn't happy about. And years later she fell back on a profession that she knew could make money fast."

"She worked as a prostitute?" I guess, looking him in the eye.

He's tapping his fingers together in agitation. "I don't like that term. I prefer 'sex worker.' It's still work, whatever anyone says. And it's not the sex workers who are at fault but their bloody customers. All the perverts of this world who take advantage of someone in a weak, vulnerable position."

"I see."

"That sounds judgmental, Pearl."

"What? I haven't said anything! All I said was, 'I see.' "

"Just your tone of voice. Have you any *idea* how tough it was for Sophie?"

"No, I haven't," I say carefully. "I can try to imagine but I cannot put myself in her shoes." I nearly say, *I have never fallen so low,* but instead come up with, "Life has never gotten that bad for me."

"Money is important to Sophie. She's terrified of losing everything we've built up. Scared shitless of going back to being poor, or in a compromised situation."

"Look, I don't know much about your finances, Alexandre, but it seems to me that you could both sell up and never work a day again for the rest of your lives - if you ever chose to."

"Tell me about it. Not a day goes by when I haven't considered doing that."

"Well, why don't you?"

"I can't just abandon her – we're business partners."

"You'd hardly be feeding her to the lions, Alexandre. She'd be set for life. You both would. You said yourself, it's all about deals now, and the creative process is over. You could start another company; create something new if you wanted. I mean, if you're not happy–"

"I am happy. Please, let's drop this, Pearl. Let's go swimming."

The water is heaven and it washes away that unpleasant conversation. The sea is smooth and refreshing but not cold. Rocks glimmer beneath us and we dip and dive about each other like children. Alexandre is a strong swimmer – thank God. I'm glad I'm not disappointed in that department. Snotty, I know, to care about something like swimming, but I do. A bad swimmer could be a deal breaker. How ridiculous is that?

Afterwards, we sun ourselves on the rocks like salamanders.

He has a dark tan and doesn't seem to need sun-cream at all.

"How come you already had swim trunks with you?" I ask.

"I always keep an emergency overnight bag in my car. Dumb, really. It started in LA having to be ready in case of a fast getaway after an earthquake. I got caught out once and it shook me. Call me a geek, but I like to be prepared. Next time, I'll pack for you, too."

I smile. 'Next time' – I like that. "So what else have you got in your bag of tricks?"

"A shirt, shorts, jeans, cash and so on."

A man prepared for anything. I have a feeling this has less to do with any earthquake than a little boy of seven having to leave home at a moment's notice, never to return.

"We can have dinner here later, if you like," he suggests. "Watch the sunset."

"I'd love that." I start to giggle.

"What?"

"Already thinking about dinner, Monsieur Frenchie, and we haven't even had lunch yet."

"Just to prove I'm really French, I carry a corkscrew in my car, too."

We are back in our luxurious suite drinking chilled champagne (my no-drinking resolve didn't last a second) – I'm lying naked on the bed, admiring my tan.

"You can always tell an American girl," he observes, "by her tan mark."

I look up at him.

"Tits like vanilla," he explains.

"You think I should have taken off my top, don't you? Like the European women."

"I don't know about that," he says, running his eyes along my body and biting his lower lip. "It's sexy. Provocative. Those arrogant little breasts are asking to be sucked and played with, just asking for it."

I take a cube of ice from the ice-bucket and circle it around my nipples until they go hard. "Like this?" I tease. The melting water is trickling down my breasts and onto my stomach. "And what about my pale-skinned bottom and–"

"Your little, cream-colored pussy," he interrupts, coming over to the bed. But he doesn't touch me, just continues to drink in the view of my sun-kissed body. "All of it is asking for it," he notes, narrowing his eyes. "Asking to get fucked."

I take another cube and slip it in between my legs, up inside myself. I gasp at the chill but then it feels welcoming. I trace my finger up along my wet slit and watch his expression. He can't keep his eyes off me. I run my tongue around my lips, staring at him as I do so. He takes off his swim shorts and I watch his huge phallus spring free. It, too, is paler than the rest of him. Also, asking for it. Begging to be ridden. To get sucked. I want to get on top of it, feel it deep inside me. I want it to make me come again.

He takes a gulp of champagne, holds it in his mouth, and straddles me so his hard penis is resting in between my breasts. I am pinned to the bed. He leans forward, pressing his thumb on my lower lip, opening my mouth and then kisses it, letting the champagne run down past my tongue. He slowly licks my mouth.

"It's so good to see you naked in the full light, Pearl. A few freckles have come up on your face, you look beautiful."

I look into his green eyes flecked with gold highlights, rimmed with black lashes. "You…you look like….sex," I whisper in his ear, the words falling out incomprehensively, and then I nibble his lobe which tastes of salt. I breathe in the smell of Mediterranean sun-on-skin mixed with Alexandre; a perfume designed just for me. I claw my hands about his butt and draw him higher, closer, and take his smooth erection in my mouth. It, too, tastes of the Mediterranean. I close my eyes and suck on it. It smells of sun and sea. I let my tongue flicker, rim and slap its round tip, sucking off the pre-come, tasting the love I have for this man, the surge of sexual desire and the hunger I feel, like an ache, to have all of him inside me, his soul, his body – all of him.

"Kiss me again," I demand. He pulls his hips back and grazes his lips along my throat, then lifts my wrists in the air and licks me under the arms. The sensation is so erotic and I sense my clitoris swell with excitement. I expect him to go to my breasts next, but he doesn't. His tongue journeys south all the way down, stopping to lick my thighs yet avoiding my pussy. Oh, no, not that again…the slow, tantalizing torture. It's throbbing now, my hips flexing and bending, wanting attention in that core centre, but he leaves it be. Instead, he lifts my legs high, one at a time, and licks me behind each knee. He carries on down my legs and takes my salty toes in his mouth, sucking each one, slowly. I am so relaxed, floppy as a soft doll.

I pop my finger inside myself and feel the heat, slick with desire. I tell him about last night's dream with the black horse.

"You want to ride me again, baby, is that what you want," he says, his face between my thighs. He is kneeling on the floor now, staring up at me from between my legs. His tongue flicks just once on my clit but not again. Teasing me. I can feel its pulse.

"Please fuck me," I beg. "I need it deep inside." I'm wriggling on the mattress.

He gets back on the bed and slips underneath me, lifting me up with his muscular arms, placing his head in between my feet, and he hauls me close to him so my legs are either side of his torso. He pulls my back up so I am sitting on top of him.

"Swivel round," he instructs, and he maneuvers me so I am straddling him, my knees either side of his hips. I'm sitting on his crotch but facing away from him. His view is my ass and I am looking at his feet.

"Now ease yourself on top of my cock."

I kneel up to position myself and take his erection in both hands. I aim it inside me, rimming it about me first. This feels great.

"Won't this hurt you, being at an angle?" I ask, slapping his hard rock against my clit and rimming it up and down and around the lips of my opening.

"No, this feels….delicious," he murmurs with a groan, pushing his hips forward so he is closer and slipping all the way inside me. "They call it the Reversed Cowgirl. You're in control, Pearl. You call the shots… with your pistol…with your pussy pistol."

I smile. I start riding him slowly, easing myself up and down. This is novel; I have never tried this before. His hands are on my waist, guiding me. I am looking at his strong calf muscles, his elegant feet. He has a bird's eye view of my curvy buttocks.

"Your ass is out of this world, oh yeah, keep that rhythm, this feels great, chérie. Love that peaches and cream ass, love that tight, wet pearlette moving so sweetly."

I lean forward now and slip my hand under his balls. I can hear his breath in gasps. I keep riding. Up and down. Up and down. Then I lift myself off his cock completely and squeeze his erection in a tight grip. "I need to get smacked about," I say, and I begin to slap his cock against my clit again, guiding it around my hot entrance and back on my clit. Oh yeah…this feels amazing. I observe my nipples darkening like crimson rosebuds. Then I ease myself on top of him again and press down so his erection slides deep, deep, deep inside.

"Rodeo me, baby. That's right, you Wild West American Cowgirl."

I want to laugh, but the sensation feels so intense, all I can do is concentrate. I'm pulling almost all the way out now, teasing my entrance and then making circular movements with my hips.

"You lak this?" I say in a faux Texan accent. I graze my thumbs across my nipples and they harden like bullets. I cannot see him but I can hear his murmurs. Oh yes, he does like this. Then I rest my hands back on his legs, impale myself upon him so he is deep inside me again, and I start to rock back and forth. He's stroking my butt cheeks with his hands, and just knowing how turned on he's getting, is making me hotter. I can feel that G-spot getting rubbed…oh yeah, this is nice. I arch my back. Alexandre lifts his hips a touch and….ah, he's hit that spot. I rock forward once more and start…

"I'm coming, Alexandre. You're making me come." I clench my muscles tighter and feel another wave roll over me. He's pumping now, his hips rising from beneath in hard thrusts.

"Me too, I'm coming."

Feeling him thicken inside me brings on another surge of pleasure and I slam down on him. As I do so I press my clit with my middle finger and feel an intense roll of orgasm rush again to the surface. "It's happening again," I scream out, hardly believing this is real. Ripples and spasms rush through my body like patterns.

"I think I've accomplished my mission," he says in a low voice.

A wave of panic engulfs me. Does that mean it's over? *He's made me come with penetrative sex again, so that's it?* But I don't say a word. The aftershocks are making my body tremble. I'm like putty.

Alexandre is in my bloodstream like a drug.

While my nerves are still tingling, he pushes me off him so I'm kneeling on all fours. He grabs my hips from behind and shoves his huge erection into me from the back. I gasp. *More?* I hold onto the bead-stead as he fucks me so hard my head bumps up against the padded part. He's literally growling like an animal, ramming me from behind, punctuating his words with thrusts.

"Love. Fucking. You. All I can do is…. fuck you, Pearl. All I can think… about is… making you….come."

Then he pulls out slowly and starts sucking me so gently, so softly, his tongue darting between my thighs in tiny, almost imperceptible sweeps. The rough and now the smooth, the combination and surprise of it has me on the edge again. I find myself willing him silently to fuck me hard once more. And he does.

"This ass is….driving me…. crazy. This round, silky-smooth ass is…." he doesn't finish his sentence, just rams himself into me and starts pumping hard again. I feel another wave building up. He cries out in French and then more words that I don't understand. His hands are cupping my butt tightly, claiming it.

Possessing it. "This ass belongs to me," he roars. He's thick and rock hard inside me. And then… he stills. Stationary. All I can feel is his throbbing, the rush of his release. It's filling me up. He's still, motionless, and the sweet soreness I feel inside me and the big pulse of his cock has me about to come. I can feel it. My head is down on the bed, my butt high in the air, his still erection pounding like a slow drum beat inside me. I touch my clitoris softly with my fingers, and feel the double-hot sensation build up, and I climax once more.

I'm quivering all over. "Oh, Alexandre," I whimper. "What are you doing to me?" I'm moaning and he starts moving gently back and forth again.

"I'm coming again, baby," he whispers, and I can feel a new surge of his release pulse through me. "Je t'aime."

He just said he loves me! But I don't reply. It's the moment of passion, I know - I can't be really sure if it's me he loves, or my body parts. Either way, my psyche is jumping up and down for joy. I remain still, lapping up my post-orgasm spasms.

Cool, calm and collected.

That's me.

16

We are having lunch overlooking the sea, and I am quietly meditating on what just happened. If I had read about my experience in a woman's magazine, I would have thought it was an invented fantasy to sell more copies, but it happened – it really did - multiple orgasms have rocked my world.

I, Pearl Robinson, had multiple orgasms. The notion seems extraordinary. Surreal. As if the new Pearl has been prized from her oyster shell and re-packaged as a shimmering piece of priceless jewelry. Pearl - the exquisite. Pearl - the treasure. That is how I now feel.

I think of all the wasted years in my thirties. My sexuality stagnant - sitting on a shelf like an unread classic book. Something of quality but ignored, or worse, in the hands of somebody who did not know how to read, or at least, did not know how to read me. My ex-husband - oblivious to the wealth inside my body.

It took a twenty-five year-old Frenchman to unleash my riches.

Now I feel cocooned in love. I sit here inhaling the salty sea breeze and watch a couple on their honeymoon swimming and splashing below us, next to the rocks. Once, that would have filled me with benign envy.

Not now.

Alexandre's lip is curved into a quiet, satisfied smile. Mind-blowing sex followed by grilled wild sea bass for lunch. At least, I think that's what he's pleased about, although it could be because he has arranged to pick up Rex from Paris on our way back to New York. He has, indeed, organized a private jet – Rex will be travelling in style. We're leaving tomorrow morning for Paris by helicopter, apparently. So much for Alexandre's 'ecological' carbon footprint – I have a feeling he gads about the globe this way a lot. Why did he make out he was so politically correct, never using private transport? What else isn't he telling me?

Alexandre is talking on his cell. I love listening to him chat away in French.

He slaps his phone on the table and says, "Today everything has come together," and we laugh at his double-entendre. Come together. So true.

"What else are you feeling cocky about?" I ask, smiling.

"A deal."

"I thought you were tired of making deals, that that side of things didn't thrill you anymore."

He laughs. He has a mocking look in his eye which disarms me, and I discern a slight sneer on his face. "Are you kidding? I'm making silly money. That turns me on, Pearl, as much as what happened today between you and me. A challenge complete."

My stomach drops like lead – a thousand stabs pierce my gut. Is this the same human being I thought I knew? The man with the black Labrador? The man who would have stuck by a crippled woman for love?

I feel like a gutted fish. Empty. Dead. But he's smiling away, unaware of the turmoil inside me. I am no more important than a money deal. A challenge.

"I've had too much sun for one day," I manage to say before my voice cracks. "I'm going back to the room."

"Okay, just got to make another call or two. I'll join you in a bit."

When I get back to our suite, I turn on my iPhone which has been re-charging. Five messages. The latest, from Anthony, who received my 'Madonna is here' message – although I can't be sure - still haven't seen her with my own eyes. I called him this morning, S.O.S as a joke. He's hysterical, wanting to know if I've done what he asked, namely, to chat her up and become her New Best Friend. Another two messages from him. Next, Natalie asking me to bring her a towel from the hotel, 'So chic,' she raves. 'So iconic. Must have.' My dad has also left a message, harping on about Natalie, wondering what happened. Men are so clueless. I really don't want to play piggy in the middle to their drama. Then, a voice I don't recognize, at first. Then it dawns on me who it is. The dagger voice - Sophie. She and her brother have something in common. They can slice your heart open with just one word.

"Pee-earl," she begins. "I don't know what the fuck you sink you are doing wiz my leetle brozzer almost twice is age, old enough to be is muzzer - but I sink I should warn you, you are barking up ze wrong tree. Ee does not give a fuck about you, you know? Eet woz a bet we made in ze coffee shop. Ee said zat he bet he could make you crazey about im, fuck you on zee first date. Zen ee told me ee ad a challenge wiz you. I know all about your sexual problems, Peearl. Your frigidity. Eet woz a game ee play wiz you. Game is over, stalker woman." There is a crackling on the line and then the Simon and Garfunkel song, *Mrs. Robinson* begins playing in the background.

Wow, what a bitch.

I stare blankly at the wall of this zillion star hotel. Dazed, out of focus. Alexandre has discussed my private secrets with his *sister*. It makes me feel nauseous. As if there has been some incestuous tryst between them. How dare she know about my sexuality? How dare he tell her? A bubbling heat is consuming me, too furious, now, for tears. I rummage about the room and find what I am looking for: my bag with passport and the clothes wrapped inside a plastic bag. The suitcase would have been too big to bring by bike courier. Never mind, they brought all the essentials. I grab it all, put on the same 1950's dress I arrived in, and some flip-flops. I run out of the room. I dare not even ask for a taxi at the front desk. They could alert Alexandre. I race from the grounds, leaving the scent of pines, the chirping crickets and the Mediterranean paradise, behind me.

I am now at Nice airport. Luckily, there is a flight to Paris and I can change there with just a few hours wait for a flight to New York. I'm listening to Beyoncé on my iPhone – *If I Were a Boy* –

you tell'em, Beyoncé. I wish I could understand how certain men's minds work – how some will stop at nothing to puff up their egos even if they know they're breaking someone's heart.

Just before take-off, I do the decent thing. I call Alexandre to let him know I have left. Just in case he reports me missing to the *gendarmes* or something. Thank God his voicemail picks up and I can just leave a message.

"Alexandre – what can I say?" I start in a small voice. "I have left. Obviously. I received a message on my cell from Sophie who seemed to know every intimate detail of my sex life. I'm glad your 'challenge' worked out for you, and for me, too. It was a real eye-opener, an experience of a lifetime. It was beautiful. Beautiful because I believed in it. But… now I have found out that it was all a game for you, I know that it could never be the same between us again. As you said yourself, the biggest sex organ is your brain. And my brain is shot to pieces right now. Goodbye, Alexandre. Good luck with Rex, shame that cute dog and I will never meet. Bon voyage."

I end the call, sit back in my economy seat and let the tears fall. The catchy tune to *Mrs. Robinson* is playing over and over inside my head like background music to my misery – a tune I used to love.

A reminder of who I am.

And what will never be.

17

When I walk into my apartment, its walls feel like a fortress - a welcome haven, safe from the evils of the outside world. Whatever happens (God forbid, a tsunami should strike New York City), this is my security. My nest.

I haven't even turned my cell back on. I don't want to know what Alexandre's reaction may be. I just need to feel at peace. It's four in the morning European time, ten pm here – time for bed; I have to go to work tomorrow.

I keep going over everything in my mind; could there have been some sort of mistake? No, Sophie knew intimate details about my sexuality. I feel humiliated as if I were some sort of experiment. Not to say I didn't enjoy being Alexandre's guinea pig - I cannot deny that, but I feel dishonored by him.

I call Daisy, give her the lowdown on my latest drama and ask if there's any way she can do an early breakfast tomorrow. I need to talk to someone – get a second opinion about this whole crazy mess. We are meeting at 8am at the café next to my workplace.

I run a bath and rummage around the kitchen for something to eat. I land on some potato chips which I dunk into cream cheese. I scoff the whole packet. Comfort food. I'll need to watch myself in the next few weeks. No bingeing – I'll get rid of those calories tomorrow with a long swim.

The bath feels soothing, only, it reminds me of our time together. Will I ever get this French bastard out of my system? I hear the house telephone ring. I'll ignore it. The doorman? Anthony? Who cares – I can't be dealing with any of that now.

I mull over the sheer arrogance and inflated ego that Alexandre seems proud to own. A cliché of his own making. Yes, French men have a reputation for being great lovers but also, arrogant shitheads. Why was he playing games with me? To feed his vanity? I dry myself and moisturize my body all over, and then look through the playlist on my iPod. I find the perfect song for him. "This is for you, Alexandre," I shout into the air. *You're So Vain* blares out and I start to dance about the bathroom. I feel energized. I can get through this.

By the time I flop into bed, I'm exhausted. Did I dislocate my shoulder blade by punching my fist into the air too hard?

I fall into a deep sleep which feels like five minutes. The alarm on my iPhone goes off and I get ready for work. I have failed both Anthony and Natalie. I did not become Madonna's NBF and sorry, Natalie, I did not feel inclined to pinch a towel from the hotel. You can buy one online, my dear, from their E boutique.

Daisy has lost weight in the space of one week. Incredible. Less Annie and more Nicole Kidman. I order a bagel, lox and cream cheese for my breakfast (uh oh) - and she, a fruit salad and tea.

"Well, you look great for someone who has just had her heart broken," she observes, glancing me up and down.

"Don't be fooled by the tan."

"Look, you had a good innings. Inning? Innings? I never know if that word should be singular or plural."

"I don't know either," I say. "But you're right, it lasted longer than I expected."

"Did you get to keep the pearl necklace?" she inquires with raised eyebrows.

"No, I left it at his house and he never gave it back."

"Oh well. You win some, you lose some."

"What would you have done?" I ask.

"If I still had the necklace?"

"Yes."

"Tough call. Pride would make me want to return it, but then…well…there is such a thing as severance pay."

I laugh. "Anyway, I don't have it - so luckily, I'm not in that predicament."

"How are you feeling?"

"Humiliated. But strangely grateful."

"Don't sell yourself short, Pearl."

"Look….sex," I whisper, lowering my voice, "was out of this world with him. I am now hoping that he has awakened something in me. That I can find another great relationship with someone else. In the future. I'm also more open to younger guys, something I never would have dared to consider before."

"Watch out, mothers, lock up your sons, here she comes! Just teasing, Pearl, don't look so horrified."

"I'm just a little sensitive to the cougar insult that Sophie spat out at me, that's all."

"Not every woman can pull a younger guy."

I squint my eyes at her.

"Pearl! Where's your sense of humor?" Daisy takes a large mouthful of strawberries and banana. "So, what's Plan B?" she asks with her mouth full.

"Do you think there's any way all this was a mistake?"

She shakes her head. "I doubt it. Those two are as thick as thieves. He obviously confides in her. Sorry, Pearl, I'm just giving my honest opinion. Bitchy as Sophie has shown herself to be, there must be some truth in what she said, or how would she have that information about you? I'm sure she made it sound worse than it was, but still. She knew stuff about you that she shouldn't have been party to. Can you imagine telling Anthony intimate stuff about your boyfriend?"

"Eew, gross, no!" I glug down the rest of my orange juice. "You know what gets me more than anything?"

"What?"

"Not hanging out with his dog, Rex. I had visions of us all together - walks in Central Park, you know, the whole family dream thing."

"Were you imagining a real family with him, too? Babies and everything?"

I haven't told Daisy about the condom-less sex. I know she

would disapprove. A faint shiver runs through me and then I take a deep breath. *No, Pearl, that ship has sailed.*

"Well, you know, a girl can have her flights of fancy," I say.

"It all seemed so on the cards, Pearl. Until this sister crap messed it all up. I'm surprised. No, shocked, actually. I really believed he was into you. He had me fooled."

"You never met him, Daisy."

"I didn't have to. The pearl necklace spoke volumes, the trip to France et cetera. It seemed he went to extremes to make you happy – he didn't have to do all that, he still could have accomplished his 'challenge' without all those extra trimmings. The truth is, the more I think about it, it doesn't add up. But then….he is French, I suppose. Maybe he wanted to do it all with flourish and style."

"I guess we'll never know."

"Hasn't he called you a million times?"

"I don't know. My cell is switched off. Between him, and Anthony obsessing about Madonna, I don't dare listen to my messages."

"You'll need to give Alexandre a chance to at least explain."

"Explain what? That his only sister is a psycho bitch from hell who once stabbed her father in the groin, and who has it in for me? To be honest, maybe it's better like this - I'm well out of it. Do I really want her on my tail? Sharing my life with her? I mean, she's his sister and they're business partners. I wouldn't want to test her temper."

"Alexandre did say, though, that the father was a monster, didn't he? Maybe he deserved to be stabbed," Daisy reasons.

"Whatever - I don't want to be on the wrong side of her. Perhaps it's best I keep well away from Alexandre."

"Probably. If you see him, you'll only get tempted again. And this Sophie character sounds like bad news, whichever way you look at it." Daisy checks her watch. "Crap! I'm really late! We'll speak this evening, okay, Pearl?"

"I'm late, too. Thanks for listening, Daisy. Thanks for being there for me. And you look great, by the way. Ten pounds slimmer."

"Don't exaggerate, Pearl, but thanks."

We both get up from our seats, pay the check and dash off our separate ways.

When I get home from work, Luke, the skinny doorman who I thought had been fired, presents me with a box. I recognize it – wrapped with the same type of white velvet ribbon in the gray box. I think I know what it is. My heart is thumping through my chest, adrenaline pumping through my veins as if I'm preparing to run from a wild beast. Funny how nature has adrenaline kick in whether we like it or not.

I have a quick shower to ease the day away and when I pick up the box again I am a little calmer.

Déjà-vu. I set it on my bed and open it. The pearl necklace wrapped in one of his T-shirts which I pick up and smell. Bastard. He knows just how to get to me. He hasn't washed the shirt and I can smell him all over it. Sunshine, salt, the odor of his skin. I inhale it and feel a surge of desire sweep through my body. There is a long note in his handwriting and attached a typed, printed note on different paper. It reads:

Darling, precious Pearl,

You are my pearl, you are my treasure. Don't deny me this. Don't deny me the love I have for you.
When you left my heart broke in two. The Spanish describe their soul-mate as 'media naranja' the other half of the same orange. And that is what you are to me, the other half of me, the perfect half that matches me. I have never felt this way before about anybody. Ever.
You think I betrayed your trust. No, I would never do that. Sophie snooped at my iPad and saw my personal notes. They were written in English so I never imagined she would bother to translate them. Call me a jerk, call me a nerd for making notes concerning you. But here they are. (I have copied and pasted this). This is what she saw:

Problems to be solved concerning Pearl:
Needs to reach orgasm during penetrative sex. (My big challenge).
Needs confidence boosted - age complex due to American youth worship culture.
Need to get her pregnant ASAP due to clock factor. (Want to start a family with her.)

I feel embarrassed showing this to you but it is the only way I know how to explain myself. I write lists and notes – I write them for everything – you know that.
When I first set eyes on you in that coffee shop, I was

smitten, instantly. I remarked to Sophie how beautiful you were. Sophie commented on how easy American girls are, how they jump into bed with anybody at the drop of a hat. I told her, that in your case, I thought I stood very little chance – that you looked sophisticated and classy. (Given that I had never been with an American woman I had no idea if what she said was true). It was disrespectful of me to discuss this in French with her while you were standing right there before us when we were all waiting in line. I apologize. But that was then.

This is now.

Now I have found my Pearl I do not want to let her go.

I will fight for you. I want you in my life.

I have made a decision. I am giving over HookedUp to Sophie. I will still keep shares but will no longer be involved in the daily decisions of running it. I'd like to start up a new enterprise – a film production company and I will be looking for someone to run it (production skills mandatory). I wondered if you would consider yourself for the job?

Here is the necklace. It belongs to you, and only you.

A squadron of kisses,

Your Alexandre

P.S Rex has arrived and wants to meet you.

P.P.S For the present time my family members will no

longer be staying at my apartment when they visit New York.

I smell the T-shirt again and go all weak. His natural scent is like an elixir of love. Before I have a chance to consider the contents of his note, the telephone rings. It's Luke, the doorman.

"Ms. Robinson, did you call the Fire Department?" he asks nervously.

"No, I didn't. Is there a fire in the building?" My voice flies up two octaves.

"Not as far as I know, Ms. Robinson, but a firefighter is on his way up to take a look. Somebody must have called 911."

"Well, it wasn't me. Mrs. Meyer from the eleventh has been known to call emergency services. They came once to retrieve her cat from the fire escape - did you ask her?"

"I'll call her now."

"Or that guy on the second floor, what's his name? Oh yes, Mr. Johnson. He is always burning his food."

"Okay, ma'am, thank you."

I go to the kitchen and look out the back door to see if I can hear a commotion. Nothing. All is silent up and down the back stairs. Why only one firefighter? Usually they come in pairs. I hear some clanging outside my kitchen window and I look over with a start. The firefighter is right there on the fire escape, peering into my apartment. Is he about to smash my window? I race over to open it – I don't want shards of glass everywhere. I lift up the window, raise my eyes and cannot believe the vision before me. I break into a smile.

Hot. Hot. Hot!

But not from any fire.

"Excuse me ma'am," the voice exclaims, "I heard there was fire in this apartment."

I observe the sexy outfit, the dark pants with yellow stripes. But the firefighter isn't wearing a top. His muscles are ripped, shining with perspiration, his cheeks dark with yesterday's stubble. Any girl's fantasy.

I open the window wide and his big black boots jump down into my apartment followed by his drop-dead gorgeous body.

"You nearly had me fooled," I laugh. "But your accent gave you away."

Alexandre is standing there, legs astride, holding a Fire Department helmet. It's not such a crazy idea - the electricity between us really does have me on fire.

"I heard there was a lot of heat coming directly from this apartment," he says with a big grin on his face. He takes a step closer and stares into my eyes. I can feel his breath on mine. Mint, apples, sun, Alexandre. He takes my chin in his hand and lets his lips graze my mouth. I respond with a gasp. I can hear him take in a gulp of air, inhaling the scent of me, of my hair. It feels like a century has passed since we were last together, yet it was only one night away. I open my mouth a little and his tongue finds mine, letting the tips meet. The connection, like lightening, goes straight between my legs.

"A lot of heat is coming from right down here," he tells me. He palms his large hand on my crotch and I feel a rush of blood pump through me. "I'm sorry, ma'am, but I'm going to have to put out this fire any way I can."

He gets down on his knees and places himself underneath me. He unzips my skirt and lets it fall to the floor. He pushes my legs apart and hooks his fingers inside my panties, peeling them down. Very, very slowly. He blows softly in between my legs, then flicks his tongue for just a second on my clitoris. Then he blows again.

"If you knew anything about fire, Mr. Firefighter," I gasp, "you'd know blowing on a flame just gets it more excited."

"True," he murmurs, letting his tongue lap along my slit. "Perhaps it needs some help cooling down."

He presses his tongue flat against my buzzing V-8 and I hold onto his head, my fingers running through his soft dark hair. I push my hips forward, pushing myself so the lips rub up and down against his mouth. I am so stimulated - so hot and horny. I'm moaning. I am still wearing a bra, nothing more, and I look down to see my breasts held like cupcakes in a demi push-up. I pull out one breast and play with my nipple, watching it turn hard. Alexandre begins to stand up and circles his right arm around my thighs, lifting me up over his shoulder in a fireman's lift! He's so strong - the way he does it so effortlessly makes me feel as light as a feather. I'm hanging upside down over his shoulders, gripping on to the waistband of his sexy fireman's pants with one hand, and with the other, cupping his cute, tight butt. He's taking me to the bedroom.

"Are you abducting me, Mr. Fireman?"

"I need to teach you a lesson, Ms. Robinson."

"What kind of lesson?"

"To teach you not to play with fire. To trust me, and not play silly, girlish games. Or you could get burned."

He lays me on the bed. As he does so, the telephone rings.

"It could be the doorman," I say. God knows what chaos Alexandre has caused.

"Answer it. Tell him I'm showing you some fire safety tips."

I laugh, and do as he suggests. Poor Luke is confused. Half of the building is in a panic. I assure him there is no fire here, that everything is under control but he did the right thing letting the firefighter into the building.

Alexandre stands on the edge of the bed and undoes the zip of his pants. Like a cobra, his erection comes free, proud and magnificent. The black pants, the big heavy boots, the clinking of the bits of metal on the waistband have me mesmerized in a Playgirl Firefighter Fantasy. I walk on my knees and take his erection in my hands, letting my loose hair brush back and forth, swishing across his shaft. I kiss him there, up and down, mini nips and kisses all over, and on the tip.

"It's beautiful," I breathe, and I mean every word.

I take it in my mouth, rimming my lips about his hard shaft and look up at him from under my lashes.

"Turn around," he says and swirls my body using his hands to control my hips, so my butt is facing him. I am on all fours.

"I'm going to have to spank you, Pearl You did wrong abandoning me in France the way you did. You had me desperate, distraught. I have to punish you so you won't do it again."

He pulls my thighs further apart.

He's into hurting women, after all, I think. I brace myself. How bad can a spank be? He pulls me closer to his pelvis. I'm waiting for his hand to come down on my ass. Instead, I feel a thud right up between my legs right at my entrance. I don't know what he is doing, exactly, but it feels so erotic, the thud, whack, thud. I bend my head all the way down and push my head under my thighs. I look up from under myself and see his cock slapping me. His dark pants against the color of his smooth flesh, has me throbbing with excitement.

"Pearl, I'm going to have to bite you now. Bite that creamy ass of yours." I feel his teeth nipping into my flesh, all over my butt, and then at my wet entrance where he gently tugs my lips with his mouth.

"Keep punishing me," I murmur in a faint whisper. "This feels incredible."

"Greedy… (bite)… Girl…. Greedy…. (slap)…. Girl."

I'm groaning.

Suddenly, he lifts me off the bed, holding me in his arms like a baby. *What? Don't stop now!*

"You've been punished enough," he says seriously. "I want to make love to you now. I think we've fucked enough, don't you? I think we need a bit more commitment from one another. No more games."

"But I am committed," I protest.

He sets me back down so I am sitting on the bed, and he gazes deep into my eyes. "Undress me, Pearl. Get me out of this gear. I feel claustrophobic trussed up in this outfit."

I smile wickedly. "Not so fast, Mr. Fireman. I think Mr. Firefighter needs a little dance first. A little lap dance to ease his tension." I find my iPhone and go to my play list and select the most sensual song I can think of - a French song - *Je T'aime….Moi Non Plus.* I start slowly gyrating my hips to the rhythm of the music, the deep voice of Serge Gainsbourg, the breathy, ecstatic sighs of Jane Birkin – a love song if ever there was one.

Alexandre's erection is jutting out from the uniform pants and I dip down on it, parting the lips of my cleft as I do so, sitting on it then rising up, pressing my pelvis against his stomach, rising all the way up and impaling myself on him again to the beat of the music. But he grabs me tight, his hands immobilizing me.

"Pearl, that's enough now. Get me out of these. Game's over. I don't want my future wife doing a lap dance for some dirty firefighter."

I burst out laughing. "But *you're* the firefighter."

He's trying to suppress a grin. "Some dirty firefighter who broke into your apartment uninvited."

I smile, realizing what he just said: *future wife*! I unbutton his waistband and pull the pants down over his hips, stopping to gaze at his navel, kissing it, tugging gently at the hair there with my teeth. I peel the pants down past his muscular thighs and stroke his arms until my hands are resting on his. He holds my hands, squeezing my palms and caressing my fingers. There is a stillness about him, a calm. I see such tenderness in his eyes – an expression I have not noticed before. I bend down and unlace one boot, and then the other. Then I stand up, and push him backwards onto the bed with a hard shove. He topples back and laughs with surprise. I tug each boot off and throw them, one by one, on the floor.

"Now you're free," I say.

"Take off that bra. I want you naked. Naked the way you were at Cap d'Antibes. Let me see those pearly breasts that are trapped inside."

I unhook my bra and throw it across the floor but carry on with my dance. I can't stop, the music is making me feel very sensual. *Future wife….oh yes!*

"Be still," he beckons with an intense look on his face. He steadies my moving hips and pulls me to him. "Lie beside me."

I lie down at his side so we are facing each other. He is motionless - just gazing at me. He strokes my hair and lays his long fingers on my shoulders, fondling me softly, studying my face.

"You're unique, Pearl. I've fallen in love with you."

I say nothing, just watch his expression.

"I want to marry you. To start a family. Is that what you want, too?"

I nod. My heart is beating so loudly he must be able to hear it.

He draws me close to him, pulling me into his arms, hugging me tightly, and plants small, whispery kisses on my neck and shoulders which send shivers all over me. He smoothes my wild hair away from my forehead and traces his finger along my eyebrow, my nose. I curl my arm around him and stroke the small of his back, tracing my nails lightly on his coccyx and on the cheek of his butt. I edge up closer to him. His breath is coming in long, slow sighs. Sighs of contentment, of feeling at peace.

His fingers are stroking my inner thigh with such a light touch I can hardly feel them and then they tap on my clit as lightly as the heartbeat of a bird. Tap, tap, tap.

"A little spanking," he says with an ironic smile. "For being so wayward - for escaping from me."

I edge up the bed higher so his erection is resting at my entrance and I sense the head there, soft yet hard. I clench my inner muscles into mini contractions, needing him, wanting him – I know he can hear my desire through the pattern of my breath.

He eases himself into me, stretching me open and I cry out in surprise. He feels huge.

"So wet," he whispers, pulling himself back out so he is only an inch inside me. He stills, doesn't move again.

I use his biceps as leverage to move myself in little circles so he is rimming me. I have this carnal need within me but the look on his face is about love, tranquility. I keep moving, his tip is soft on my clit, then my entrance, all the nerve endings - the nexus of pleasure connecting my entire body - are alive with hot desire. He kisses me softly, parting my mouth with his tongue. He flexes his hips towards me which makes him enter another inch. I hold the pulse between my legs. He is still gazing at me.

He narrows his eyes slightly, and says, "Will. You. Marry. Me. Pearl?" When he says each word he gives tiny punctuation thrusts which are like mountains moving inside me. I grab his butt and pull him deep into me so he is close. He stills and I can feel his throbbing. Something about his heartfelt words bring on a rush of pleasure, fireworks inside me, the waves of bliss roll through me, the unexpected orgasm upon me now in flashes of white stars. Intense. Sublime.

I cry out, "Yes, oh yes."

He juts his hips forward and I feel his release, filling me. He holds me tighter, closer. "Yes, what, Pearl? What are you saying yes to?"

"Yes, Alexandre. I will marry you."

"That's what I wanted to hear," and he kisses me again.

Teaser for *Shadows of Pearl*

(Part 2 of *The Pearl Trilogy*)

I'm lying between the glorious Egyptian cotton sheets in Alexandre's bed, relaxing against the plumped-up, down feather pillows. I feel satiated. Complete, both physically and spiritually. Beyond satisfied. More glorious love-making has left me feeling like the luckiest, most appreciated woman in the world.

Of all people, I know what it's like to be stuck in a sexual desert – without another human being to fulfill my needs. For almost twenty years I had convinced myself that work could be a substitute. I'd given up. I'd learned to be self-sufficient in every way – yes, in *every* way - and I never, in a million years, believed that at forty years old I would meet anyone special, let alone a man fifteen years my junior. And not only a younger man, but ridiculously successful, kind, devastatingly handsome, and last but not least, a veritable god in bed.

And to top it all off; completely in love with me…

Alexandre Chevalier.

I still feel as if I have walked into a modern day fairy tale.

It's tough when you're riddled with insecurities the way I am. Hard to believe that a man so gorgeous can covet you and feel the same intensity of passion that you feel for him. Yet, there he was, Alexandre Chevalier, co-founder of the Internet sensation HookedUp – a company which has taken the world by storm and, at the tender age of twenty-five, has made him into one of the wealthiest men in the world. There Alexandre was - wanting to date me.

And if that wasn't enough, he has chosen me, Pearl Robinson, a forty year-old with my just-above-average, girl-next-door looks, to be his *wife*.

Yes, I do believe I'm dreaming.

I look now at my left hand which I'm turning this way and that and admire my diamond engagement ring - proof that all this is real. It's glinting, catching rays of morning sunlight which are pouring in through the long bedroom window. The ice-blue silk drapes are half open. Alexandre hates to sleep with them closed - as if darkness could swallow him up at dawn.

I've learned a lot about Alexandre in the two months since we've been engaged. There's a shadow that lives within - a mood which can encompass him at times, and it frightens me. I can never be sure when it will possess him but it is there, deep inside his soul. He's a damaged man - that much I know. Yet he seems to be an expert at hiding the phantoms which lurk within.

So far, I have only seen glimpses.

I too, try to hide any gremlins from my past. Some things are better left unsaid. We are still getting to know each other.

I can hear him now, next door in the en-suite bathroom. The faucet has just been turned off. I picture him in my mind's eye; water trickling from his lightly tanned chest, his biceps flexed deliciously as he dries himself, his strong, muscular thighs, the ripples of his stomach and his wet, almost-black hair - wayward and mussed-up - which frames the even features of his handsome face.

I think of our lovemaking just ten minutes ago and a shiver of lust shimmies through my body. I cannot get enough of him. He possesses my psyche. I have never needed anybody as I need him. But I try to keep myself cool, calm and collected, even though I'm on fire inside. He mustn't know the apprehension that envelops me - fear that I could be flung back again into the desert, abandoned with no water - on my own once more. And when I say 'on my own' I don't mean literally so. No, you can be with a man and feel like an island – as I was with my ex-husband, Saul. I blamed myself for my frigidity, my inability to reach orgasm through sex which, if I remember correctly, happened in my early twenties after I'd split up with my first boyfriend, Brad.

I thought I was a lost cause until I met Alexandre. He intrinsically understands me and my body. Maybe that's why I'm hooked on him. Sexually. Mentally. But I try to keep that to myself. There's nothing like a needy woman to scare a man away. Especially one as hot as he is. I have to hold onto my independence, my self-possession.

Or I could lose him for good.

My fiancé saunters into the bedroom and fixes his eyes on me, running them along my naked body with approval. I cannot believe he is actually mine. *My fiancé.* How I relish those words.

I'm now willing him with my gaze to come back to bed, just for ten minutes, but I know that his drive and ambition rarely lets him lose restraint. He has a plane to catch – a business trip is waiting; clients hanging in limbo with baited breath for a decision to be made, a deal to be signed. I've learned that Alexandre is a ruthless negotiator, a tough cookie when it comes to business – nobody gets to be as successful as he is by accident.

I drink him in. A white towel is hanging about his washboard abs. Beads of water are gathered about his buffed-up chest. His green eyes are gazing at me.

"Come with me, Pearl," he says, his French accent full and rich.

"I told you, I really can't."

"I'd love to show you my favorite haunts in London, take you to the theatre, a walk along the South Bank by the River Thames."

He moves over to the bed and sits beside me, fondling my chin with his long fingers. He tilts my head back a touch and presses his lips to mine. His tongue explores my mouth, the tip of it gently probing, running along my lips. He holds my head in his hands and teases my tongue with his. I feel the electricity of it - tingles shoot between my thighs. I groan. My sound makes his kiss more intense, hungrier. The towel moves - his huge cock is flexing against it. I rest my hand there and feel how stiff it is. Always ready for me, even with just a kiss or at the sight of my naked body. Nobody has ever desired me the way he does.

"Why are you tormenting me like this?" he whispers. "You know I don't like us being apart."

"I can't just leave Anthony alone – he's come all the way from San Francisco to visit. Besides, I told you, I have that important meeting this morning."

"It's just work, it can be postponed."

"No, it can't. Samuel Myers has flown in from LA. You can't start up a company for me, Alexandre, and then expect it to run itself. HookedUp Enterprises needs me more than ever right now – it's my baby."

"So têtue," he teases, his French accent rumblingly deep.

"What does that mean?"

"Stubborn."

I laugh. "I know you, Alexandre Chevalier. You told me once yourself, that the last thing you wanted was a woman to be hanging onto your 'every word, your every movement' – that's what you said. You'd get bored of me if I didn't have my own projects, my own life."

"Perhaps, but sometimes I think you push it, Pearl. Like the wedding, for instance. Why are you making us wait until December? It's absurd – we could get married as soon as I get back from London." He grazes his tongue along my lips and kisses me again.

"I told you - I've always dreamed of a winter wedding," I whisper.

"The ice princess."

I trace my fingers along his cheekbone and smile. Let him think I'm the ice princess. Let him think I'm cool. He can't know that my insides are made of marshmallow – that my need for him is more than life itself.

"You'll be late," I warn, running my fingers through his thick, soft hair.

"What I like though, is when I fuck you I make you melt," he murmurs, his hands trailing down my back along my spine. "I love your dimples, these adorable dimples in your back, just here…and here." He makes circular motions around my little dips and then runs the tips of his fingers further south, cupping my buttocks in his large hands.

I feel the tips of his fingers as they lightly, so very lightly touch my cleft, lifting me off the mattress, pulling me towards him. "So wet," he says. "Even when all I do is kiss you. Funny how you and I get each other so worked up - you've made me rock hard."

"Yes…isn't it?" We both laugh.

"Shit, damn it! You're so tempting, Pearl. Damn my meeting." He nips my lower lip softly between his minty teeth.

The tease - I'm used to this. He keeps me in check – always

leaving me begging for more, my heart racing. I throb with desire, aching for his return – even before he has departed. Or even when he's right beside me, I'm on red alert, ready for sex at a moment's notice. Alexandre says he likes it this way. My resolve must stay intact, though. I need to stay strong. I cannot lose myself in him one hundred percent.

Or he'd swallow me whole.

I study him. It's not just sex that has me in his hold. It's the way he is inside; his kindness, generosity, his sense of humor, the love he has for me - even his damn French pride which makes him a touch possessive and jealous. Not too much - no, but just enough to make me feel desired and treasured. All this makes up a complex personality - a character I'm still trying to work out.

He walks over to his closet and opens the door. That same closet where, just three months ago, I hid myself behind rows of hand-tailored suits and racks of silk ties – where I childishly played Hide and Seek. A tremor fills my body now, remembering that sexually-charged moment. Alexandre caught me and then tied my legs to the bedposts with two ice-blue silk ties, splaying my thighs apart. I thought he was going to play bondage and he did. His style. Sweet - but terrifying as I couldn't imagine what would happen next. I had nothing to fear; he 'beat' me with a Kingfisher feather and tied my wrists together behind my head with the priceless Art Deco pearl choker he bought me in Paris. The excitement tipped me over the edge – the trepidation, the lust, the sensitivity all mixed together in a delicious cocktail of sex. A cocktail which has turned me into an alcoholic of love. A drink which I need every day just to function at my best.

I am addicted to him.

I watch him now. Six feet, three inches of pure, virile male.

What is it that makes me want him to take charge in the bedroom? To overpower me? I love being beneath him, strong and dominant as he is – on top of me, pushing me to my limits, making me scream his name when I come. He has control over me sexually and he knows it – I can't let him also dominate my life. He's testing me. I can sense it. Testing me to see how strong I can be. He made it clear that he wants an equal. I have to match him; I cannot let myself sink into oblivion. He once told me he was attracted to me for my maturity and that he was into 'women not girls' – I need to act my age – keep my composure. It's a battle I fight every day. I still feel like a vulnerable child inside and sometimes find myself acting like a teenager with her first love. Passion is a powerful thing – hard to control.

"What's it to be today - T-shirt and jeans, or a suit?" I ask him.

He pulls on a pair of boxer briefs over his tight, perfectly formed butt. My eyes then focus on that fine smooth hairline that goes from his abs down to his groin. He still has a semi-erection bulking out his underwear. He looks at me. "I don't know, what do you think?"

"Both are sexy. The second you put a suit on I want you to fuck me, though - you fully-clothed with just your cock free. You could take me up against the wall. I love it when I'm naked and you're dressed in one of your chic, tailored suits. I love it when you slam me from behind." I bite my lip. "Hard as a rock. Just thinking about it makes me so–"

"Stop tormenting me, baby, or I'll have to put you over my knee and spank you." He winks at me.

"That'll be the day."

"You know I could never do that, Pearl, not even in jest."

I observe him as he pulls out a pair of jeans and a black T-shirt from the rack in the closet. "Jeans it is, then," he says assertively, "or I'll never get to London on time."

"Bastard," I say with a grin.

"It's not as if I haven't asked you to come with me. It's not too late to change your mind."

"No, I'm staying."

"Sure? Last call–"

"I'm sure," I say, already regretful.

I slip out of the bed and glide towards him. "I'll miss you." I place my arms about his warm, strong torso and hold myself close to him. I breathe in his faint smell of lavender, hand-picked from his fields in Provence - crushed into heavenly oil - and the famous wish-I-could-bottle Alexandre smell - his natural odor that has me completely intoxicated.

As if on cue, Rex bounds his way into the bedroom, excited from his morning walk. He often barges in on our intimate moments. His black Labrador-mix tail spins about like a windmill; his tight muscles rival his master's.

"Oh Rex, how I'll miss you my boy," Alexandre says, bending down to hug his dog. "Look after him for me, Pearl. Don't let Anthony spoil him with too many treats. I'm late, I have to rush. See you in a couple of days." He embraces us in a family trio and then looks into my eyes and says, "I love you, Pearl. You're my everything - my light, my future. Take care now." He plants another kiss on my lips and makes his way down the corridor to the elevator where his ready-packed case is waiting. I don't follow as I'm still naked. Anthony is staying in one of the guest rooms – God forbid my brother should see me with no clothes on.

Anthony is in his element. He arrived late last night and

couldn't believe that Alexandre's chauffeur was there to meet him at the airport. He tells me that he's moving in (joke). Or is it? Anthony could get used to this lifestyle. Not to mention his boy-crush on Alexandre.

I get dressed and find breakfast waiting in the kitchen. Coffee, cereals, home-made yoghurt and jellies, fresh fruit and a spread of croissants and pastries sit temptingly on the table. I begin to set things on a tray to send up to the roof terrace. Sun is streaming through the windows and the sky is crystal blue. The perfect Fall weather. Cool, sunny and crisp but warm enough to still eat outside. Patricia, one of the staff, finds me rummaging about the kitchen and a look of dismay shadows her face. She's wearing a neat, black and white uniform – her choice – she says she feels more professional that way.

"Ms. Pearl, please, what are you doing? You'll make me lose my job if you insist on serving yourself."

"I doubt that, Patricia. I thought Anthony and I could sit on the roof terrace, have breakfast up there, today, but I don't want to be a nuisance."

"That's what the Dumbwaiter's for," she says with a wink.

"Best invention ever," I agree.

She loads everything into the mini-elevator which sends food or forgotten cell phones up and down between floors. Anthony has not yet set eyes on this marvel. I can hear him now in the living room screaming and yelping.

"Thanks, Patricia. I'm going to take my excitable brother upstairs."

I find Anthony sitting on the piano stool, breathless, his mouth open so far that his jaw is practically horizontal to the floor. He catches my eye as I'm standing in the doorway.

"Oh my GOD!"

"I know," I reply simply.

"Pearleee—"

"Do you want me to call 911?"

"Oh my freakin' God!"

"Yes, I think God has gotten the point."

"What is this place? A *museum*? I mean, this room is the size of mine and Bruce's entire apartment in San Francisco!"

"It is pretty awesome."

"Awesome does not even begin to describe this *palace*."

I watch his eyes scan the room; the walnut wood paneled walls, the delicate cabinetry and integrated bookshelves, the parquet floor, the picture windows with views of Central Park on one side and of The Plaza on the other - and the massive marble fireplaces. Rex is wagging his tail as if in agreement. He came from humble beginnings - from a dog pound in Paris – where the poor thing was waiting on Death Row. I get the feeling that he, too, appreciates his luxurious surroundings. Anthony is now caressing the piano keys; whimpering sounds are emanating from somewhere deep within his body as if he were sick with fever.

"Can you imagine having a grand piano like this?" he gushes.

"I don't have to imagine it, Anthony – it's a reality."

"Have you pinched yourself? Are you sure you're not just dreaming?"

"Sometimes I do wonder."

"A Steinway? Seriously? I really do have heart palpitations - you need to call an ambulance."

"Play something, Ant."

"Are you talkin' to me? Are you talking to *me*?" he jokes, imitating Robert de Niro in *Taxi Driver*. "Are you talking to *me*? Well,

I'm the only one here!"

I burst out laughing. Anthony couldn't look more unlike Travis Bickle if he tried. My brother is heavy, blonde – okay, not heavy - he is actively overweight. And when I say actively, I mean he cannot stop eating, even though every day he swears he has started a new diet. I've missed him – he does make me laugh. Except when I'm the object of his humor, which is often.

He begins to play and within seconds my eyes well with tears from the beauty of the sound. The way he strokes the keys with such a whispery touch makes me remember what a novice I am compared to him in the musical department. He has so much talent I find myself holding my breath.

"Mom used to sing this to us to get us to fall asleep. Do you remember?" He's playing *Lullaby* by Brahms.

"I miss her so much," I tell him quietly.

But he doesn't reply. His answer is all in his playing. His fingers caress the keys and his eyes, half closed, speak of nostalgia for a life cut short; a woman we both loved beyond measure who was taken from us too soon – her bones ravaged by that evil disease which begins with C and ends in heartbreak. Before I know it, I'm weeping, as if all my pain has finally unleashed itself. Pearl, the Independent One can finally let loose her pent-up sorrow.

"Why her?" I mumble. "Why her…"

Anthony stops his playing short. "I know. I know."

I take his hand and try to change the mood, "Breakfast, come on! You think this room is cool? You ain't seen nuthin' yet," I joke, "wait till you see the roof terrace."

I lead him upstairs, Rex excitedly at our heels, and listen to Anthony's oohs and ahs as he flips out about the décor, the priceless antique furniture and works of art. His eyes settle on a giant, red, heart painting with a multi-colored background. "That's a Jim Dine," he observes, "isn't it? A. Goddam. Jim. Freakin. Goddam. Dine!"

"Alexandre gave that to me a few weeks ago. An engagement present."

"Oh, so like, the rock of a diamond solitaire you're wearing on your finger wasn't enough already?"

I laugh. "Obscene, isn't it?"

"Well, it is *big*, to say the least."

"It belonged to a Russian princess."

He raises an eyebrow. "Of course it did."

"The diamond was part of a pendant and Alexandre had it made into a ring."

Anthony's reaction to the roof terrace with its real lawn, trees and sumptuous views across Central Park and the Manhattan skyline is even more extreme than mine was the first time I laid eyes on it all, back in June. "So the view wasn't enough… there has to be a freakin' *park* on top of this roof *as well?*"

"All for Rex," I say.

"I'm going to dress up as a dog."

I pull my cardigan tighter about my waist. "It's a little cool, let's go into the orangery and have breakfast."

"Don't we need to take Rex for a walk in the park first? Do his poops and stuff?"

"Don't worry, he's been out already."

"You took him out this morning so early?"

"No, Rex has a kind of nanny. She comes every morning at 7am sharp. Then again at eleven and every four hours if some-body's home. If I'm at work then his nanny – her name's Sally -

she hangs out with him. Rex is never alone."

"You're kidding me."

I giggle. "No, really. Rex lives up to his name. He's a king."

"I'll say."

"Come here, Rex, let me see that new collar you're wearing." He wiggles up to me sporting a smart, electric blue collar. He's wagging proudly. "Sally must have bought him that; she's always getting him gifts."

"So who else is running the show, besides Rex's nanny?"

"The housekeeper, Patricia, two or three cleaning ladies, a chef who comes and goes if Alexandre isn't in the mood to cook and–"

Anthony interrupts me with a waving hand. "Stop! I've heard enough, I can feel myself turning green."

I pour some coffee for us both and he's staring at me as if dissecting my very being. Uh, oh, what now…

"Pearl, what is wrong with you?"

"Excuse me?"

"What the hell are you playing at with this winter wedding bullshit. Winter - hello - is two months away. What are you waiting for?"

"Look, Alexandre and I have only known each other for just over four months. I want to be absolutely sure."

"Sure of what? That you're even luckier than Kate Middle-ton?"

"I don't want to make a mistake. I want for us to really know each other, warts and all."

"You want him to know about your *warts*? Are you crazy? Snap him up now before he realizes what's happened. You don't want him to see your goddam warts or he could change his mind!"

"Thanks for the vote of confidence, Ant. Actually, that expression is kind of gross. Let's just say I want us to be great friends as well as lovers before we tie the knot. I want to be open about everything and anything concerning my past and for him to do the same with me."

"Are you *insane*? Keep your goddam mouth *shut* about anything at all that makes you seem less than perfect. Keep any skeletons you may have locked firmly in the closet. You cannot jeopardize this golden opportunity."

"I want us to be honest with each other."

Anthony doesn't hear me – he rattles on, "Okay, I get the whole fairytale wedding thing in Lapland. I do. The whole reindeer pulling the sled, the white, silk-velvet ribbons on their antlers, the powdery snow – I get it, but please, don't be a fool – you need to get on with this marriage already and stop dithering about."

"You want me to settle for a quick wedding just in case my fiancé changes his mind? If he changes his mind, then I would have done the right thing. If he's that mercurial I shouldn't have been thinking about being with him in the first place."

Anthony rolls his eyes. "What's the worst that can happen? The marriage fails and you end up with a nice settlement, thank you very much."

"No, Anthony, that is *not* the plan. I would never marry for money, you know that. I refused to take a dime from Saul. In fact, I ended up lending him a ton of money which he never paid back and I never even asked him for it. I've suggested to Alexandre that we do a pre-nup. That way, it's clear from the outset that I don't want a cent if it turns out we aren't made for each other."

Anthony buries his head in his hands. His exasperation is palpable. "Please, Pearl, stop. I just can't *bear* hearing you throw your life away."

"I'm being practical. Realistic. Strong."

"You're being a dumbass – burning all your bridges. What does Alexandre say about this pre-nup nonsense?"

"He says no, and that he doesn't even want to discuss it."

"Phew, that's lucky."

"Try one of these Danish pastries – they melt in your mouth," I say, offering him a platter of tempting goodies, knowing that's the only thing that will shut Anthony up - at least for a while.

But all he does is stuff the pastry in his gob and talk with his mouth full. "And what's with all this business you've started together, this HookedUp thingamyjig?"

"HookedUp Enterprises."

"Yeah. Why can't you be content with just being a trophy wife, so to speak? You'd never have to work again in your life."

"That is *so* not my style and you know it. Besides, Alexandre secretly likes me being into my career. He bought up Haslit Films. It's all under the umbrella of his new company, HookedUp Enterprises, run by me. And he and I are the directors of it, except he's a silent partner. He doesn't want any say in how the company's run day to day – it's all up to me. So he *says*, but I'll need his help. I want him there – I'm not that proficient with the business side of things. We've started doing feature films, keeping on Haslit for the documentary side."

"So where does that leave your boss, Natalie?"

"She's on board, too. She came with the package."

"So wait, that means you are now technically Natalie's boss

and the tables have turned and you're like, some big shot who's going to hang out with Tom Cruise and Matt Bomer and all those sexy TV and movie sirens?"

I laugh and breathe in the heady scent of winter jasmine entwined about the trellises of the orangery. "Who knows where it could lead – it's exciting though."

Anthony taps his finger on his nose. "Just exactly how rich is your husband to-be? That is, if you move your skinny ass and hurry up and marry him and don't blow it all, somehow."

"Alexandre is a very powerful man. Much more powerful than I had first imagined."

"Not to mention drop-dead gorgeous. If he wasn't going to be my future brother-in-law, I swear I'd–"

"Anthony, please – you'll shock Rex."

"Sorry - go on, you were saying…"

"I actually had no idea how wealthy he was – his T-shirt and jeans look kinda had me fooled."

"Doesn't he wear a suit to meet clients?"

"Very rarely. Only if the clients are way older."

Anthony narrows his blue eyes. "Isn't everyone way older? I mean, he's only twenty-five, right?"

"He's very laid back about the way he presents himself. On the outside, that is. But I've overheard him speak business on the phone. I wouldn't want to cross him, that's for sure. Although he never raises his voice and he's always polite and friendly, but there's a kind of chilling power he holds over people. I can't explain it."

Anthony is still devouring his Danish. "A computer coder, huh?"

I take a sip of coffee. "That was what he led me to believe

when I first met him. He's very modest - it's his French upbringing. He never discusses money or boasts about his wealth. He likes to make out he's just a regular guy."

"And what about Psycho-sister – does she get a stake in this new company of yours?"

"Sophie? No, this has nothing to do with her." I look at my watch. "Oh my God, Anthony, speaking of my new company – I need to run or I'll be late for my meeting. Will you be okay on your own?"

"Hell yeah, are you kidding? I get to play king of the castle."

"Sorry, that's Rex's role, isn't it sweetheart?" I say cupping Rex's wide black head in my hands and giving him a kiss on the snout.

"Ha, ha, Rex means king in Latin – very cute."

"Be good, big brother and don't get into mischief. If you need anything Patricia can help. See you later."

"Later, baby sis."

Shades of Pearl Playlist

Pierre Bachelet and Herve Roy - Emmanuelle

Come To Me High - Rumor

Air - Bach

Under My Thumb - The Rolling Stones

Gymnopédie No.1 - Erik Satie

At Last - Etta James

Prelude in E-Minor - Frédéric Chopin

Black Cherry - Goldfrapp

Nothing Compares 2U - Sinead O'Connor (written by Prince)

Black Coffee - Julie London

Sex Machine - James Brown

Is This Love? - Bob Marley

What A Wonderful World - Louis Armstrong

Crazy For You - Madonna

Mrs. Robinson - Simon and Garfunkel

If I Were A Boy - Beyonce

You're So Vain - Carly Simon

Je T'Aime Moi Non Plus - Jane Birkin et Serge Gainsbourg

To listen to the Shades of Pearl soundtrack:
http://ariannerichmonde.com/music/forty-shades-of-pearl-sound-track/

Sign up (ariannerichmonde.com/email-signup/) to be informed the minute any future Arianne Richmonde releases, go live. Your details are private and will not be shared with anyone. You can unsubscribe at any time.

The Pearl series:

The Pearl Trilogy bundle (the first three books in one e-box set)

Shades of Pearl
Shadows of Pearl
Shimmers of Pearl
Pearl
Belle Pearl

I have also written *Glass*, a short story.

Join me on Facebook
(facebook.com/AuthorArianneRichmonde)

Join me on Twitter
(@A_Richmonde)

For more information about me, visit my website
(www.ariannerichmonde.com).

If you would like to email me:
ariannerichmonde@gmail.com

Made in the USA
Middletown, DE
29 August 2015